THE BALLAD OF BARNABAS PIERKIEL

THE BALLAD OF

BARNABAS PIERKIEL

—— A NOVEL ——

MAGDALENA ZYZAK

HENRY HOLT AND COMPANY   NEW YORK

Henry Holt and Company, LLC
Publishers since 1866
175 Fifth Avenue
New York, New York 10010
www.henryholt.com

Henry Holt® and 🂠® are registered trademarks of
Henry Holt and Company, LLC.

Library of Congress Cataloging-in-Publication Data
Zyzak, Magdalena.
    The Ballad of Barnabas Pierkiel : a novel / Magdalena Zyzak.—
First edition.
        pages cm
    ISBN 978-0-8050-9510-4 (hardcover)—
    ISBN 978-0-8050-9552-4 (electronic book)
I. Title.
PS3626.Y93B35 2013
813'.6—dc23   2013010978

Henry Holt books are available for special promotions and
premiums. For details contact: Director, Special Markets.

First Edition 2014

Designed by Kelly S. Too

Printed in the United States of America
1   3   5   7   9   10   8   6   4   2

This is a work of fiction. All of the characters, organizations, and events portrayed
in this novel either are products of the author's imagination or are used fictitiously.

CONTENTS

THE BALLAD OF BARNABAS PIERKIEL

PROLOGUE

PEOPLE OF MY COUNTRY, ME INCLUDED, CAN BE COMPARED TO THE FARMER in the old Slavic joke, who, walking with his wife along a road, encounters a Mongol on horseback (the Mongol informs the farmer he will dishonor the farmer's wife and asks the farmer to politely hold his testicles because the road is dusty, and when the Mongol rides away, and the wife gets up and furiously demands, "How can you be laughing?" the farmer says, "Because I got him in the middle of it, and he didn't even notice. His balls are covered in dust!"), even if such a comparison must be considered rude.

I saw Barnabas Pierkiel only once, at a distance, in a coastal town, in the spring two years after the war. I was walking by the sea, inspecting the occasional defunct piece of artillery . . . before I describe Barnabas, why not say a bit about Scalvusia—a nation that existed and then, by the time of my seaside stroll, did not—in which, long ago, men with such imposing names as Perun and

Porevit blazed the forest paths, and women named Zorica and Danica rode bareback and kindled birch fires and ate horse. For hundreds of years, Scalvusia spread from the Black Sea to the Baltic. The peaks on the eastern border were, as long as Porevit and Zorica did not run out of mead, sleeping giant knights, said to rise to protect the people, were we ever in need.

Scalvusians were a bright and tolerant people, as you will see. Storks nested in our chimneys, and our babes were found in cabbage fields—a veritable nation of immaculate conceivers. Friends and enemies drank arm in arm, under a sky the permanent gray of which seemed bluer with each passing vodka. Were I a poet, not a self-effacing bureaucrat, I'd here provide lost Scalvusia a most grandiloquent epitaph, but, in light of my meager faculties, and considering I'm translating my own original from our dying tongue to English (so forgive my idiomatic oddities and pray the apparatchiks do not learn of my interest in your taboo tongue, or worse, intercept this manuscript as it makes its way west, copied out between the lines of a copy of *Concepts for Screw-Cutting Lathe Operators* in the valise of a not-to-be-named Polish friend), I will merely say: Scalvusia died of its wounds.

Then it should come as no surprise that, in 1947, two years after my country's final destruction, when I saw the noble figure of Barnabas Pierkiel, I experienced a sadness not unlike when one remembers one once had a childhood.

Barnabas stood at the end of a pier in a parka of such harsh wool as not even horseblankets are made and a pair of mercilessly worn galoshes; he stood with his head down, as if in search of some answer in that herring-infested inlet of the Baltic. He was, and still is somewhat, rather famous, albeit not at all outside our swallowed country, and to see him at pier's end reminded me that he, too, would be lost in little time, and so I decided to research and compose his history.

And why in English? Because, alas, in this part of the world, sympathies with a passionate idler such as was Barnabas Pierkiel in his youth—these are in short supply. Possibly my information has been colored by the fantasies of subversive comrades, but I have been told that in the West, especially in English-speaking countries, idleness, if not passion, remains widely valued, and the citizens labor so little that a substantial majority do nothing but organize and attend literary salons.

I did not approach him on the pier. I knew from where he'd come (I was born in a similar place): the tiny village of Odolechka, located so far from the sea and everything else that nearly no one had known it existed, that is, until everyone knew at once. I soon traveled there and, via archives and by interviewing the survivors, found myself able to fashion this report of a series of extraordinary events, in which Barnabas, though not always directly involved, seems to have been nonetheless the unwitting lynchpin.

So, I bring him to you as a gift of sorts, and as this young hero's heart is like that of a lion and also a little like that of an ass, it is my sincere hope that readers leonine and asinine may equally find in this chronicle a brief but welcoming abode.

CHAPTER I

In which our hero self-admires

BARNABAS PIERKIEL HELD HIS BREATH SO AS NOT TO DISTORT HIS REFLECTION in a pan of water he had carried from his grandmother's kitchen and laid on a more or less level stump. He murmured at his facial regularity and symmetry, a handsomeness, he felt, that was by no means superficial. So much mystery he witnessed in his own eyes that, at length, he conceded defeat. Let astronomers decipher it. He scanned the rest of his reflection and concluded he was graceful in his new and only suit, procured by way of skillful haggling at a discounted price from Kowalchyk the tailor. The jacket was a perfect fit (for whomever it had been made), "modified" to create a large torso and squared shoulders, as was the latest fashion. Above the lapels flared the wide collar of Barnabas' cerulean shirt, which contrasted with the biscuit color of his hair, treated daily with an egg yolk shine-sustaining ointment.

Yes, what better entry to a man's character than to observe

him in a moment of acute self-contemplation. Do we dare charge
Barnabas with empty vanity? Do we scold an avid art student for
resting his admiring eye on Helen's bust by Canova?

Barnabas' favorite aspects of himself included his shins (long
and straight), his lobes (of minimal flap), his nostrils (petite,
shaped like pearls), and the singular springiness of his step. Barnabas was right to venerate Barnabas. This had not always been
possible . . .

Unlike many of us, who are born either ugly or lovely and live
and die thus, bearing through the decades our crooked shins, warty
fingers, our odalisque figures and whatever else genetic fate has
determined, Barnabas, in his early teenage years, had lost his
beauty utterly. He'd only recently escaped what he considered
his "tragic era," in which so much suet had oozed from his pores
he'd been convinced he'd contracted cloven hoof disease or dis-
saffected pig disease or some other countryside ailment.

At fourteen, his faunlike childhood body had turned disproportionate, his limbs in constant competition to outgrow each
other. Then, at approximately fifteen and a half, like an overnight
fungus, his head had become so large (relative to the rest) that he
had gone to school with his grandmother's shard of mirror tied
to his brow to remind potential head-critics of their own hideous-
ness. It was not long before a *History of the Decline of Serfdom*
thrown by Burthold the bully shattered the family shard, which,
due to economic factors in our young parliamentary democracy,
was never to be replaced, thus Barnabas' pan of water.

The "tragic era," at its lowest point, encouraged Barnabas to
try his luck at suicide. One postschool afternoon, young Barnabas
inserted his enormous head into the oven, but there, instead of the
dark void of eternity, in a swirl of smoky odors he at first mis-

took for the vapors of Hell, he found a roasted chicken. Looking at the lifeless bird, Barnabas experienced an unpleasant vision of his own body plucked of all hairs and displayed with its many disgraceful imperfections in an open coffin. Instead of lighting the coals, he sadly devoured a leg and went upstairs to brood.

A few weeks later, he turned seventeen and lovely. This is where my chronicle begins, with Barnabas staring at his bacon-greased reflection in the pan, recalling with embarrassment the years he'd spent in odious form; and yet, these had not been entirely without dividend, for they had bestowed a certain melancholy sensitivity of soul.

It's true that when a young Scalvusian is sensitive and melancholy, he requires a certain quantity of drink. Among beer, mead, vodka, schnapps, and moonshine, who can say of which Barnabas had become most fond? This is not to say his introduction to liquor hadn't happened in the cradle, where, as for most Scalvusian lads, a vodka-soaked twist of cloth substituted for a pacifier.

At last, with anguish, Barnabas looked away from his reflection. He considered the landscape. Odolechka was a cheerless little place. Deep in the secluded parts of Eastern Europe, the land about the village offered nothing more than fields and trees and tonnage of manure that seemed disproportionate to the rather scant number of scrawny cows. The scent became especially intense in spring, when the western wind blew from the pastures, a scent to which Barnabas, with his delicate senses, had, unlike his contemporaries, never become immune. He felt faint every spring, sometimes staying in bed for days with a vodka-soaked rag on his nose. He had developed an almost superstitious fear of feces. Indeed, he had once attempted to resist the tyranny of this very basic physiological obligation and, as leader and sole member of his protest movement, had avoided the outhouse for six days and nights. On the seventh day, the result had been so daunting that Barnabas had pushed this memory to the very corner of his nether unconscious, where it would remain alongside his failed suicide. He kept his pigpen very clean.

At this moment, probably for the first time in his life, Barnabas was not bothered by the Odolechkan stench. In fact, he was so nervous, his sense of smell had ceased to operate. He was, however, cognizant of an oily wetness harassing him from head to foot. With indignation, Barnabas realized this wasn't dew, but that, simply and gracelessly, he was covered in sweat, not only due to nervousness (for he was about to do a thing requiring the total of his courage), but also as a direct consequence of the fact that his suit was wool, unsuitable for summer, and the only fabric Kowalchyk had agreed to spare at such a price.

Still, removing the jacket was out of the question—the way the lapels harmonized with the shirt's collar, the manner in which the six buttons more or less aligned down his front, the grace with which the pads sat on his shoulders—this refined arrangement could not be forsaken. So Barnabas targeted a patch of dry grass and carefully lay on his back, attempting to reduce his bodily functions to a minimum.

Daydreaming Barnabas did often and well. Some in the village claimed dreaming was what he did best, but I consider such opinions regular slander. Lazy Barnabas was not. On the contrary, he was eager to help, whether to carry buckets of water for some local maiden, to guard someone's flock, even to labor at the mill. It happened that work disliked Barnabas, though. Inevitably, the water spilled, a sheep eloped with man or wolf, the flour contained more dust than grain. This again was not due to ineptness, but that Barnabas was overwhelmed by lofty thoughts and thus unable to stay focused on mundanities.

AN AFFINITY FOR THE EXTRAORDINARY, AN AIR ABOUT THE BOY OF HAVING been designed for more than peasant toils, went as far back as infancy. One harvest afternoon, his mother (who, sadly, not long after that harvest, had perished, it was said, of acute incomprehension after being shown into the private back room of the tavern to identify the corpse of Barnabas' father, who had stripped nude with his drinking partners to play what later were reported as "men's games," which, harmlessly enough, began with Olek the carpenter drinking a liter of vodka from Boleswav Pierkiel's boot, but then escalated into Kazhimiezh the shepherd cutting off his own big toe with Olek's hand-cranked spinning saw. At this point, the archived police report maintains, Boleswav, not to be bested, grabbed the still-spinning saw, and shouting, "Watch this, then!" swung it at himself, to the detriment of the connection between head and neck. "It's funny," says the testimony of Kazhimiezh in the report, "when he was young, he once put on his sister's underwear. But he died like a man.") had left the cottage door ajar, and Barnabas had crawled into the fields.

The boy settled himself in the wheat, where he lay for hours without a sound. The field was reaped that day, but he, by some miracle, remained unscathed. Later that night, a magpie warped and quorked until Barnabas' mother, frenzied with worry, rushed out to scream at it and there, in a patch of skipped-over wheat, found her child placidly eating a clod of soil. The incident was puzzling, as no other patch had survived the scythes and, besides, the Pierkiel clan had always been afflicted by ill luck, the details of which will be gruelingly unveiled in the pages ahead.

After Barnabas' orphaning, his care devolved upon his grandmother, one of the few Pierkiels in the last six hundred years to achieve old age. She belonged to that strain of ox-strong women, nearly gone from our modern world, known for carrying anything from hefty men to blocks of plaster. As if in compensation for this unusual vigor, Grandmother Pierkiel was endowed with negligible imagination and no tolerance for daydreaming or other ascensions of the soul. Indeed, her soul was so prosaic that, regardless of whether or not it existed, it neither ever rose nor even snored.

NOW ON THIS SUMMER DAY IN 1939, OUR HERO WATCHED THE CLOUDS. HE gained no insight. He sat up, spat, and said, "For her, I would invade Siberia, or at the very least the northern part of Bukovina. I would publicly admit that I and Yurek are first cousins. I would give up beer, mead, vodka, schnapps, and moonshine, or, at the very least, beer, mead, vodka, and schnapps." *For her?* He certainly was not referring to his grandmother.

He vigorously scratched his chest and brushed his shoulders. How much longer could he postpone the encounter? A coward, was he? His great contempt for the unromantic, for his dreary village and livelihood, demanded he indulge in paperback legends. Would Rudolf Vasilenko sit and wait for destiny to yank him off his quaking glutes? Wouldn't Vasilenko confidently stride forth and punch Fortune in the kidney? (For those who have not heard of Vasilenko, and I would not be surprised if that includes everyone who's not Scalvusian, he was a prewar agitator, a cor-

poreal human, also the protagonist of six or seven sixth-rate nov-
els, something of a bolshevik, famous for robbing banks, escaping
capture, and dispensing money to Scalvusia's poor.)

Barnabas reached into his trouser pocket, felt the lacy keep-
sake, and his heart waltzed. He had found the dear item a few
days ago dangling from a rosebush behind *her* house. Initially, he
thought she'd left it there for him to find. Alas, he had been forced
to remind himself that, as of yet, she didn't know of his existence.

He groped the brassiere from his pocket and pressed it to his
face. What a seraglio of whiffs and emanations enveloped his
senses—mystifying molasses, hints of hidden coves and pirate ports
and cloves and peppers—a gaseous ambrosia so omnipotent that
he became disoriented, also mildly nauseated.

Despite appearances, Barnabas' fascination with the garment
was not chiefly prurient. He affixed to it a soaring, spiritual sig-
nificance. During the day, it traveled in his pocket or, sometimes,
when he was alone, wrapped around his wrist. At night, he wore
it as a sleeping mask, its cup capacious enough to obscure his face.
Two nights ago, his grandmother, discovering him in this intimate disguise, had shrieked, "Dirty!" fled back to her cot, and, the
next morning, denied having entered his vestibule at all.

He stroked the brassiere once more, returned it to his trousers, patted his pocket, and set off down the path between the
fields. He might have gone on horseback, but he wasn't yet committed to an audible approach. What if, for some unforeseeable
reason, it turned out best he not be seen or heard? He walked
and whistled and, in the minutes it took him to cross Duzhash-
vina Creek, a wheat field, then a cabbage field, his cheerfulness
increased tenfold. In mere minutes, she would know his worth,
his plans, his adoration.

The most direct route to her house was not the route an older man might choose. A gully full of stinging nettles halted Barnabas. He dimly remembered, or thought he remembered, his feeble-minded cousin Yurek looming over his cradle with nettles in hand . . . Barnabas banished early sorrows with a haughty stomp. He hurtled through the nettles like a Draguvite to battle. Little did he know the scale of the events these minor wounds inaugurated. For how can we ever foresee the outcomes of our exploits? Unfortunate feasters, unable to peep at the bottom of the broth cup clasped in our own hands! Poor Barnabas.

CHAPTER II

In which Barnabas serenades his beloved and
finds consolation in an albino peacock

HER HOUSE HAD AN UNDENIABLE SPLENDOR. NO CABBAGE WAS COOKED IN
the kitchen, and no hens pecked crumbs on the floor. Barnabas
suspected no hen had ever been inside, unless plucked, boiled,
and placed on a plate and topped with potato purée.

Barnabas had observed the house from various covert loca-
tions, for instance, behind the dog rose bush by the fence, also up
in the inky boughs of a black locust, and once atop the neighboring house's shed. The house's walls were unstained by the countryside's jaundice. In the manner of an oversized meringue, the house
appeared ready to topple beneath its own opulence. Two Greek
columns supported this volatile excess. On the triangular tympa-
num, a coat of arms (obtained by the landlord in a suspicious
transaction under a bridge) displayed a bear's paw frozen in a
honey-scooping gesture quartered with a talbot eyeing a trefoil.
Peonies, like beads of wine, dripped from the baroque balcony.

"What an ugly bulb. You shall have to be killed." A sonorous, accented voice drifted from the garden's recesses, and Barnabas dove to the ground with such ardor he nearly impaled himself on a beanpole. Then came the trumpeting whonk of a blown nose, of such force as is only performed by most damsels strictly in solitude. Far from discouraging him, this thunder merely sharpened her allure. Barnabas relished it like a voyager hearing the land-ho horn. He lay in drowsy recollection . . . of her fingers picking dry grass from her braid, the flaming inside of her mouth, a glimpse as she laughed, eating a *koroovka* bonbon, her slightly awkward high-heeled gait across the town square.

He lifted himself to his elbows, eye to the gap between fence posts. Here was a sight he had not expected: his beloved's buttocks glared at him through a cloche of heaped skirts. She seemed to be on hands and knees? No luscious pear, no ripe citrus equaled this bursting rotundity!

(I would like to point out that Barnabas would never have gone on peeking at a lady's behind had it not been hypnotically perfect.)

Barnabas composed himself and inferred from the unabashedness of the pose that his beloved did not, in fact, know of his presence . . . but then, how could she? This taxed Barnabas' thinking apparatus for a moment. Arms swooping, hair trailing, she emitted wet whispers, sugary rebukes to what looked like a patch of clover. He was used to women addressing rabbits and chickens (he himself engaged in an occasional debate with his pigs), but this long-winded tête-à-tête sent a nervous prickle through his shoulders. Perhaps it was the rumors he had heard about her garden from a gossip or two in town.

Beyond common marjoram, dark thyme, and chamomile, this

garden yielded herbs that cured warts, gallstones, scoliosis. A
pellet she made from powdered twigs, people said, had the power
to turn an honest man into a liar and a liar into a mute. Beneath
the shrubbery grew *chorluk*, that famous root that restored male
potency. Everyone in Odolechka talked about its efficacy. Terrible
chorluk had held a certain Yanko in such a solidifying grip that
his wife's odes and ululations kept the whole village awake for
three nights in the autumn of 1938.

She crushed a petal cluster in her palm and stood and turned,
a skein of yellow pollen drifting down her dress front. She swung
her basket, ambling toward him through the weigela. For one
unnerving moment, he lost her in the petals. He moved his eye to
the next gap in the fence . . .

BARNABAS WAS NOT THE ONLY MAN IN ODOLECHKA WHO HAD FALLEN TO A
state of stupor over this young gypsy, Roosha Papusha. Her house
was the property of her lover, the wealthiest, most ostentatious
man in town, Karol von Grushka. The origins of the Papusha–
von Grushka affair were unclear.

This much was known:

She had arrived with a score of gypsies in the spring of 1936,
and when their caravans left, she stayed. None knew why she
broke from the group, though many said her gypsy lover had
been killed in a dispute with a nongypsy somewhere on Kowomunak's outskirts. Von Grushka found her sleeping in his stable.
The villagers said, not without a shiver, that when he discovered
her beneath an old horseblanket (here, the accounts of her attire
vary, some claiming she wore nothing but a velvet choker), she
exhibited no shame and asked him to put a ring on her palm so

that she might tell his fortune. As soon as the gold touched her palm, it touched the bottom of her pocket.

The contents of her skirts were also passionately debated. Dzaswav the tavernkeeper, who claimed to have been given a brief peek, maintained that a rainbow of ribbons with nests at their ends swung about her knees; dark birds laid dappled eggs in these nests. Dudrovski the farmer had witnessed her hem catch (so he claimed to any who would listen) on Yerzy the butcher's broken step, exposing a hunting knife strapped to her calf. Basia the spinster vowed a gypsy dwarf magician resided in cozy seclusion between Roosha's thighs, slipping out on half-moon nights to commit mischief in the village. The sage Volodek refuted all of the above, claiming the skirts, tight at the top, capacious starting at the middle thigh, were a smoke screen of silk to obscure a radio connected to the Worldwide Masonic Conspiracy of Romani Blavatskian Anarchists.

BARNABAS ALSO WONDERED AT THE CONTENTS OF THOSE SKIRTS . . . BUT, even if a sorcerous dwarf were to attack him (he had heard of stranger things happening to decent fellows), he was unable to fear his enchantress. He'd gladly let her mesmerize and rob him. The nuisance was, he had so little that, listed, it littered less than a third of a page: one suit, some pigs, a leaning tower of food-stained paperbacks, one monogrammed handkerchief, a single cuff link with an imitation canary diamond missing, and an incomplete set of *paranchak* cards (additionally useless as Barnabas lacked a firearm), that dangerous and demanding Scalvusian national sport, in which a player must drunkenly fire into the sky approximately at the constellation least resembling the arrangement of stars on the card he has drawn while standing on one foot and spinning.

The contrast of this modest inventory with that of his beastly competitor, von Grushka, at this moment gone on his annual wild boar hunt, made Barnabas' heart and stomach twitch like a duo of insecure miniature pinschers.

A tiny yelp, appropriate for the frailest of creatures, never for a gallant of seventeen, escaped him. Had Roosha heard this intolerable unmanliness? She certainly had turned toward his hiding place. Jumbled explanations piled up in his head: of having slipped, having dropped something precious into the bushes, and / or having spotted a rabid fox. He pressed himself as low as possible, his face against the ground.

"What's this in the dirt? What's munching my marjoram?"

Here followed an excruciating silence, in which Roosha regarded our hero with curiosity, leaning over him, as if looking at a mushroom at the bottom of a ditch. He watched her through the triangle between his index and middle finger.

"What are you doing in my dog rose, dogboy?"

How could he—on his belly, face bemudded—answer such a question in the manner befitting a young gentleman of dignity?

"I saw your hydrangeas—"

"Hydrangeas? I don't have hydrangeas."

"I, in fact, it was gymnastics, *men's* gymnastics," he said, attempting nonchalance, a difficult demeanor to affect when one is prone in mud.

"What a peculiar way you have of doing it! At first, I thought it was one of the grubby muskrats devouring my shrubs." She laughed and scanned the garden, as if to be sure there weren't more young men cowering about. "If you were only doing *men's* gymnastics, then you can't be blamed, can you? Unless you were trying to rob my garden?"

"Never!"

"You'd be surprised how many ruffians do. There's such a plenty of them, sometimes two or three a night. Sometimes they sing me songs about their favorite foods, drinks, lovemaking positions . . . sometimes they bring instruments. One suitor played for me all night on a harpsichord he dragged here all the way from Prague."

"The manners of the locals are something horrific," Barnabas spouted with passion.

"They're as bad as gypsies, worse."

"They're all thieves," said Barnabas, "all Odolechkans, I mean, not the gypsies. Many of them have dripping noses! Most have crusty chins and dirty nails. They eat with their mouths open. And they drool, it's a fact. They don't change their clothing. I know a boy—nobody close to me—he won't throw away a coat until it's shreds. There's a man in this village—I won't say his name—he stores his trousers in a shed, standing upright."

She had seemed unimpressed, but this last revelation moved her. "No!"

"Yes!" Barnabas exclaimed, "The whole town is an armpit!" delighted at his poetry, but Roosha no longer appeared to be listening. He followed her gaze to a shrub by the opposite fence.

"I know," she said, "about these muskrats. They migrated from Prague some thirty years ago, and now it's an infestation. No poison dries up their nasty forked tongues. I caught one of them eating my soap yesterday, but he escaped. Not before he ate half of my ankle soap. Male, every one of them. Who can say how they breed?"

"I could help you. I have some experience with beasts." Barnabas, emboldened, rose to a squat. "My uncle was a rodent doctor," he lied (no learned men in the Pierkiel clan, I'm afraid). "He taught me about all kinds of rodents, field mice, even pigs."

"Well, while you're here, you might just pound a few. Last time I saw a muskrat, it was rummaging in the pipe."

This impressed Barnabas very much, as few Odolechkans enjoyed the luxury of plumbing.

She shuffled her red skirts like an industrious hen and ascended the stairs. She was the kind of woman in whom the parts and the sum of the parts all worked with astonishing harmony. When she walked, everything flowed and hopped; when she sat, each part arranged itself to maximum effect by way of gravity or antigravity as needed.

"Are you coming or not? Carry my basket, puppy. I saw you've been nibbling my fence. Perhaps you need a snack. I will fix you a cup of perfect soup."

He stood and followed in a daze. What was to blame for what happened next? A broken step? His shoes, inadequately crafted by a myopic cobbler? The jerking pulleys of his nerves?

Barnabas tripped and gravity was not his ally. He flailed, flung the basket (tomatoes, tulips), groped the air, and clutched the first solid object in reach, which happened to be Roosha's celebrated derriere.

"Oh!" Thus she summed up her experience. It was, to Barnabas, the song of the doves of cupidity.

A ring-loaded fist interrupted his appreciation, and when he recovered from the punch, he was gazing into the inflamed throats of weigela blooms. Twisting, he glimpsed what local gossips had in vain imagined. It was a thousand, hundred thousand, million, trillion and minus divided by power cubed (after trillion, his numerical notions were muddled) times more marvelous—from the billows of red and white silk burgeoned one goose-bumped knee, on it a ravishing bruise, also a calf of the highest quality, and one ankle crossed over the other—a vision so lovely that, Barnabas felt, the Earth itself ceased its laborious rotation.

With one cruel shuffle of fabric, all was concealed. She squatted beside him, face within a handsbreadth of his face. A flushed cheek, an eye, kohl and shadow, a pupil contracted to a point. Barnabas had evaluated many dames in the tavern's old editions of *Kinemo Review*, but not even the bewitching Beata Lantana (who had recently died when a deranged fan, after being refused an autograph, had smashed her with an étagère) could compare to Roosha. To honor Roosha's beauty, he would claim the moon for Scalvusia, steal the treasury in Moscow, serenade her in a tongue not yet invented, chop his left leg off in proof of devotion (an hereditary sentiment perhaps).

"*Cara mia!*" he beseeched her in the next best thing to a tongue not yet invented, that is, the two words he knew of Italian, borrowed from a popular ritornelle. For fewer than ten seconds, as she stared down at him, it seemed to him she was about to swear her love, maybe to suggest names for their future son and daughter.

Rather, "*Shastoyavskaya!*" she uttered the terrible, untranslatable Scalvusian curse, then, "Bastard devil!" shaking her hair in Medusan frenzy. "I thought a dog had bit me from behind! A herd of dogs couldn't be worse. I think you broke my bones, you brute!"

"It was a romantic accident—"

"Of course, and who doesn't do it on purpose? All of you do. I had one suitor try to make love to me atop a harpsichord he dragged here all the way from Vienna. The rickety thing didn't even have sheets! You carnivorous beast. You leg humper. I almost lost my teeth. Imagine me with dentures."

"Ma'am, I think they're all in the right order," Barnabas remarked shyly.

"Listen to this! He's going to tell me they're all in order, like he knows what the order is! He thinks he gazed into my mouth before, like I'm his mare or cow." Her tongue glided over her shiny teeth. "I'm nobody's cow, if that's what you are trying to imply. I am mistress of myself. Only you wait until I tell Karol, wait till he hears what kinds of skulkers come around! He'll shoot you all. The best hunter east of the Danube, and he has a room full of rifles. He has the flintlock Bonaparte carried to Vilna, and he'll shoot you like a hare! And if he doesn't, my brothers will come from the forest and snatch you in the night. They know how to deal with your kind. Or I'll put a curse on you this minute, change your dainty features to a pickled paste," she ranted on, while Barnabas, in vain, tried to interject.

The Roma camp was gone from the town's outskirts, but Barnabas knew that caravans often rolled in soundlessly, and the following day women like ravens would throng the square. Who knew where the men hid? Not even that clairvoyant Volodek could foresee the comings and goings of gypsies. Barnabas stopped trying to interject.

"Can't you speak? I don't blame you, because there's nothing to say! Nothing! And stay away from my pipes." She stomped a few times and gestured at him with her right hand, the gold-ringed pinky ominously erect.

"The muskrat!" he objected.

The silks of her skirts tumbled furiously. She went inside the house.

Barnabas, at the bottom of the stairs, contemplated the tragic brevity of their encounter, the speech he had not delivered, and felt such despair that he slapped his face, ceasing after a few slaps, fearful of damage. He stroked the darling features. But what good was his beautiful head if inside there was nothing but cabbage?

"Oh imbecile! Simpleton!" our hero cried. "Even Yurek, who eats dirt, who makes friends with goat's fleas and rocks, could do better!"

He had been rehearsing for a month. The speech had become rather long and grand. He considered it his finest work of oratory yet attempted. (Such works, to be fair, had been few, though he had, on occasion, had to make some speeches on the subject of human rights to his grandmother.) Volodek, without question the best orator in Odolechka, had been teaching Barnabas the basics of the art in exchange for a few minor labors. Also Barnabas had read more than half of Borys Polensky's *Guide to Etiquette*, determined to prove himself a man of some distinction.

He sighed and, as he was not used to so much emotional strain, remained on his side at the disaster site and, leaning on his elbow, looked at Roosha's tulips teetering on puny necks. So might Barnabas have reclined until dusk, had not something in the deeper foliage of the garden captured his attention. An opalescence stalked behind the shrubs toward the open lawn. A ghostliness rippled from shadow to shadow. Barnabas crawled toward the shaking shrubs and found himself facing a peacock in full display.

"Albino!" Barnabas whispered and made sure to breathe through his nose. He felt the slightest wind would break the bird into a cloud of drifting feathers. It was like a dandelion's pappus.

"Oh, Roosha's pet," he whispered, trying to produce as little outflow of air as possible, "I will tell you what I had prepared to tell your mistress, for to tell no one is worse than slapping my own face. I have come to court you. Perhaps you have other suitors, perhaps they give you gifts of jewelry and pigs and fine clothing. I have only pigs, but pigs are not entirely ignoble creatures. A pig can count to three, I think. My love for you is more than the love of Tadeush for Malgorzata, when, in *The Lay of the Cottonwood Lady*—have you read it? If not, I would like to bestow on you the gift of my only copy—when Tadeush throws himself from the flying ship and lands on the fool, who dies of a slightly crushed windpipe, just crushed enough that his last song sounds like a lovesong instead of the usual mockery. I would court you like no man has courted. Oh, Roosha, I will slap any suitor of yours in the face with a glove, white silk, but pigskin gloves should not be overlooked. I have read major excerpts from Borys Polensky's *Guide to Etiquette*, and so I am prepared to love you in the fashion of a gentleman."

The peacock stared back with superiority and self-importance, but not without a note, it seemed, of avian appreciation.

CHAPTER III

In which Barnabas, unbeknownst to Barnabas, is being watched

BEHIND THE PIERKIEL HOUSE, BESIDE THE PIGPEN, A DECAYING BARN LEANED more or less in the direction of Russia. At first glance, the animal that lived within resembled a cow, due to general stockiness, piebald pattern, thickness of torso, and inadequate length of limbs. At second and third glance, Wilhelm was not a heifer but a horse, and whatever she lacked in appearance, she more than compensated for in dignity. The angle at which she held her head suggested noble blood. No Arabian's tresses compared to her abundant topknot. Barnabas brushed her mane each day. As he gazed into the hazelnut shell of her eye, an uncanny sensation arose: could this animal count to three, even four?

If nothing else, the long muzzle suggested a wisewoman's ponderous visage, and the lazy flap of her tail, as she shooed away flies, suggested a stoic acceptance of life's unrelenting pestilence.

How many hours had these two spent gently blowing into

each other's noses, enjoying sugar lumps and pears? Barnabas' communication with his own species (or, to be exact, its male half) was a great deal more strained. Being from a pigherding family, he had had to endure no small amount of ridicule. Local louts, Burthold Blonsky ringleading, had snorted at him since he first attended school.

Thus Barnabas grew up to be a loner. For this, he was mocked as well. Villagers sneered when he refused to partake in the local activities (for example, groping and chasing Anechka the barmaid—who wouldn't have minded a Pierkielian grope—or, for example, ramming bottle caps into each other's foreheads) in favor of sitting astride his peaked roof and staring at the heavens. He was mocked when he hushed a rowdy crowd to hear a distant skylark. Men of Odolechka and of the surrounding towns predominantly valued knife fights over atmospheric phenomena and wildlife observation.

For it seemed that—whether due to consanguinity resulting from the village's isolation or some barometric anomaly that pushed the local blood primarily to groin and abdomen, diminishing supply to unessential outposts such as craniums—Odolechkan intelligence was rather below the national average. At school, that pitiful hovel, under the guidance of Grunvald the impoverished schoolteacher, dim heads struggled in vain over the most basic mathematical and grammatical conundrums.

Barnabas himself had not excelled at first, but a certain nimbleness of mind had allowed him to master the alphabet at the budding age of twelve, while many of the rest remained distressed or unimpressed by language in general. Barnabas' advanced capacity displeased not only the other students but the teacher, whose sense of self depended on his pupils' failure, each new stupidity reifying the fine futility of all existence. One day, as Barnabas picturesquely lingered amid daisies, he was mobbed by Burthold and his pack and bludgeoned with an abacus.

No surprise, then, that Barnabas became something of a misanthrope. The humans he loved were himself, Roosha, and his grandmother. He also loved all of his pigs and his mare. He rode Wilhelm at least four times a week. Sometimes to induce Wilhelm to move required an arcane pattern of pleas and jerks, for her tendons and joints were no longer young.

On this bleak afternoon, morose Barnabas-upon-Wilhelm followed his customary route through Yayechko's wheat field, out along a crumbling stone-and-mortar wall, the last remains of a fortress in which, a generation previous, outnumbered Odolechkans, then under Austrohungarian occupation, suffered a long siege, finally surrendering to the Russians.

In the decades since, more than one Odolechkan had been conceived in the shade on the wall's far side. Sometimes, tavern raconteurs insisted, ghastly gristly moaning from the broken stones had interrupted certain Edenic acts. Some even swore that, on sunny days, a sweet marrow odor seeped from the soil.

The period of the Siege and subsequent Odolechkan starvation was of great interest to our hero. He wished for nothing more than to have participated in those events and considered his own overdue arrival to this world a gross blunder of history. He'd searched the pitiable town library for every possible datum. Many an afternoon in his younger years he had spent snooping up and down the length of the wall, once unforgettably unearthing a shrapnel-studded human pelvis. Grandmother Pierkiel, if questioned about the Siege, liked to slap Barnabas' head and extol Grandpa Borivoi, the hot-blooded progenitor who had thrown himself at the Russians like a lion attacking early Christians, but without the lion's dental advantage (indeed Grandpa's teeth had been famously few), and whose life had been saved by a trip on an untied shoelace granting him the luck to knock himself senseless against a howitzer.

But Barnabas' maladroit moves of late were not so lucky. He considered the degree of his debacle. To plummet was possibly the worst move to perform during a courtship. His tender ego wriggled and preened, pouted and slithered, only to finally assay: the pinky finger! For there was not a doubt that she had showed him that dainty, erect digit. A secret signal certainly, but signifying what?

He wished he were better schooled in the gesticulations of the female body. Of course, an Odolechkan girl or two would gladly have demystified him long ago, but Barnabas was not enticed. I will not delve into particular characteristics, only note that the indigenous build was sensible if graceless: wide feet, turnip knees, heads nested close upon substantial torsos. In consequence, the only woman he had had the chance or desire to observe on a regular basis was his grandmother, always in a shoveling, sweeping, scratching frenzy, interrupted by the occasional shaking of a fist at the Almighty.

Barnabas' thighs squeezed Wilhelm's barrel sides, and they bounced into a gallop. Wilhelm belching out hiccuplike neighs, they sped down the hill, past old Horchensky, who, astride a fence, was stealing a pear from an orchard and, Barnabas supposed, most likely figured Barnabas an emissary from the capital. They reached the river and halted, and Barnabas washed his hands and face.

"The finger," Barnabas declared his topic: "Did she mean it

like when a *rushoolka* brandishes her wand? Some kind of gypsy curse? Will I end up with boils . . . or a wife?" he asked his horse.

"Boils or a wife. She adores me!" Barnabas made a little song of this and sang it for a while. Then, seating himself on a warm slab of rock, he indulged in some elegant brooding. Her finger was a symbol of resentment of her situation, of desire to be freed from Karol von Grushka. Barnabas decided he would liberate her. Didn't Rudolf Vasilenko liberate the poor?

Having reached this complex conclusion, he reclined on the slab, looking better than he felt. It was no brocade divan, yet there was a certain glory to this pose, he thought, one hand submerged wrist-deep amid the glossy stones and minnows.

WHEN BARNABAS HAD BEEN ASLEEP A WHILE, THERE EMERGED FROM THE rushes a strange and suspicious shape that at first might be confused with a gourd or melon, if only ripe cucurbits sprouted so fast. This shape was followed by a neck like a heron's, then a puny torso. This anatomy belonged to none other than Barnabas' addlepated cousin Yurek, the infamous stinging nettle tickler.

What was Yurek doing here? Your humble chronicler has no idea. According to three learned doctors, Yurek Pierkiel should have been safely locked away in the mental asylum at Troshku. One medic in particular, a man so ruined by his notorious patient that he had once pulled out tufts of his hair at a mere mention of Yurek's name, had begged a scholarly symposium that Yurek be straitjacketed interminably.

But Yurek, though deranged, was something of a charismatic fellow. What eyelash flutters, what sweet murmurs, what blushes he affected to trick the asylum staff. After long years of vain efforts, one particularly weak-willed nurse, a childless and lonesome woman, yielded. I shall not abuse you with the details of what this poor Giulietta did. Enough to say, our crafty Romeo escaped. Why did nobody pursue such a dangerous bedlamite? Because, you see, our young democracy, ruined by centuries of wars and partitions, was not yet completely recovered. Thus most departments of public service were on strike six months a year, and, besides, insanity, that faithful companion of troubled lands, was rather too common to be properly accommodated.

But let us return to our scene. It can't be said to be a pretty one: Yurek's mouth, an orifice perpetually and mindlessly ajar, betrayed a thorough disinterest in the physical matter that fell therein and thereout; his eyes did little to compensate, being in expressiveness equal to two mouseholes.

This baleful personage strode forth, leaned above sleeping Barnabas, and gurgled softly. It was like a hundred distant turkeys, with marbles for gizzard stones, had suddenly burped into choral song. A greeting? A threat? Nearly all family reunions have menacing consequences. Barnabas slept unaware of the bubbling above him. It would seem something awful was nigh, some moist revisitation of the terrors of childhood, and yet, just then, Yurek straightened and, in an awkward trot, disappeared into the willows.

CHAPTER IV

In which Kumashko the priest imbibes too much
and officiates a ruckus

EVERY JUNE, IN HONOR OF THE LOCAL PATRON SAINT VIESHA'S BIRTHDAY,
Odolechka hosted a bazaar. Preparations dominated the preced-
ing week. New garments were purchased, bicycles cleaned and
waxed, men's faces shaven, and women's hair abused into incred-
ible arrangements of bouclé curls then still the fashion in rural
parts. If one happened to have a new horse, bicycle, or wagon,
one tried to keep it secret until the day of the bazaar. Families
arrived in the company of milkcows followed by geese. One year,
a man carried about a new sewing machine strapped to his back.
Trinkets, even ordinary houseware objects such as colanders
and hammers, swung from belts and hats like festive bells. The
bazaar was a site not only of exchange of products, but of
glances, jealousies, and sundry minor follies. Barnabas himself
had attended last year with a passel of pigs so carefully scrubbed

they resembled a cluster of peeled radishes. This year, however, he had in mind an endeavor that would not brook the company of pigs.

Scalvusian custom dictated important events be inaugurated by a mass or at least a rushed benediction. Accordingly, on this blithe morning, before the bazaar, most Odolechkans were gathered in the unventilated church. Though they hymned with devotion, their ecstasies likely arose from expectation of the day's profits and purchases. Barnabas fought to not nod off. He knew all there was to know of the heavenly master and had no intention of bothering Him as long as He kept his distance.

Barnabas, leaning on a splintery pilaster in the narthex, indifferent to promises of eternal salvation scrawled on the announcement board beneath a picture of what seemed to him a veal chop ringed by a crown of thorns, became enchanted by his own reflection in the glass that covered the board. His tresses, tamed by a half jar of brilliantine, were slicked into a glossy shell. He turned left, right, chin up, chin down. Such depth, such angularity! Meanwhile, the priest touched on topics as various as shepherds, flocks, fishes, asses, deserts, oceans, wine, thou shalt not commit to thy wife, a man teased by children for being bald, one hundred Philistine foreskins . . .

Yany and Sabas, men about town, stood next to Barnabas, clad in identical, nondescript Sunday bests emitting nebulae of naphthalene. They didn't look at Barnabas, not one admiring glance, their eyes on their cuticles. Barnabas became impatient and hot. Itchy wool harassed his back. Cursing Kowalchyk the tailor, he exited the church.

BARNABAS, OBLIVIOUS, HAD NOT STOOD LONG OUTSIDE, FLAPPING HIS lapels, before the church routine came to a radical halt. While your historian, faithful to a notion that life is too short for brooding on the dark, often gruesome rituals that take place inside churches, would rather follow Barnabas and watch him eat a sausage or a salted herring, indeed would rather chronicle almost anything other than lengthy agrestic theology, one feels obliged to report the following events, as they catalyzed a scandal such as comes only once or twice a century to a town like Odolechka.

The priest, Kumashko, in a sermon on the hopes of this year's crops, supported vaguely by the story of Job, stopped suddenly and stood as if in philosophic reverie. This behavior was uncharacteristic, for he was no Bishop of Hippo. Even in times that should have been committed to reflection, he always found a sensible occupation, such as polishing crosses, painting church walls, or dripping wax onto the floor.

So the priest stood, and when he had had enough of thinking, instead of distributing Holy Communion, he gulped a glass of wine, wiped his mouth, suppressed a small updraft of stomach gas, and stared at the tabernacle with a mystified expression. An anxious murmur spread through the crowd, the Holy Communion being a great favorite, indeed the most anticipated moment of the whole service, when one was finally allowed to have a bite.

"What's this?" came from the Police Chief, who had awoken. He was in possession of a vast, uncompromising abdomen and an infallible nose that detected edible material in all forms, no matter how insubstantial.

The priest noticed neither the Police Chief's exclamation nor the discontented faces. He turned from the tabernacle to the flock with profound slowness. "Sinful folk!" he erupted, "Sinful! Sinful!" prolonging each *s* with a serpentine flourish, which was inappropriate in general but appreciable in context, considering, if one had in mind the paradisiac mise-en-scène, the priest's face resembled a ruddy apple. A few eyebrows rose, a few heads nodded, a few cast accusatory glances at neighbors. There were also a few who felt betrayed, especially those who had recently shared some *koolski* or a game of pick-a-stick with the cleric.

"I have been watching, I have been watching, and I can hold still no more!" he thundered, raising a fist that had, at myriad invitational teas, always held cream puffs so daintily. Many a brain convulsed—what had Kumashko seen? And where? Through whose window at what time of night?

"Sinful, dark as a figleaf submerged in sin and swampy pudding. Hellish! Olid quags and bogs and the rearmost wind. Infernal pits of arms, licked by tongues of the kitchen fires, intestine of the lamb-horned infant of the earth, the nostril of the Babylonian whore!" Here he took a breath, while the flock stood and sat in awe, and one or two women considered fainting but opted not to, anxious not to be found guilty while unconscious, whatever the sin might be.

"Look at your faces!" Kumashko flapped his hands. Some ducked behind their prayer books. "Sharp chins and round! False smiles and genuine. Faces scrubbed and unscrubbed. Curly mustaches and smooth upper lips. Pink cheeks, white cheeks, yellow cheeks. Exodus 33:23! 'And again the Lord said, behold! There is a place with me, and thou shalt stand upon the rock. And when my glory shall pass, I will set thee in a hole of the rock, and protect thee with my right hand, till I pass: And I will take away my hand, and thou shalt see my *back parts*: but my face thou cannot see!' "

Some who had been sitting stood. Some who had been standing sat.

"Freckled noses, red noses, swollen noses! What lies underneath? Rotten rot rotting! The smell of it reeks so much of Hell that I can barely stand to share this sacred bathhouse with you!"

At this, some pressed their arms to their sides, guilty as they were of skipping their Sunday bath. The priest took another draught and replenished his cup from the decanter.

"Gluttony!" he pronounced with satisfaction, and there was a general tensing of abdominal muscles, especially in the front pews, where the Police Chief, with equal parts nonchalance and difficulty, produced a paper-thin slit between the back of the bench in front of him and his ventral rotundity. Only two weeks before, he recalled, he'd devoured twenty-seven schnitzels in a competition with the Head Clerk. But hadn't he starved, when the Russians had come, during the Siege?

Self-consciously, he pressed a fist against his solar plexus, but the priest seemed to look right into his intestines, where, the Police Chief imagined, some schnitzel remains still lay in state.

"*Nimis* and *ardenter*!" roared the priest. "Filling the stomach as if it were a leathern pouch! A feedbag for my horse Mr. Konskipysk! A bucket for the unwashed masses! Juicy chickens, greasy pigs, and crispy livers, fatty *pierogi* and distending *bigoses*, tripe stews and lard from the jar! Off into the gastric voids. Mark 11:12! 'And the next day when they came out from Bethania, Jesus was hungry. And when he had seen afar off a fig tree having leaves, he came if perhaps he might find any thing on it. And when he was come to it, he found nothing but leaves. For it was not the time for figs. And, answering, he said to it: May no man hereafter eat fruit of thee any more for ever. And his disciples heard it. And they came to Jerusalem. And Peter, remembering, said to Jesus: Rabbi, the fig tree, which thou didst curse, is withered away. And Jesus, answering, saith to them: Have the faith of God.'"

Absolved thus, the Police Chief let his stomach loose in a significant but charming (so his Secretary reassured him) bulge. He even began to enjoy himself in a way men do when witnessing a piquant row, though he made certain to retain a stern expression.

Kumashko, having once again attended to his glass, redoubled with "Abomination to our Lord, our Lord who watches through that eye of his donkey-herder!" and pointed at his own eyeball. "The sloth that some of us know so well!"

At these words, no one felt particularly guilty, as Odolechkan lives, as understood by Odolechkans, were replete with excruciating toils.

And yet, Kumashko demanded, "Corn, wheat, and millet? No, you'd plow over your own great-aunt, had she happened to lie there, as she surely would, because she is slothful as in Bethania! Oh no, it is not just the young! It's the young and old, the dead and even the unborn! When out in the field, do you think of that coulter, of that chisel? Of that gentle ox? No! The hole in the rock! First it's just the hand, not even—a finger! Soon the whole palm, every knuckle stroked and stroked, and then—the elbow! And shoulder and then! Oh, abundant waterfalls, the figs of Babylon, hanging from the withered tree. Lechery!"

The husbands looked down and so did the wives, and the youth scrutinized their toes, recalling bushes, haylofts, pastures, even a bed or two. And even the gentlest virgins turned shades of rose, and so did several females of advanced age, who rather preferred to wilt than bloom.

The priest by now was positively *en flamme*, thrusting himself all over the chancel, making exclamations, many in mysterious Latin, known only to two learned members of the community, who asked not to be mentioned by name in this chronicle.

"*Luxuria, gula, avaritia, superbia, ira, acedia! Avaritia!* All this, all this . . ." Kumashko here attempted to climb the communion table, stumbled, and fell. It wasn't even Latin now but a guttural, primal, rapturous tongue that resembled nothing so much as Schweitzdeutch mixed with Pigmy and perhaps a dash of Eskimo-Aleut. "And now I'll tell you, and now I will pronounce!" And then he chuckled and grew quiet.

The speechlessness of the laity was so entire that borborygmus here and there was heard. A few began to clear their throats, and finally the Police Chief, being in charge of Odolechka's safety, spoke these brave words, "What shall we do to get the absolution, Father?"

The Mayor, in the first row, woke via a hard pinch from his spouse, Apollonia, a woman very near the coloring and posture of Lot's wife in her post-Lot years. But, as the Mayor was a shy man, reluctant to undertake any form of public performance, all she managed to elicit from him was a faint "oyoy?"

"Sacrifice!" The priest flung himself backward onto the priedieu and looked about with basilisk eyes.

What and/or who could be sacrificed? Visions of martyrhood

blossomed in many a head, especially those of certain religious and elderly dames. Who can say what self-mutilations might have followed had there not now occurred a loud thud, the source of which was not immediately apparent. Pious eyes looked to the heavens (or, as it were, the scaffolding for the forever-paused ceiling repairs); others fearfully glanced at the tattered kneeling cushions.

The thud turned out to be of noncelestial nature: the Mayor had merely collapsed on the speckled stone floor in the t-shaped languor of one cut down from the cross. This position inspired awe. Everyone gathered and leaned over the limp Mayor. Apollonia stood over him with Pontus Pilatic coolness . . . then realizing some reaction on her part was expected, she nudged his head with her slipper. A few spontaneous zealots started chanting. The baker's wife beat her breast in a floury flurry. It was hard to remain unaffected by the spreading elation. Apollonia's eyes, those slits of pale water-green, flared with inspiration. A little stroke, perhaps? Something to do with the Divine Design? Her sufferings rewarded, her prayers answered?

She knelt and took her husband's hefty head and turned it toward her own. Promisingly, only his eye-whites showed, but alas, his eyes then fell open, and he gazed at her with all of his familiar basset hound consciousness. A mere faint! She dropped his head. But not all was unhappy—a source of strength, the bulk of a Roman soldier, materialized beside her—the Police Chief! Unreluctantly, and not without a frantic pressing of her lissome hip against his thigh, she yielded her place by the convalescent. Soon her husband was pulled to a sitting position, the Doctor knocking on his knees and checking his teeth. That the

Mayor was undamaged disappointed everyone and undermined the priest's performance. The wailing stopped, the baker's wife ceased her breast-beating, and a scattered sniggering ensued, while some began to use the commotion to sneak toward the exit.

"Wait!" screamed the priest, but the doors had opened.

CHAPTER V

In which Barnabas ogles *groshkikrazny* melons and more

LET US DO A VOLTE-FACE TO BACK WHEN BARNABAS EXITED THE CHURCH. With due hauteur, he looked about his town in its beggarly glory: cottages of rotted wood, stork nests on the roofs, the central square of mud, the tavern and well at the square's center, the moldy stocks that had not been a form of punishment in decades, and the square full of stands and stalls, some already open, populated by the not-so-pious. Barnabas whisked to a food stall, where he speedily consumed a sausage and a salted herring and, thus fortified, prepared to begin his rescue of Roosha from the bestial robber baron Karol von Grushka.

Dreamily, he scanned the neighboring fruit stand's gooseberries and melons, looked away, then felt an eeriness at the edge of sense . . . something was amiss at the heart of being. He looked again into the fruit. Something amid the ruby *groshkikraznys* troubled his attention. Rows and rows of unassuming globes, then why did he feel he had entered a bad dream from childhood? Had he just seen Yurek's head? A glimpse of Yurek's streaked tiger eyes? A drooling chin glistening in the noonday sun? Clutching a sausage skewer, Barnabas tremblingly searched the fruit. No, it was just *groshkikraznys* after all. Yurek, Barnabas recalled, was safely incarcerated at the Troshku asylum, a windowless fortress surrounded by a moat, hundreds of kilometers away.

"Pierkiel!"

The sea-urchin hair and powdered face of Celestyn the barber approached across the square.

"Who's that?" Barnabas feigned shortsightedness.

"You good-for-nothing wretched good-for-nothing!"

This was not what a man liked to hear after eating his herring. Indignantly yet nonchalantly, Barnabas moved a bench between him and the barber, who was about to lunge at him across several crates of strawberry pottage. This barberous assault was thwarted by the appearance of Odolechka's three respectable spinsters, Basia, Daria, and Zhmiya, whose coiffed nods and handshakes Celestyn was obliged to return, but he did so glaring at Barnabas above the spinsters' heads and gesturing at Barnabas' gleaming hair.

"Oh that," muttered Barnabas with scorn. If there was one thing he despised, it was the greediness of local vendors. What carnage they were ready to cause for a few jars of unpaid-for brilliantine. Was it a man's fault that he had to style his hair? Was he to be publicly whipped for needing a shave? Obliterated for a drop of cologne and a puff of talc? Such sociological musings led Barnabas to where many thinking men arrive in the course of critical inquiry, that is, the tavern.

The square was filled with screws and scrolls and hooks, coal-mining picks and hammers, lace collars made by the blind Honorata nuns atop Tchjornamatka Mountain, bison-shaped crystal vases, pictures of the holy family with hydrocephalic Jesuses in the laps of pea-headed Josephs, zircon engagement rings, *matryoshkas*, amber and glass rosaries, fruits, vegetables, meats, knitted shawls, ear-flapped hats, and defiant farm animals—everything yelping, mooing, clanking, quacking, banging, knocking. An outsider might have been at risk of mental schism, but to Odolechkans, it was pleasantly melodious.

Not so to Barnabas. All this was no more than a nuisance slowing down his amorous pursuit. But it would not serve to be obvious. He would loiter at the bazaar's center and let Roosha come to him. As it happened, he had little time to loiter. Entering the mudflat front "garden" of the tavern, he accepted a stein from Anechka (whose beery bodice he ignored for the nine-hundredth time), watched her fill it with the local tannic brew, and drank until the sun of the stein's bottom burned above him.

He prepared to order more; meanwhile, in the no-man's-land between the beergarden and the bazaar proper, a buzzing agitation mounted. An old peasant narrowed her eyes as she leaned over her display of serviettes. Another affected extreme preoccupation with the tick in the ear of her heifer. The three spinsters clutched their six hands. Bags were unnecessarily shuffled and tables rearranged.

Roosha reentered her stall by the well, returning from who knew what mysterious errand. Barnabas, not to be distracted by the custom of paying for beer, leaped up, then, realizing he clutched the beer stein still, returned it to Anechka and set off again in

Roosha's direction, as unsteadily as a walking Pisa tower upside-down-cake (an idiom impossible to translate from Scalvusian), and feeling more and more like the time he had swallowed a putrescent crayfish tail.

So Barnabas stagger-sauntered toward her, prepared to produce, like a gem dealer his cabochons, the rehearsed and polished words of apology and devotion. Alas (not to disappoint the Pierkiel tradition of plummeting to Earth at least semi-regularly), just as he came within range, some thing or body struck him from behind.

CHAPTER VI

In which Odolechka is introduced to the automobile,
a technology hitherto largely in the domain of rumor

THERE ARE MEN IN THIS WORLD WHO DO NOT SIMPLY EXIST BUT WHO EXUDE
implicit challenge to the existence of other men, animals, even
certain objects. Karol von Grushka did not *sit* in a chair but
brought it to a state of complete submission. He did not *pet* his
hounds but throttled them good-naturedly. An action as ordinary as gripping utensils was an assertion of von Grushka's
thumbs and index fingers over inanimate matter. His clothes did
not simply cover his frame but yielded to it. This attitude found
its physiognomic reflection in his bulldog jowls, pectoral breadth,
and orange hair-tufts blazing from his ears.

On this day, having slaughtered two wild hogs, he had
returned early from his hunt, bathed, changed, arrived at the
bazaar, instructed his driver to park by the church (so that the
automobile would be conspicuous to those soon to exit the service), proceeded on foot to reconnoiter Roosha, and, in passing,

trampled Barnabas. Von Grushka had not particularly noticed this collision, accustomed as he was to objects exiting his path as quickly as they there appeared. He was, instead, ensorcelled by the sight of Roosha weaving a basket in her stall. Wicker swans and squirrels lay piled up by her sides. Her nimble fingers, Daphne-like, blurred into the willow wands she wove. Von Grushka longed to lick those fingers, suck the sap from their slender shafts, but to be too long even in the general vicinity of Roosha here, in sight of all, imperiled his reputation. To be considered were his dying wife, his hoped-for knighthood, and the good opinion of the village dignitaries, even if they all, combined, had a lesser net worth than he; that is, if the combined net worth of the Doctor, the Head Clerk, the Mayor, the Police Chief, and Kumashko was, as von Grushka had this morning casually calculated while sawing the tusks off a boar, approximately seven hundred billion thallers.

He arrived at Roosha's stall. "Morning," he mumbled, taken by the sudden inarticulateness that, it seemed, befell even the mightiest Odolechkans in Roosha's presence. Without waiting for a response, he beetled off and stooped behind a hay wagon, feigning a need to retie his shoe, a fine shoe of polished horse-leather, assembled at his factory a few kilometers upriver. Didn't he spend billions of thallers (Scalvusia was, in 1939, in a state of mori-bund inflation) on her upkeep? He visualized the velvet pumps in which she had planted some odious herbage, the cashmere shawl she had ripped off her neck during one of their quarrels and tossed beneath a moving oxcart.

"I, a military man, who just might someday enter politics. Do not cast pearls before gypsies!" he mussitated, walking on, and did not stop until he reached the churchyard, where he faced a peculiar sight. The Doctor and the Police Chief appeared to be carrying the Mayor bodily from the church. This failed to improve von Grushka's mood. Why was this man paraded about like a sultan? Von Grushka stepped backward, not eager to be associated with the grunting procession.

"The Mayor collapsed, pushed by God's thumb itself!" cried Apollonia.

"What's that?" said von Grushka, a little relieved to learn the occurrence was of a spiritual nature, a sphere in which he had no interest. He embraced the Mayor and kissed him on the cheeks five times, as the ancient Scalvusian custom dictates. Disengaging from the Mayor's three-day-old scruff, von Grushka glanced at his new automobile parked on the church's sacristy side. It was the only such machine in Odolechka, where everyone traveled in wagons or on horseback or assback. Oh, the sight of his new automobile, not two weeks off the assembly line! Indeed, von Grushka was nearly an auto-erotic, if you will allow me to sell you a second-hand pun.

"A miracle!" Apollonia spouted.

"Isn't it?" von Grushka said, considering the curves and lines of black metal and glass and chrome.

"The venerable father has conjured a sermon to make the angels tear out their angel hair!" she continued. "Some electric ghost o'ertook him, and he orated as no orator ever has before, not since Saint Peter. I saw the seraphs and God's own holy golden wheel of entirely silver fire above my head."

"My dear woman," said von Grushka, "one gold wheel? Four wheels of industrial rubber work so much better."

"My eyes blurred. My nose itched. I felt something stirring right in here." She pointed to her womb.

"God's will," confirmed the Mayor.

"Hold your tongue," Apollonia hissed in the ear of her despised spouse. "God comes speaking, and you faint."

"What was I supposed to do? Wooziness came upon me . . . There's no denying what's happening in the hay around the village, one would think it's some sort of heatwave." The Mayor rubbed his shabby chin with consternation. "As for the rest, it's everyone on their own."

"Everyone on their own! That's not my definition of civic responsibility!" she said, smiling at von Grushka. "We're all going to Hell!"

"To Hell?"

"To Hell, my dear poor Karol! The infernal gates opened before our eyes, and the Devil lured us toward the depths," Apollonia croaked. "The Devil whips, ties, and gags us."

"If we must go to Hell, let's all go in my new machina." Von Grushka placed his hands on the Mayor's shoulders, maneuvering him so that he faced the automobile. To von Grushka's embarrassment, the three spinsters, who had wandered from the tavern to the church, stood pressing their bosoms against the auto, believing it could bring good luck or husbands at last at least (these two were not to be conflated); meanwhile the Doctor, having passed the Mayor into von Grushka's hands, had arrived at the auto and, with a professional air, inserted his finger into the exhaust pipe. Von Grushka's bandy-legged driver Ivo, until yesterday a stableboy, feinted at the spinsters with a cotton candy stick to no effect, then climbed into the cockpit.

On the Odolechkans, being the better part of a century behind the rest of Europe in technology, Ivo's starting of the engine had an effect like Rozier and Marquis d'Arlandes' balloon had had on the Parisians when, in 1783, it soared above the Seine.

"Thisa . . . thisa . . . ," said the Police Chief. A crowd had gathered.

Von Grushka snorted with pleasure and dropped the Mayor entirely. "A Gippopotam 260394TYDCLS Suprasupra! Four-cylinder engine. 2545 overhead valve!"

The spectators received this oratory with the same stupefaction they had not long ago granted the priest.

"Large!" yelled someone.

"Black!" yelled someone just as clever.

"Valve?" said the Doctor.

"So impressive!" Apollonia twirled, delighted at her own accordion reflection in the waxed surface.

"It seems highly appropriate that we should take a ride," remarked the Mayor, regaining his feet.

Von Grushka took the front with Apollonia and Ivo. The Police Chief thumped onto the rear seat, his daunting fundament obliterating two-thirds of the available surface.

The Mayor fit himself in with less ease. (He and the Police Chief were two of the town's most imposing personages not only in terms of social status but also in terms of diameter.) "Could you please shift left a bit?" He poked at the Police Chief's thigh.

"Fraid not," the Police Chief said.

Perhaps because of Ivo's drunkenness (at the traditional level for carriage driving), perhaps because Ivo had been, until yesterday, a stableboy, they drove off the rutted red road into the admiring crowd, which dispersed like a gaggle of geese. They nearly hit the priest on his way out of the sacristy and, at the bottom of the church's lowly hill, knocked over a stall dedicated to the trade and sale of marinated meats.

CHAPTER VII

In which the Pierkiels consent to sell a duchess to a gypsy

WE RETURN TO OUR HERO, WHOSE PERSPECTIVE THE NEGLIGENT AUTHOR keeps abandoning. You will admit, after what has already come to pass, that Barnabas was not born lucky. The time has come to unveil some of the inauspicious events that the Pierkiel clan had endured since the Late Middle Ages, which is as far back as their lineage is traceable. The list is long and grueling and starts with the plague, when Fendrel Pierkiel, jaundiced and emaciated, one of the three Black Death survivors of his parish, was killed by one of the first dim rays of the Renaissance just as he made his second convalescent step from his hovel. His orphaned son Brom, one of the other two survivors, prospered in the survival business until the age of nineteen, when, not long after impregnating Genovefa the scullion, he was struck by lightning on a cloudless day while navel-gazing in the family radish field. Brom's son, Fendrel the Second, was lanced one balmy summer night by

a barmy Teutonic knight. Sudden deaths continued for the next
two dozen generations. Appendixes burst, hearts stopped mid-
snore, horses reared under riders.

Death wasn't the worst of it; limbs had a tendency to abandon their hosts, if not in a battle, then in a public square. One
unfortunate Pierkiel, a butcher's apprentice, lost an arm while
napping on a block of uncured ham. There was no shortage of
birth defects either. Antoniush Pierkiel was born with an extra
head atop his own, but with so little brains, one head would not
have been well filled.

In short, nothing terribly good happened to the Pierkiels, perhaps with the exception of Barnabas' great-great-grandfather,
who, though born a serf, was emancipated in 1848 and awarded
a barren (once radish-yielding) patch of land from his landowner
(the very same land in the family's possession now), but even
that came with such a high tax that it brought the whole family
near starvation.

No surprise, therefore, that von Grushka's shove sent Barnabas
face-first into the mud and thoroughly bescumbered Barnabas'
best and only suit. Our hero's body was undamaged. His pride,
however . . . he spent the next few days with his pigs, avoiding
human company.

Despite his years of shame on their account, he had a mature
and personal relationship with his drove. He spared no effort in
making their short lives as pleasurable as he could and even took
care to christen each animal after Scalvusia's royals, and not out
of disrespect to pigs or royals; to Barnabas' despair, the monar-
chy had been abandoned in the late nineteenth century in favor
of humdrum democracy, with only a few powerless princes still
rooting here and there.

Barnabas spent many an evening deep in such national classics as *The Eggcup of Countess Kurpuchnik*, the touching *Life of War, Life of Agriculture*, also *Corsetius: A Romance of the History of the Time of Stumpiswav the Brave*. A fictionalization of the life of Empress Sisi had inspired him to believe that, had the Habsburgs not fallen, he would have found his way to her court somehow. Indeed, in these monarchic moods, his equally fervent sympathy for Rudolf Vasilenko's populist antics did not seem to him particularly contradictory.

Lacking higher opportunity, Barnabas held his own court. There was rowdy King Gustav and tiny Princess Pelagia, longtailed Princess Kunegunda and Duchess Dorota with udders like black grapes.

Abject, having plummeted now twice in Roosha's presence, Barnabas mused on whether the mucky existence of Prince Kshyshtof was superior to the ignominious existence of Barnabas Pierkiel. It was time to return his pigs to their pen, time to complete the spring cleaning, which his grandmother had begun at dawn.

Barnabas sighed. All the comforters, pillows, the dirty old tapestry, and the musty carpet had to be beaten, the floors swept and cleaned, walls whitened, his suit washed, windows polished and furniture dusted, and, no matter how much work ensued, no later than a week from now, everything would return to its general muddle.

"Where you been, you scrawny finch?" His grandmother brandished a pair of pliers.

He ignored her, ushered the pigs into their pen, and then, on the southern side of the fence, where the pines grew in uneven clusters, he saw . . . a wood haunt, a woman?

"Here was I, pulling my tooth"—Grandmother clacked the pliers—"when *she* came. Standing there and staring at the pig-pen, mute as your dead great-stepmother Halenka, she is!"

A rag cloak covered the visitor from neck to dirty toes. Beads and amulets trailed from her wrists, and a fuzzy stack of brown-black hair collapsed onto one shoulder. Recognizing her as Tsura, Roosha's sister, Barnabas nervously licked his finger, smoothed his sideburns, and advanced toward her across the yard, halting at a safe distance. Uncanny stories circulated about Roosha's sister; some said she had been a changeling child, found under a pile of peas. She, it was gossiped, not Roosha, was the one more skilled in secret *magiya*. With one glance at a person's tongue, she was able to tell what he had put into his stomach. She judged souls from looking at tonsils and threw handfuls of enchanted bulgur on a chosen victim's doorstep. But to see her person was a rarity in Odolechka, as she hardly ever left Roosha's house, and if so, then only to roam the woods and pastures.

"I'd ask you in, but the southern gate's broke since that Horchensky got drunk and stole my wire to build rabbit traps," said Grandmother, wary as she was of hocus-pocus.

"I saw a black stag in the daisy field," said Tsura. "Blacker than what happens to who looks sideways at my sister."

"A black stag?" whispered Grandmother.

"There's been one rummaging around," Tsura said.

Grandmother crossed herself and spat.

"Right by Umarlu Grove," said Tsura, "and it jumped at me, so big I thought it was the *turlak*."

"I'm sorry you suffered a fright, Miss Tsura. Normally, it's best to travel with a man in that part of this part of the world," Barnabas said, quite gallantly he thought, at the same time noticing the pigpen exhaled an unbearable odor. "Out by Umarlu Grove, you shouldn't be alone, not when you're a lady, that includes yourself, because you are one, a lady, naturally."

"Barnabas, hush. What's the *turlak?*" Grandmother triple-crossed herself thrice.

"The *turlak* is what happens to a baby, not one of ours, a Scalvusian child, when the mother speaks beneath her breath about what happens in the caravans. The child dies and wakes up under the roots of the churchyard weed called *turlachvast.* Roots of the weed dig up the child. And the child grows long and large. *That's* a *turlak.*"

"What happens in your caravans?" asked Grandmother with diminishing fear and increasing suspicion.

"Don't ask, or your baby boy here might wake up with the tendril of the weed root in his pretty nose, tickling him from a sleep that's black as stags."

"Get your curses talk away," said Grandmother. "We don't want any weed baby or what you say."

"Roosha wants to buy a sow," said Tsura. "The maddest one you have." As if upon some mystical insight into the speech of the superior species, Duchess Dorota, asleep in slurry, woke with a grunt and raced across the pen and struck her forehead on a post.

From reading the romances of Lady Kurpuchnik, Barnabas understood that mercantile pretexts, possibly even pig purchasings, were, in certain cases, used by women, those elusive creatures, to lure desired suitors.

"This one." Tsura confirmed, pointing at the Duchess. "Roosha wants it now."

Grandmother said, "She has money?"

Seeing the pile of wrinkled cash Tsura gathered from her skirts, Grandmother rushed to the gate. "You come in!"

"No thank you, *bobochka*." Tsura passed the money through the fence and glided toward the woods.

Barnabas, inside already, buttoned his best shirt, donned his jacket, lamented the loss of the family shard of mirror so many years ago, and, despite the urgency Tsura had suggested, spent close to twenty minutes examining his face in a pan of water, and then another half hour engaged in anti-pen-odor ablutions from that very pan. Even Borys Polensky, that gentleman of genius and decorum, would have been proud.

CHAPTER VIII

In which no man who hath his stones broken shall
come nigh to offer the offerings of the Lord

"AM I NOT THE SLAVE OF GOD?" SAID KUMASHKO THE PRIEST TO HIS
schnapps, then emptied the bottle into himself. "Deuteronomy
15:16! 'If, however, a slave is content to be with you and says I
shall not leave you, I love you and your family then take an awl
and pierce it through his ear to the door and he will be your
slave for life.' "

Kumashko searched his bedroom for an awl. He opened the
armoire, pulled out its four drawers, and emptied them onto the
floor. He dug through the objects there deposited—his wrinkled
priestly apparel, a calf-whip given him by Daria the spinster for
anointing her dachshund, two sardine cans, myriad empty and
half-empty bottles of schnapps, a coil of inedible hemp rope given
him by Lechoswava the sausage-rope maker as a thank-you gift
for blessing one hundred *kielbasas*—but there was, to be certain,
no awl. Finally, underneath one sock, this being a present from

Kowalchyk the tailor for marrying his sister to a Russian Orthodox shepherd, Kumashko found a mangled fork.

He gripped the fork in his spasmic hand, lurched to his bedchamber door, and, in one motion, forked his ear to the door and screamed for a minute.

Now he stood immobile, half whimpering, half relishing the holy anguish in his earlobe. But the worrisome thoughts about the fig tree and Jesus' reasons for killing it returned soon enough. Kumashko's moral downfall had been triggered by this very inability to reconcile certain contradictions in the Good Book. "Why did he kill the fig tree?" he wailed, ripped the fork free with a jerk of his head, and banged his head against the door, the fork hanging still from his ear. "Why did Jesus kill the fig tree?" He repeated this centerpiece of his discontent, a discontent that had been deepening for several months, approximately since his thirty-seventh birthday. He felt old, too young to be a wiseman, unrespected, undervalued, brilliant yes, but fettered by circumstance. Something had darkened and soured in the once-limpid depths of his brain. Paranoia had set in. He wondered if the Faith had somehow dwindled since the fifteenth century. Why hadn't he traveled the world in his twenties and seen if this was true? Why hadn't he, or any priest he knew, gone barefoot to Rome?

Sinful images of distant female nudity, proximate female nudity, upper female nudity, rear female nudity, upper male nudity, and rear male nudity crusaded through his battered head. He envisioned Anechka the barmaid, as he had seen her once through a keyhole at her father the Doctor's house (he had been there to see about his laryngitis, and having grown bored of the Doctor's reading material, primarily blasphemy of the technical sort, had opted to peer about), pulling her stocking back on and smoothing it along her thigh.

"Sinful!" He dropped onto his hands and knees and obtained from beneath his bed the bulletless heirloom blunderbuss he kept there in case of intruders. He rolled onto his back and held the blunderbuss in one hand and his cassock aloft with the other, preparing to crush his genitals with the blunderbuss-butt.

Wistfully regarding said genitals for the last time, he remembered a passage that had always made him feel strangely hopeful, as it did especially now: "Deuteronomy 23:1. 'He that is wounded in the stones, or hath his privy member cut off, shall not enter into the congregation of the Lord.'"

With a moan, he dropped the blunderbuss onto the rug, jumped onto his bed, and thrashed impressively, then sat on the bed's edge and looked around his room with quiet disappointment. It was hardly an ascetic's chamber. A table that displayed the Good Book was adorned with carved pineapples. Any pineapples in Eden? What relation the pineapple to the fig?

"Why did Jesus kill the tree?" he asked Beelzebub, who surely, he reasoned, was present, invisible, and listening. He took from the sideboard another schnapps. His dipsomania, pacing his paranoia and depression, had progressed over the last few months, and yet had brought no progress in the question of the fig tree. Beelzebub evidently harbored little interest in this or any other theological problem, but rather sat, Kumashko imagined, swinging his hooves from the edge of the pineapple table and picking his sixth and seventh noses with the points of his scorpion tail. The priest snatched the Good Book off the unholy table and, drinking schnapps, rescrutinized some passages marked with strips ripped from a *Krool Gazeta* (the best, worst, and only periodical our erstwhile capital boasted in 1939), passages that would not leave him any peace.

Genesis 17—he read aloud: "And when Abram was ninety years old and nine, the Lord appeared to Abram, and said unto him, I am the Almighty God; walk before me, and be thou perfect. And I will make my covenant between me and thee, and will multiply thee exceedingly. And Abram fell on his face: and God talked with him, saying, 'As for me, behold!' "

Kumashko beheld. He stared at the chair across the room and grew hopeful for a moment, noticing a very real depression in the cushion, until he remembered the Police Chief had called on him yesterday to ask about the Lord's opinion of onions and other "light" foods.

Deuteronomy 23 still in mind, Kumashko turned to another marked passage, Leviticus 21: "For whatsoever man he be that hath a blemish, he shall not approach: a blind man, or a lame, or he that hath a flat nose, or any thing superfluous. Or a man that is brokenfooted, or brokenhanded. Or crookbackt, or a dwarf, or that hath a blemish in his eye, or be scurvy, or scabbed, or hath his stones broken. No man that hath a blemish of the seed of Aaron the priest shall come nigh to offer the offerings of the Lord."

He scuffed in his socks to the mirror and, with growing horror, examined the beginnings of a cataract in his right eye. He noticed also that, though he was only arguably dwarfish, he looked more than a little scurvy, but how was that his fault, when Artur the greengrocer hadn't stocked citrus in over a year?

"Blemish of the seed of Kumashko the priest!" screamed Kumashko the priest at the priest in the mirror, who, he saw, had scabs on his forehead from stumbling home from the church, drunk after midnight the night before, and, it could not be denied, the nose in the mirror was flatter than a *nalashnik* and probably superfluous. As to the stones . . . why not complete his damnation, if everything else on him was aberrant. He veered drunkenly and tried to smash his left testicle with a new half-empty schnapps bottle, but it was hard to target. He swung and swung, battering his thighs, the precious schnapps pouring out with each blow.

He gave up and regarded his schnappsy rug with new, profounder melancholy, until a yet profounder thought began to manifest. He was entering some antechamber of understanding with regard to the fig tree. He sniffed in the direction of the pine-apples of Eden. "Why *did* Jesus kill the fig tree? The only tree I know of truly is myself, for who can say more than *cogito ergo sum*? And why am I the tree? Because I bear no fruit!" He sprawled on his rug, digesting this revelation, which led him to recall from Revelation 17: "And here is the mind which hath wisdom. The seven heads are seven mountains, on which the woman sitteth."

"Sinful!" he said, then crawled across his rug and bent over the contents of his armoire and picked up the calf-whip, the sardine cans, the coil of rope, the sock, and crawled to the table and stood and took the Good Book and left his house, then returned, picked up the bloody fork, and left again.

CHAPTER IX

In which Barnabas receives a lesson on the subject of *the will*

PIERKIELIAN LUCK HAD IT THAT JUST AS BARNABAS, AS CONFIDENT AS SAINT George en route to the dragon, rode toward Roosha's house (just as Kumashko was leaving his own), Karol von Grushka sped, with greater speed and style, from the direction of his residence on the respectable Right Bank of the Viluga River. His wife had leeches put behind her ears and committed herself to bed for the day, and von Grushka had decided he'd sneak away for a quick rendezvous with his concubine.

Roosha had driven von Grushka beyond the Pale of Unsettlement, if you will, well into the Imperial Russia of Frustration. When, last week, he had arrived to take her to the Philharmonic in the capital, he had found her buried under a duvet in a mood as sour as *piklovanegzhuby*, so that, instead of the divine Popin's First Piano Concerto, he had spent a delightful evening listening to her mellifluous sniffs. Ailments she had not cared to describe or name had prevented her mouth from being kissed. She had presented him, interchangeably, with hand and foot, then sent him off to town on foot because she absolutely needed camphor and bonbons, and upon his return (with only camphor), he had found her, kind soul, resuscitating Yoosef the postman (who had clearly fainted, probably in admiration of the Gippopotam, while delivering the "evening mail," which, Yoosef had explained, was a new National Scalvusian Postal development) in the tulip bed.

"If Yoosef weren't a peasant," von Grushka ruminated out loud in his cockpit, "I might imaginably be suspicious, but no one of lower social status than myself could put the antlers on von Grushka."

As von Grushka drove into the muddy lane, he saw a boy forcing a sow through the garden gate. A young, handsome fellow hard at work! Nothing inspired von Grushka more than energetic youth. He stepped from his car and aided our hero by solidly planting a boot in the Duchess' hindquarters.

"Fine specimen. Good speck! Good gammons," he began, offering a specialized judgment of the animal (too detailed and pedantic to be given further length in this chronicle), which now attacked Roosha's garden in a frenzy of nibbling and sniffing. The boy, though undoubtedly opinionated about pigs, stared in silence at his ragged shoes.

Von Grushka was accustomed to making strong impressions on young country boys. He smiled indulgently. He thought he'd try a simpler style of pig discussion: "What is this you've brought here, then?"

"A pig."

"How about this pony here? Is it for sale, too?" Von Grushka indicated Wilhelm.

"What pony?"

"This fine tall one here." Von Grushka patted Wilhelm's flank.

"Not a pony. Not for sale," said Barnabas.

"There's a price for everything. As I learned in military school, when a boy's pants are stolen at night by the other boys—"

"There's no price for my horse," interrupted Barnabas. "And if you continue in this mockery, sir, I'll demand satisfaction!"

"Feisty youth, feisty! That's the attitude I like." He thudded Barnabas on the back. "You remind me of myself when I was your age."

"You?!"

"Yes!"

"Impossible! From which side?" Barnabas offered his left profile, then his right.

"Piss and vinegar and *benzina*! I like your demeanor."

"My what?"

"I'm jesting. I'm fiercely fond of animals, too. Even rats and muskrats. I enjoy the cultivated pleasures of hunting. The soft doe tasting the clover, the sulfur aroma after the bullet's been fired, the doe mangled at your feet. To take her into your arms. To count her little bones, to play with her vertebrae. Superb. Venison with noodles, for example."

Roosha stepped out onto the balcony. "I see you've brought your entourage."

"Greetings! What a splendid barometric pressure we have this afternoon!" Von Grushka bellowed. "A day on which a headache is impossible."

Roosha leaned against the railing. No detail was lost to von Grushka's connoisseur eye: the outward bend of her knee in her skirts, the delicate line of her neck, the Carmen carmine of her mouth.

She raised her hands to her hair and gathered it into a knot. "Is it?"

"Is it what?"

"So splendid?" She allowed her hair to fall. "Barometers are tedious. Who's been to the Dead Sea?"

Von Grushka glanced at the boy, who turned pale and shuffled his feet bizarrely, almost like an old woman stomping grapes in a barrel. Did this boy know about his affair?

"Well, Miss Roosha, if you don't mind me saying, seeing you on such a lovely day would lift the most miserable and slavish spirits. Look at this perfectly adequate sun!" Von Grushka pointed at the clouds. "Look at this fauna below your feet." He pointed at the dust-bathing Duchess. "I hope there's nothing ailing you, Miss Roosha. Not even a Russian could suffer on a day like this." He glanced at Barnabas. Certainly the boy was too dim to be any trouble. No one knew. (Everyone did.) But was this pigboy all right? Stomping and shuffling one moment, the next leaning against the fence with theatrical dignity, the boy did look a bit deranged. Mouth and foot disease?

Von Grushka took a prudent step sideways away from Barnabas and said, "I always like to come here and collect the rent. Miss Roosha is as good a tenant as a man could ask. Who says the Romani don't rent?!"

"I don't bother with suffering. I simply refuse." Roosha trailed her ringed hand along the railing. "I take after my grandmother Tschilaba. She was an unfortunate woman. As a child, she was accidentally fed a spoonful of cursed moose's milk. She never fully recovered. Then she pushed a bean into her nostril. She saw the best gypsy laryngologist in Sarajevo, but he couldn't get it out. She spent her life suffering, the bean blooming in her nose every spring. I never heard her utter a complaint, it's a matter of disposition. She was also buried twice, the poor *bobochka*. Luckily, the first time she had a rope tied to her toe. It was attached to a bell, and the graveyard guard heard her. That was the first luck she had in her life. Then of course, she died a month later, this time successfully."

"Just like *my* family!" Barnabas exclaimed from the fence.

"This young man here delivered a pig!" Von Grushka pointed at the Duchess rooting by the fence.

"Oh?" she said to Barnabas. "This family of yours, are they a stumbling lot? Often to be found at low altitudes?"

Barnabas mumbled.

"So your folk are from the lowlands," interpreted von Grushka. "Swineherds, I presume?"

"For generations." Barnabas nodded. "Before that, they were radish farmers."

"Starvation and poverty? Pest and filth? People living together with livestock in one barn? Poor young man. Courage! There is a way out of an offal heap," said von Grushka, "with hard work and perseverance."

"I eat every day," the boy protested. "I eat from a tureen. With fork and knife."

"Tureen, indeed. It wasn't easy for me either. Especially during my school days. When I was a young boy, someone stole my ink bottle. Twice. Then, at the Akademy, right before my final examination, I accidentally sat on an anthill. By the time I was aware of this, I was in front of the learned commission, but I carried out my will. Will! Do you know what that is, what *the will* is? I didn't betray myself with one twitch. I knew that each man faces a trial. He fails or not. He proves his worth or doesn't. He's a man or a weakling. A winged hussar or a tit-sucking babe. I remember, like yesterday, the question was about the April Insurgence. Not that the ants didn't burn and itch, but I spoke at length. I spoke of Shavanchak, that supreme commander, and by the time I got to his arrest by the czarists, tears, not effeminate tears, but tears for the loyal dead, were streaming down my cheeks. But I didn't scratch myself, not even once! I turned the enemy into the ally, you see—" Von Grushka stopped in astonishment.

Roosha had gone inside.

"Young fellow," said von Grushka, "I have an important professional business to attend to upstairs, but I see you are in trouble. Remember, whatever bothers you now, it will build your stamina tomorrow. Whenever you doubt, think about my anthill ordeal. If you'd like to hear the rest of the story, please come by my factory." He dug into his pockets and shoved a messy ball of wrinkled cash into Barnabas' arms. "For the pig, also the piss, vinegar, and *benzina*."

CHAPTER X

In which Barnabas discovers an arboreal abomination

IT WAS AFTER TWO A.M. WHEN BARNABAS WALKED HOME. NOWHERE HAVE I witnessed nights as black as those in Odolechka. Even a sober Scalvusian would have had trouble navigating in this gloom.

Barnabas, after a liter of Kashak's moonshine, swerved left to right, front to back, front left to back right, and so on. "Who? Mr. Andryoshka? Never heard of you. Need anything? M-medicine? I am a shoe maker. A shooo maker." He tripped and cackled. "Just don't come too close, Mr. von Grussso. I can't answer for myself. I'm a pugilist, no?" Barnabas' knees mutinied, and he knelt on the path. What a noise! Had someone opened an armoire? He blessed thrice his burbling stomach, his knees, and the forest path. "True, I hurt my leg getting the water out of maaa ear. Sprained it, jumping over an anthill. Ants ... Wilhelm? Where are you?" He felt the ground in search of the harness, vaguely remembering he had left Wilhelm back at the tavern. "I'll come and get you, little Wilhelm, yes, like a meteoroot that fell from the heavens." But Barnabas was queasy and required a brief rest. "Tie a knot on the side of his head, and he'll be just fine, side of me heaaad." He was asleep across the path.

I will use this moment, while poor Barnabas grapples with Morpheus, to assure you our hero was a man of strong morals. Tsura had already paid him for the Duchess. Besides, he'd never have accepted money from an enemy. After von Grushka had gone inside Roosha's house, Barnabas disdainfully tossed the thaller notes into a tulip bed. And yet, was it wise to leave money out for the Duchess Dorota to chew and the peacock to trample? Should von Grushka be permitted to *accumulate* until the mints run out of paper? Didn't the precious thallers rightfully belong to the disadvantaged, the morally wronged? The forsaken? The unappreciated? Wouldn't Rudolf Vasilenko himself agree? Volodek certainly would. (A pleasure or not, you shall meet Volodek before long.) Money in the mud was money for all. Persuaded thus, Barnabas had stealthily retrieved each note, taken these public notes to their natural habitat, the public house, and had not risen from the tavern's splintery stool until Anechka's bodice contained the total worth of one twice-sold pig.

Barnabas woke with a sneeze, stood in the predawn gloom, said thoughtfully, "Sprained my ear," and walked off the path, across a pasture. *Sprewzhyna* grasses' tight loops caught his ankles, and he stumbled, stood, and zigzagged on until he reached a long wall of oaks. A wooden structure stood with its back to the oaks, divided into quarters by what seemed to be a pair of great black wings.

"Lived here my whole life, haven't I?" Baffled, Barnabas stared at the building. "Maybe it's a haunted ... oh, the mill."

He giggled. Just the old windmill, on the other side of which was the ditch in which Kashak had crashed his bicycle the same year the three spinsters' now dead goat gave miraculous birth at the age of nineteen. And yet something was the matter. It was as if Barnabas had seen something disturbing and had looked away and now refused to let himself admit what he had seen. His stomach twinged, as if from fear.

"That's where they make flour. Just ground grains. Nothing to fear. In maa ear." He was a brave man. The mill didn't frighten him. He had devoured loaves every day with perfect composure. He remembered, years ago, his mother kissing a scrap of bread after it had fallen onto the ground, an old Scalvusian custom.

"Lived here my whole life." And yet, he felt as he had at the bazaar, when he thought he had seen Yurek in the melons. It was something in periphery . . . to the left, off in the oaks. He looked, belched, quickly looked away, and felt as if he'd seen a thing that could not be and thus had seen no thing at all. This nonseeing grew stronger and stronger. What was he nonlooking at? He approached the anomalous shape. It looked as if a human foot were growing from a rotting trunk.

One of the dead Russians rumored to haunt the woods? Just last week Volodek had reported a sighting of one of them loading a handheld cannon with a corncob.

"Corncob," Barnabas whined and nearly fled, but nothing can deter a curious Pierkiel. (For example, Bzhezdobna Pierkiel followed Napoleon's army across the Nemen River, not because she was a camp follower, not at first at least, but because she was dying, literally, as it turned out, to know what so many Frenchmen would do when it began to snow.) Barnabas invoked all twenty-three apostles. The wind shifted the boughs; there was a quiet thunk. Approaching, he saw, to his relief, it was no more than the pale fruiting body of a tree fungus. Barnabas bent forward with interest. Perhaps it was edible. He squawked, jumped back in revulsion, then bent forward again. It was a fungus *and* a foot.

Five toes. A heel. A human foot! Barnabas stared at the misplaced appendage. It seemed to levitate a centimeter above the fallen trunk. The heel of it touched a tree fungus, such that they seemed a single fungus. Barnabas tasted beer, garlic, rye bread, paprika, beef, cheese, cabbage, sausage, and a few other things he had eaten. He dared not think what was above the foot. He dared not think of the pale calf, knee, and thigh and then . . . he had seen a corpse or two in his life: Uncle Gregosh, who had fallen from his roof and snapped his neck while trying to sneak back into the house without waking Aunt Malvina, also Grandfather Borivoi, when they had finally reassembled him in his coffin. Barnabas preferred relatives, and persons in general, to be not dead when he saw them.

"Rye bread," he whined, wishing he were still at the tavern. How gladly he'd welcome the damp refuge of Anechka's cleavage now. "I saw nothing. I went to the tavern, then fell asleep somewhere."

But he could not stop looking at the foot. Was a stranger's foot dangling in the woods his responsibility? "No. A man is responsible only for his own feet and his pigs . . . and his lady love's feet, maybe . . . and her pigs, if she has any."

A hem of black fabric hung above the ankle. Barnabas, to his own supreme surprise, gripped the ankle and pulled. It felt like

touching the cold slab of pork fat that Grandmother hung outside for tomtits in winter. Barnabas let go of the leg and furiously
wiped his hand in the underbrush. The body was somehow
caught, not to be pulled down, but it swayed now, in and out of
the shadows, and Barnabas glimpsed a face in the oakleaves. Its
features had become those of a squeezed rubber doll, but it was
not beyond recognition.

CHAPTER XI

In which the Police Chief must perform
a duty of some importance

THE POLICE CHIEF AWOKE SLOUCHED ACROSS A MILKING STOOL IN THE
corner of his office. For ten or so minutes, he listened to the morning lament of his intestines, distressed as they were by a new dra-
conian diet, entirely of radishes and lard, forced upon him by his
Secretary. He had been a large boy who'd become a rather larger
man. He had been subjected to sundry Scalvusian weight-loss
techniques since childhood: his mother had hung him from the
ceiling by suspenders, coated his belly in mustard, forced him to
spend at least two hours per day in the outhouse. Nothing could
help him. He stretched his back (sore from hauling the priest
down from the oak and then from passing out across a stool
with too much vodka in his gut) and stood and leaned above the
Mayor, who lay snoring on the sofa. Wasn't he a little lamb?
Perhaps the Police Chief should not disturb the sleep of this
innocent.

He sat down at his desk and began the day's work by envisioning Kumashko starving in Hell. Inspired by this, he dug under a stack of police reports (all of them affairs of some importance, especially the recent rash of unsolved, high-speed horseback moonings on dark country roads, also the disappearance of the barber Celestyn's nannygoat), in search of a stale knish. Here it was. With stealthy tenderness, glancing at the door behind which his Secretary surely snooped, the Police Chief sampled the knish. Mastication brought a certain clarity of thought: what would be the demoralizing consequences of Kumashko's action on the Odolechkan citizenry? This had to be handled with delicacy, assurance, and exactitude.

"Mayor." Gently the Police Chief stroked the Mayor's scruffy cheek.

"Sensual mouth, fisherman's boots, and voluptuous arms," the Mayor mumbled, slapping the Police Chief's hand.

"What?"

"Good morning," said the Mayor, now awake. "Where is my tripe porridge?"

"What do we do with this? Worse than the scandal of Ahab and Jezebel," the Police Chief said, retreating to his desk to pick a few uneaten knish crumbs off it. "Something—how do you say it?—*political*, by which I mean the opposite of everybody knowing all about it, must be done."

"I don't see how. Dead is dead. What specks of what are you eating there? Where is *my* breakfast?"

"But how? And why did he do it? Also who could be so troubled in this town?" the Police Chief asked, pointing with authentic feeling at the landscape in the window: a strand of murky sky, three middle rungs of a ladder leaned against the window, and hectare upon hectare of cabbage fields crammed with manure. "And how do we interpret the cow-whip wrapped around the sardine can? Who takes such a thing with him up into a tree at night? If such a thing got out to the public . . . what does it say of our community? I'd be ruined. You'd be ruined. We'd be disreputated."

"Listen," said the Mayor, "I don't know about you or your disreption, but God spoke through me last Sunday." He scratched his pate. "Maybe that swineherd who found him left the cow-whip. Maybe we can say it was a pig-whip."

"I will solve this, or I am not worthy of my ancestors, the nomadic Kooza shepherds." The Police Chief picked his baton up and thumped it against the sofa's arm. "Also don't worry about that swineherd. I explained it to him. He told me he wasn't even there, that he was sleeping on his horse, whatever that might mean. The boy was drunker than we were last night, anyway."

"Stop talking about it," the Mayor moaned. "You're hurting my kidney stones."

"Perhaps this can be to our advantage, handled right. Remember when Jesus, three years ago, showed his image in Mrs. Yayechko's curd? Oh, how we feared excommunication then!"

"Yes, though it was I who identified the Savior!"

"Remember," said the Police Chief, "how the bishop from Krool gazed at it through his monocle and confirmed it was our God's only true son, flesh and blood! Those were the days of glory for Odolechka."

"Only if that blasphemous Yayechko hadn't devoured the curd." The Mayor yawned.

"What does it matter now? No other miracle will be sanctified in a village where priests hang from trees."

"We'll be the disgrace of the voivodeship!" the Mayor chirped.

The Police Chief, at this moment, noticed and envied his friend's suspenders, far finer than any he now owned or from which he had hung in childhood. "I'll tell you the truth, Mayor, we just can't afford a new scandal after you-know-what." He made a troubled, bovine face, referring to Migdawovynos the convict, who had managed to escape the one-room village jail. "How could we have known he was hiding in the sheepfold, I ask you? A disgrace to my ancestors, the nomadic Kooza shepherds. What am I, clairvoyant? How embarrassing they'd catch him the second he crossed into Poland."

The Mayor hid behind a piece of paper he had fetched from his trousers. He pretended, the Police Chief saw, to study it with pouty diligence. There was no text on it, however, only *Parovchaki* written across it in yellow, a brand of frankfurters. The Mayor emitted an incoherent exclamation, very much like a sob.

"Friend!" said the Police Chief with concern. He knew the Mayor was a shy man, hesitant to trust people ("except he does trust the Police Chief, me, that is," the Police Chief thought), and that the slightest criticism threw the Mayor into frantic states of self-effacement, during which he hid in his shed. "Mayor, don't despair! You can rely on me. You know that. I've proven it to you over your many terms. I am an able man. How did I become the Police Chief? I've always had my plate the right side up."

The Police Chief's Secretary kneed open the door, bringing on a battered tin tray his breakfast of two larded radishes. Also on the tray was a sealed envelope. He was about to toss it into the

pile of unopened mail behind the rhododendron when he noticed
a greasy thumbprint on the missive. He tore it open at once.

I challenge you to the bigoses contest in one hour.
                                            —Head Clerk.

The Police Chief eyed the radishes. "I must perform a duty of
some importance," he announced.

CHAPTER XII

In which Apollonia wrestles with her soul
and with Nanushka's husband

"PRINCE OF DARKNESS," APOLLONIA GRUNTED, PERFORMING HER TWENTIETH
chin-up on the overhead bar. She dropped to the floor, starched
knickers and burlap corset damp from her exertions, and walked
to the bed. She stroked her favorite dress, a mourning frock that
her paraplegic grandmother Mshchiswava always wore when
crawling up nearby Virgin Maria Mountain on her annual pilgrimage. Today, touching the sanctified garment did not quite
provide the spiritual enrichment a pious woman requires. Apollonia sniffled, picked up from the bedside table a paperweight figu-
rine of a human heart, and threw it at the portrait of the Mayor's
great-grandfather Anatol. She could not, at this moment, bear the
sight of any man's face, except the sweet, emaciated visage of the
Lord on the crucifix on the opposite wall, with whom she now
exchanged tormented smiles. The struck swaying portrait of Anatol fell onto *The Melancholy Labors of the Spleen: An Account of*

the Surgical Profession, Its Triumphs as Well as Its Best Efforts.
Not even her favorite tome, normally so pacifying, could appease
her now. She was an abused woman. Apollonia picked up a garlic
head from her bureau and bit into it. This, too, failed to uplift her.
She exited the house and kicked her gander in the neck.

"First the priest damned, now the Police Chief. May God save
the reeking vapors of their souls! *Someone* has to keep Kumashko's torch lit in this village, damned or not, *someone* must relate
the Good Bad News." She waved her hand, as if to disperse some
hellish effluvia. She ran inside and counted her ribs in the mirror
in the foyer, recalling the events of that morning . . .

She had stood, in the holy Mshchiswava's dress, near the
washbasin, in Ludvik the grave digger/notary's shack, the Doctor
tapping the deceased priest's knees with a petrified egg affixed to
a hammer-handle, the kneecaps protruding from the greenish
legs like two *Amanita muscaria*. (All Odolechkans were cursed,
that much was clear. But Apollonia sensed Hell had prepared for
her a damnation uniquely heinous. She visualized a winged scro-
tum flying through Hell's sleevelike tunnels of bloody lace.) Just
then the door to the grave digger's shack had opened, and in lumbered a Golgotha of flesh. Her hands flew up—some *michnook*
gust entered her womb, propelling her forward, so that she
pressed against this monstrosity, this mountain.

"Excuse me, Apollonia, good morning," said the Police Chief.

"How dare you shove yourself against me."

"What?"

"Like this!" She pressed her hipbones to his stomach.

"Jezebel! I did no such a-thing."

"You did, you did, I saw it in your walrus eyes," she said,
rubbing up-up and down-down against the Police Chief's front.

"Hanged!" The Doctor pronounced his verdict from the bed where Kumashko lay stiffening.

"Is that all?" The Police Chief dared to maneuver away from her.

"Well, no," said the Doctor, "also, one ear pierced. Four times."

"You have sinned, originally and unoriginally," Apollonia croaked . . .

But that was all this morning. She resumed counting her ribs, examined her torso for injuries resulting from the filthy interaction with the Chief, returned to her boudoir, donned Mshchiswava's garment, and proceeded to the kitchen. The Mayor had gone to play glass *koogel* with von Grushka's wife, and Apollonia had sent her maid home early as punishment for having failed to clean a mousetrap. She looked in the icebox—nothing of interest—and went out the kitchen door to the veranda, determined to find a practical occupation to ease her agony. A brief fuss with her collection of sacramental wine corks? A jog to, up, and down the Tchjornamatka Mountain? Stomping around the town square with ash on her forehead?

She decided on a quick *matioshka-dig-a-dig*. She put on her clogs and clogged to her garden, where, from amid the tomato plants (last year's winner of the much-coveted Smerdeck's Prize at the voivodeship annual fair), she picked up her *matioshka*. She dug until her arms gave out, then sat on the edge of her ditch, studying the crop of worms, trying not to think of the tortures awaiting her in the afterlife. Apollonia clutched the *matioshka*, tears on her chalky cheeks.

Ah, the ambience of Odolechkan dusks: the cries of hungry goats, Kashak's distant drunken wife-berating, and the whistle of the train that flew by the edge of Dudrovski's farm, never to stop in the stationless village. Underneath all this, she heard an unfamiliar cooing, as if somewhere someone were reciting love poems?

Even in the face of eternal damnation, Apollonia was a genteel soul. She listened carefully . . . determining, to her terrified delight, the recitation emanated from her chicken coop. Wielding the *matioshka* (for defense, of course, as poets have been known to do ungodly things), Apollonia crept across the lawn, along the carrot beds. She jumped over the cauliflower patch. Here was the bard! Hands raised, hair in disarray, he stood on the coop's roof.

"Shekspier?" she inquired.

The poet kicked her in the eyebrow. She fell, and he hopped onto the ground beside her. Apollonia, merely momentarily stunned, clasped the poet's foot and performed what they in wrestling patois call a "banana split." After some violent grappling, she managed to immobilize the poet's head between her thighs. When he stopped wriggling, she bent and looked at him upside down—not at all what a woman liked to find under her dress. His hair was a nest of kasha, dried blood, duck feathers, tar, and insect eggs.

"No more kicks or verses!" she threatened.

"Burp," he said.

"No fancy allegorizing."

"Brings his wife," came the muffled response.

"Your wife? Where is she? In the coop?"

"Her is she." He pointed to a figure Apollonia had not noticed during the combat. There stood the wife, beside the coop, brown-haired and green-eyed. Though Apollonia was not impressed, I must say for her husband's sake, the bride exhibited a certain noblesse of visage. Folded over the ribbon tastefully tied around her head, a pair of longish ears contributed to her allure.

"This nannygoat?"

"We just us married."

"What were you doing atop my coop? Stealing hens?"

"Honeymoon, ur-bum," he whined.

This excused him somewhat. Romance was romance, even to Apollonia. "What's your name?"

"Yurk."

"What's *her* name?"

"Nanushka."

"Yurk and Nanushka." She sighed, and something stirred in her womb. This organ, though past fifty years of age, remained emotional, opinionated.

"Kick me again, and I'll smash you with my *matioshka*." She loosened her thighs from his head. "My husband is the Mayor, and my protector is the Police Chief."

"Urb," said Yurek and crawled to his wife. Apollonia and Yurek measured each other in silence, while Nanushka ate a weed. Apollonia stared at his yellow pajamas, covered in mud smears and purple splotches.

"Poor creature! Poor man. I am incited to detest you, but I am benevolent. I forgive you for kicking me, because I could not possibly hate another son of Adam! I see from your pajamas you are one of the meek, who inherit the Earth, whereas I, a publican's wife, am damned. My husband, the Mayor, is a nincompoop, a potato-rind. The Police Chief pounced on me this morning. My best friend, the priest, is burning in Hell as we speak and I"—she suppressed a small sob—"I know we're strangers, but . . . are you hungry?"

"Yurk ate rag."

"Can I trust you enough to tell you what I saw today?"

"Neeenene blrpp . . ."

"I knew I could. I saw my own death in my ribs in the mirror! Twelve ribs for the twelve signs of the zodiac. I am doomed in Capricorn!"

"Yurk eats a corn."

"You're saying you, too, feel the presence of the four beasts tramping on their own entrails? The priest, too, was gnashed in their teeth!" She approached and knelt and pressed her face against the poet's dirty trousers, leaving a teary smear. "Look, just like the Ladlochka Shroud!"

"Yurk ties wife on the rope."

"So you do know about the priest's hanging?"

"Yurk ate with his rabbits."

"Oh? Aha? A metaphor? A prophecy perhaps? A clue? Are you my Simeon the Holy Fool, you who extinguish the lights and throw nuts at women?" she cried into his trousers with great piety.

"Tickles." Yurek giggled. "Gypsies have *black* goat . . . brown." He pointed at Nanushka's leg.

"Aha!" said Apollonia, leaping up, "aha, you need not say any more. You've come to the right public dignitary with this disclosure."

And so, in possession of the "disclosure" upon which Odolechka's future hung, she led Yurek and Nanushka Pierkiel into the Mayor's shed.

CHAPTER XIII

In which Barnabas discusses politics and economics
with a theorist and a peddler

HIS GRIM DISCOVERY OF KUMASHKO AND SUBSEQUENT INTERROGATION
by the Police Chief and the Mayor had led Barnabas to understand that life is too ephemeral to be lived without guidance. Thus,
for the first time in his heretofore frivolous life, he committed to
a truly thorough study of Polensky's *Guide to Etiquette*, reading, with well-earned fatigue, all sixteen pages of it in a single
morning. He read Polensky walking to the tavern to collect Wilhelm, then read Polensky on horseback back to his home. Our
young scholar found this study epiphanically rewarding. He comprehended that his mistake had been wooing his beloved empty-
handed. Rereading select passages, he emerged from behind the
partition into the kitchen, where his grandmother was making
black bread.

"Finch," she said, "pull on my gouty toe, it's jammed," swinging her bony leg at him as he passed.

"Polensky strictly forbids touching one's toes within a two-meter twenty-three-centimeter radius of the stove. Have you seen my monogrammed handkerchief?"

"Didn't see any hankers. Not in this house," she responded indignantly.

"Strange. Polensky also says, if I recall correctly, *Lick your spoon before passing it to a neighbor*," Barnabas recited, accepting a blood sausage from Grandmother. "Or was it after?" With his free hand, he shuffled the wrinkled pages. "*Do not blow your nose with the hand you hitch your pants with*," said Barnabas, examining his appendages, lowering himself onto the dining bench. "But this confuses me. Which hand would it be? Left? Right? Polensky says, *Don't slurp!* What could it mean?"

Grandmother sat beside him on the bench, pulled up her skirts, and began tossing the dough from thigh to thigh. "Let me see." She stretched her neck to see the book. "Manners I never got. Your grandpa Borivoi had them, in plenties. He never passed a flower without sniffing it, though his nostril was scooped in 1918. Had a canary, and he *always* blew up its rear end. Didn't skip it once. He always shook everyone's hand, even if his right hand's fingers were exploded in the Russian-Japanese-Napoleon war. All he had was stubs. Many unmannered ones wouldn't shake them, but he wouldn't leave till they shook all three fingers, insisted."

"Polensky says, *A gentleman doesn't chew with his mouth open*. How, then, does he chew?" Barnabas held the sausage in his fist, examining potential angles of approach.

"Polenskunky's right," Grandmother said, "best not to open your mouth. Banes float in the air like victoria."

Barnabas slapped the sausage down and pushed away his plate in resignation.

"No Pierkiel's ever refused the blood sausage!," Grandmother yelled after him.

A THOUSAND METERS UP THE ROAD, HE PASSED A GAGGLE OF GIRLS CARRY-ing laundry to the river. It was not unheard of for scheming maidens to throw themselves under a bachelor's horse. "Good day, fair laundresses," he saluted, galloping by.

On the other side of the river, he dismounted and tied Wilhelm to the fence of Volodek's garden. The door to the cottage was open, and within, atop a stool, Volodek's wife sat cleaning a goose. She waved it by the neck at Barnabas. He waved back and walked past the cottage, past the earth heaps that marked each of Volodek's buried manuscripts, to a slab of unevenly poured concrete, adorned with such finger-carved axioms as *Volodek* ♥ *Volodek* and *abandon ye all glee*. Set deep amid that wisdom was a rotting boot. Barnabas removed his shoe, placed his foot into the boot, and laced it up. He lifted his leg, and the concrete slab slowly lifted with it, exposing the narrow opening of a bunker.

"The surplus value produced by a given capital is equal to the surplus value of an unforgiven infidel," Barnabas shouted the password.

"The simultaneous employment of a large number of laborers effects a revolution in a small intestine," a nasal voice responded.

"The exchange value of a small infidel is not raised by its use value," Barnabas finished, unlacing the boot.

"A room where twenty weavers work at twenty looms must be larger than the room of a single weaver with two intestines," Volodek confirmed. "Did anyone see you?"

"Nobody."

"Come in, if you must," said Volodek, and Barnabas lowered himself into the cubic hole.

"These idiot deviant and quasi-deviant quasi-proletariats lollygag," said Volodek, "playing grab-ass, and do they *think* for a second? Do they see the fiat currency storm in the vicinity of their noses? The German dungfork about to pierce us all? Try hiding in your whore's knickers! Hah!"

I'd like to point out that, in this Odolechka of many false prophets, Volodek was, at last, and sadly, a true one. Upon his return to Odolechka from the Great War, he had appointed himself town seer, philosopher, and economist. For decades, he had prophesied all manner of disasters, especially after heavy dinners. After his most recent vision (of a biblical/inflationary flood, during which the Odolechkans obediently squatted on tree branches holding wads of thallers) failed to manifest, Volodek lost much of his reputation.

"With just a little reinforcement, it'll be better down here than in my cottage. Look here, my fellow social animal, a regular latrine!" vociferated Volodek. "I dreamed last night of a wolf with the horsepower of a dozen men and women working together, their collective workday equaling a hundred and forty-four hours, and a wild German witch riding it naked and cackling through the night sky, a one-thaller coin in her mouth."

"A hundred and forty-four, yes," Barnabas said, "but, about that coin . . ."

"I don't pay you good thallers for standing around like a cripple. The wall has to be mortared." He pointed to a heap of broken bricks.

"About those thallers . . ."

"That's what they said at Garda in the Great War! First, we met for breakfast. Shot at each other for two hours, finishing in time for lunch. Had some cannoli. God curse Franz Joseph for preparing the self-determination of Central Europe with too little salt!"

"All that you say is right," said Barnabas, "but I've been working for you for two months and haven't been paid."

"I've paid you in wisdom, you bourgeois pork merchant! All you think about is lucre."

"You gave me a bag of lentils!"

"Ah! As soon as the laborer begins his labor, his wife gives birth. The value of labor, reversed, is an expression as imaginary as my wife!" and Volodek reached into one of the barrels behind the pile of bricks, gathering a fistful of rice. "I will give you this."

"Rice?"

"Don't yell, or you'll waken my manuscripts. I can give you one fist more, only *don't accumulate*." From a hole in the floor of the bunker, camouflaged by a flung-down anorak, he gathered a bundle of wrinkled notes.

"It's only twenty million," grumbled Barnabas, but Volodek turned from him and began to weigh rice on a postman's scale.

Barnabas climbed from the bunker and, ignoring Volodek's imaginary wife, who flapped a goose's foot at him as he passed by the cottage door, galloped away in search of Boiko the traveling peddler, who was, this time of year, in town. He did not find him in the square, nor in the tavern. Finally, he found him at the rear of the church, by the hitching posts and horse trough.

"See the daisies in the churchyard? They're Jesus' sweet little brooches," Boiko said, wiped his hands on his trousers, and finished chewing whatever his mouth contained. "How can I help you on this beautiful day commemorating the birth of St. Kokoschka?"

"I would like to buy some gifts," said Barnabas.

Boiko opened his greatcoat, displaying an array of merchandise pinned to its lining: coils of *kielbasa*, kneeling cushions, rabbit-wire tiaras, hair clips made of chicken wishbones . . .

"I don't know what to choose. There's too much." Delighted, Barnabas peered at the products.

"Is the recipient of your gift a feathered seraph?" Boiko shuffled his coat in a wingish manner.

"How did you know?"

"I saw it in your heart. In the aorta, on the throne."

"That's right. I feel it here!" Barnabas pointed at his chest.

"I'm intuitive, see. I have to be." Boiko swayed, and the *kielbasas* swayed in countertime. "I have a few items she might like. This, for example." From his breast pocket, he fetched a ball of semisolid glue. "You throw it at the wall and it sticks, and it slowly rolls down."

"But what does it do?"

"It rolls down. Then you pick it up, throw it, and it rolls again. I bought it in Krool. I see you lack the gentility of the spirit to appreciate it. I see you're not up there with the angels."

"Oh no, I'd like to take it. It's fascinating, really." Barnabas accepted the ball, which promptly glued itself to his finger.

"If you don't like it, I have others in line who will."

"Oh no, I do," said Barnabas with quiet awe.

"This is not all. I have something better." Boiko wriggled his pelvis to get at the deeper zones of the coat. "Here." He presented Barnabas with a punctured metal bucket, a pheasant feather affixed to its rim.

"Is it a colander?"

"Only a swineherd would say such a thing." Boiko pushed

the *kielbasas* to the side, snatched the bucket from Barnabas'
hand, and attempted to tie the item back, where it had initially
hung behind his legs.

"Wait, I'd like to see it again."

"Only if you don't disrespect it." After some hesitation, Boiko
passed it back to Barnabas.

"It's very pretty. Shiny, rather." Barnabas turned it in the sun.
"What is it?"

"Unarguably a hat."

"Though it seems very hard." Barnabas tried it on.

"It's medieval."

"What's that?"

"*Populus vult decipi, ergo decipiatur!* The people want a hat,
they will have a hat. But if you don't want it . . ."

"I think I like it."

"Only it doesn't matter if you don't. Others will. Only decide
soon, because I have to go home to my orphans."

"You're a father to orphans?" Barnabas removed the hat and
peered through the hole in it at Boiko.

"I and my wife have a whole brood of them. Hungry, ragged,
thin little things. I have to feed them before the Solstice Celebration, or else they'll be too weak to participate in the festivities
and sleep in their tiny cribs, making St. John himself cry."

"They're babies?"

"All seven of them. Each night, I throw them a dry crumb,
and whoever is fastest gets to eat."

"I've decided she shall have the hat," said Barnabas.

"A circumspect choice. But there's one other item. I'm not
sure I can show it to you. I don't think you'll be able to afford it.
It's the ladies' very favorite."

"I'd like to see it at least," Barnabas pleaded, stealthily trying to unglue the ball from his thumb without it sticking back onto his finger.

Boiko shrugged and patted his sides. "I don't know if I can find it. I'm afraid I can't. I'm ruined if it's gone." He reached into his trouser pockets, and his hand was visible in the vicinity of his knee. "Ahh, we're saved." He fetched a tiny box, the size of a thimble, with SNUFF printed on it. Boiko kissed the box.

"What is it?"

"Powdered herring snuff."

"It's very small."

"It has to be. It's a precious heavenly dust. Jesus himself may have used it. There are textual reasons to believe he did."

"Did he?" Barnabas weighed the box in his hand.

"Jesus bought it for his wife."

"Do you know Volodek?"

"I keep away from him," said Boiko. "Why?"

"He just was telling me about *his* wife, and I myself am interested in getting one . . ." Barnabas became bashful and silent.

"That's very well, but do you want this precious snuff?"

"If Jesus' wife used it, I probably want it. She must have had the best there was."

"I see you're a Christian. I wouldn't even show it to you if you weren't. If you weren't a literate Christian, I wouldn't think of selling you this here God-beloved merchandise, for a truly Christian price. It comes all the way from Bethlehem, you know, where Jesus walked on wine."

"I'm not sure I can afford all three, but the snuff is my favorite." Barnabas perused the treasures. "How much is it all together?"

Boiko picked up a stick and started drawing lines in the dust.

"I can give you a good price, only because I know you took communion last week. Did you?"

"Yes?"

"Well, in that case, I'll give you all of them for one billion."

"One billion thallers?"

"Do you think it's too much? Do you know what my wife said to me this morning?"

"No . . . your wife is real, right?"

"Is what?! She said: 'Boiko, now I think the orphans will be fine if you throw them a dry crumb once every *second* day. I just think they'll be fine.'"

"She said that?"

"Just this morning. Though a Christian, she never could have a hat like this. She never dreams of herring snuff. She knows I have to sell it to afford our crumbs. She's not a decadent."

"I'd like to take all three. But I don't have one billion. May I pay you later some of it?"

"What do you have right now?"

"Twenty million, more or less."

"I will bestow the grace of usury upon you, then," said Boiko, "as a more or less true Christian. The rate shall be set at eleven percent per annum. Do you understand?"

"I do." Thus Barnabas gave Volodek's wrinkled cash to Boiko and signed an IOU on a piece of the *Krool Gazeta*. The peddler left with a satisfied look, and Barnabas sat down to admire his purchases. He smelled something horrendous.

"I know that smell . . ." He sniffed each of his armpits. It wasn't a Barnabas smell but something terribly *familiar*. The water of the horse trough rippled in a faint wind. There, in the algal water, was our hero's visage, and, smell or no, a moment of physiognomic admiration was in order; this consumed him for about half an hour, so that he forgot the items he had lined up at his feet amid the daisies. His attention was at last demanded by the lingering smell, the main note somewhere between boletus mushrooms, boiled eggs, and well-aged kasha, with an afternote of something else unnameable . . . the smell of the flaw at the heart of the universe.

He looked around for the source of this terror and saw his gifts were missing. "Robbed!" he cried and ran along the trough and looked beneath it. A sudden calm despair brought Barnabas' antics to a halt. He sniffed again . . . "I *know* that smell."

CHAPTER XIV

In which Apollonia dispenses tutelage and witnesses
a thing unmentionable in a chapter title

"YOU ARE *UNHELPFUL*," APOLLONIA SAID, PAUSING AMID RECREATIONAL
coal shoveling.

"I'm *trying*." Friend and protégée Kryshia, a woman two-
thirds Apollonia's size, lifted a shovelful of coals and, arms quiv-
ering, transferred it from one pile to another.

"Look, it goes like this." Apollonia scooped coal from pile
number one and jostled it into the air with a flourish, landing it
on pile number two.

"Not everyone has your virile strength. Not everyone's teeth
can cut rope."

"I don't see why not."

"Are you ready to tell me yet?" Kryshia panted, attempting
the maneuver without success.

"What I'd like to know first is your progress on *The Melan-*

choly Labors of the Spleen: An Account of the Surgical Profession, Its Triumphs as Well as Its Best Efforts."

"Something about the extraction of the stone of madness . . . ," Kryshia mumbled, shoveling with newfound strength and urgency.

"Aha, that's an illuminating chapter, is it not? Is it not! Have you gotten to the leech-farming wig-barbers part?"

"I don't remember . . . probably. Perhaps I'm not there yet."

"But that's in the beginning! Something tells me you're not paying due attention to this masterpiece. What, thus far, have you learned about gangrenous wounds?"

Kryshia rubbed her nose, unwittingly turning it black, and said, "There are three kinds. *Blue, mysterious,* and *cryptic. Blue* gangrene occurs in moister tissues such as mouth, bowel, lungs, and vulva."

"Very good!"

"*Mysterious* gangrene is when a bubble of hydrogen gas inflates a toe or finger."

"Yes, the affected part is dark, soft, putrid, edematous," Apollonia paraphrased from memory, digging into pile number one. "The treatment involves antibiotics and, more classically, flying maggots. I personally think the classic methods are often best."

"Maggots, yes." Kryshia wiped sweat from her ear-to-ear eyebrow, turning it from blond to black. She pointed to the wisp of light beneath the cellar door. "Couldn't we at least go outside? Chop some wood instead?"

"And *cryptic* gangrene?"

"I don't know. I get confused without light. I don't remember."

"No one does!" Apollonia, shifting from her favorite book to her second favorite book, quoted from the Scripture: "'A poor man named Lazarus was laid at the gate, covered with sores and longing to be fed from the rich man's table.'"

"But even Lazarus wouldn't—"

Apollonia thrust the shovel into pile number two. In a high voice, she continued: "'Even the dogs came and licked his sores. The poor man died.'" Apollonia smiled at this rhetorical victory, kicked off a clog, and, with studied relish, stomped her bare foot onto some coal shards.

"I don't have your erudition, I could never walk across cold coals with my bare foot," Kryshia said.

"It takes practice. Try it."

"Oh, I'd rather not."

"You're being *un*helpful."

Kryshia removed her sandal and grazed a shard with her toe, which, although somewhat plump, did not appear at all *mysterious*.

Apollonia bellowed, "Harder!"

Kryshia grazed it again.

"With zeal! Like this!" Apollonia lifted her skirts and trampled the coal's sharp chips with the lanky determination of a mad giraffe trampling its dung. "Aha! Not even a scratch!" She presented Kryshia with her unmarred sole. "Follow the saints, my sister, and you will end in Heaven. Take the example of St. Zuzanna. When a pagan betrothed to her complimented her eyes, she poured boiled milk into her eyes!" For emphasis, she thumped the shovel on the cellar ceiling. Kryshia closed her eyes and stomped her tiny flat foot onto the coal shards.

"Aik!" She collapsed.

"See? It wasn't awful."

"I require a bandage right away."

"All you require is practice," said Apollonia, propping the shovel and wiping her hands with her apron. "I think the time has come. It's up in the garden. I made it beautiful with branches, the envy of all the trees of Eden." She half carried Kryshia up the hewn stone stairs into the daylight.

"I don't know how you step on that coal without cutting yourself."

"It's faith," whispered Apollonia, "the further evidence of which I am about to reveal to you, o my sister who bled for St. Zuzanna."

"Yes, what is this secret secret thing? The giant parsley crop you mentioned?" Kryshia asked, and, following her mentor's example, stooped to sniff the tea roses in the Mayor's garden.

"I try to turn you into a sophisticate," said Apollonia, "but perhaps you'd rather go back to the cellar to repractice stomping?"

"No, I unreservedly, I *spiritually* desire to see the secret thing, whatever it is."

"Then you are ready?"

"Fanatically, utterly," said limping Kryshia.

"I have found a method by which to prevent our souls' damnation. I have learned what every mind in Odolechka struggles to fathom."

"What?!"

"A secret."

"But what kind of secret is it if it can't be shared?"

"A *cryptic* secret."

"That's like keeping your best dress in the closet. A secret that's completely secret is practically useless."

Apollonia considered her best friend and protégée with new

respect. "I see my training has not been in vain. Fine, I will tell you. I have a pilgrim in my shed."

"A man?"

"A Simeon the Holy Fool." A period of awed silence followed, and the two zealots gazed at each other amid the thorns.

"Why is he in your shed?" Kryshia trembled.

"I found him atop my coop, reciting Bible verses. Then we prayed together. Then I filled the bathtub for him, the one where I keep the Christmas carp, and bathed him, like the Baptist did."

"You bathed him?"

"That's not all."

"You're frightening me!" Kryshia whispered. "What else could there be?"

"It's best if he tells you in his own words. He's very learned. Fix your hair, you look like a carpet sweeper."

"Now?"

"Just don't make any *womanesque* motions, if you understand my meaning. He might jump onto your earthly body. It is from his oversaturation with the Holy Spirit. If he does, the best thing is to grab his head and squeeze like this." She held her fist between her thighs and strained mightily.

"Perhaps you are right that I am unworthy."

"Arise, my sister!" Apollonia lurched toward the hallowed shed, dragging Kryshia by the elbow.

All was quiet in the shed. Garden tools stood in the corner by a heap of hay. A few tumbled blankets lay on the ground, a small iron bathtub, a piece of blackened pipe. No Simeon-Yurek, however.

"Perhaps he's continued his pilgrimage," Kryshia said.

"I was good to him!" Apollonia almost sobbed, moved by her own goodness, as she groped the hay in search of evidence.

"I wish I was so good," said Kryshia.

"Years of practice and suffering. One doesn't arrive at goodness without sacrifice. Yurk would never continue to Jerusalem without bidding me farewell. Shhh! What is this sound?" They heard a dreadful panting, and the back wall of the shed seemed to be shaking.

"What could it be? I don't like it at all. Sounds like a Kooza goblin," Kryshia whispered.

The women crept out of the shed and toward its rear. A splotchy canvas hung here from a laundry line tied to a hook on the shed's outer wall, the very fabric used by the Mayor, in his monthly dress-up romps, as the toga of Emperor Commodus.

"Perhaps he's saying the rosary. I wouldn't like to miss that for anything on this Savior's planet!" whispered Apollonia, and pulled at the canvas.

I should, in advance, warn you that the sight revealed to Kryshia and Apollonia was worse than crude, and this passage might well be omitted without great sacrifice, except that the indecent sight was just enough to distract Apollonia, for the moment at least, from divulging what she called her "secret," the eventual divulgence of which, you will see, became the catalyst of Odolechka's ruin. I proceed apologetically.

What the two women saw in the shade of the shed was nothing less than Yurek Pierkiel dishonoring his wife. I will not indulge in gratuitous detail, only mention Apollonia experienced a heady collision of equal and opposite feelings, and Kryshia pulled at Apollonia's kilt, and clutching said kilt, lowered herself onto an inverted bucket and stared.

Kumashko's last oration and subsequent martyrdom had convinced Apollonia: if not Apollonia, *no one* would take Kumashko's place, and thus would Hell arrive on Earth, in Odolechka, far sooner than otherwise.

"Any animal that has a cloven hoof that is completely split into double hooves, and which brings up its cud, that one you may eat! But only Simeon the Holy Fool may marry it," Apollonia professed to the four winds.

CHAPTER XV

In which Barnabas reports a theft to every
law enforcement officer in Odolechka

BARNABAS TIED HIS HORSE TO THE LEG OF THE STATUE OF THE FIRST MAYOR
(or possibly of Police Chief or Head Clerk, no one was certain)
of Odolechka and climbed the stairs of an unimposing yellow
building that doubled as Town Hall and Police Headquarters.
Grigor the janitor, sweeping the top step, seeing Barnabas approach,
doubled his pace, sending dust and paper bits down onto Barnabas' legs and shoes.

Barnabas smiled at him, entered the building, and stopped
by the stacked apple boxes that served as the Secretary's desk.
Her swollen cheek indicated a dental problem (cavities were to
Odolechka as locusts were to the Egypt of *Exodus*). She did not
look up, occupied with a careful, possibly even tasseomantic,
examination of the coffee dregs in her cup.

"Good day, and is the Chief in?" Barnabas inquired.

"He's in, but it's as if he isn't."

"He is then?"

"He is *but*."

"He isn't?"

"Correct. He isn't, *but* he is."

"Then how do I report a theft?" asked Barnabas. She pointed to her cheek. He peered at it across the apple box. Alas, no clarifying message on this cheek. An appleivorous caterpillar crawled between the box slats to the edge of her saucer, and Barnabas tickled it, then looked into her cup, but no enlightenment dwelt therein. The Secretary was no help.

There were two doors. PANTRY was painted on one, OFFICIAL OFUCE the other. The choice was confusing. Where was the Police Chief needed most? In a pantry or an official ofuce? What if he has unofficial business? Now if there were someone hiding in a pantry, in that case the Chief could be investigating . . . Usually there are shelves in a pantry. A robber or two or even three, if all of midget stature, might fit easily enough amid the marmalades. Barnabas reached to open the pantry door, but a cough from inside the official ofuce shattered his conviction.

"Ofuce, it must be, then. I remember now, Uncle Gregosh had one of these, ofuces, and it was robbed once, too, before he died." He knocked.

"Come back tomorrow!"

Encouraged, Barnabas looked for a handle, but there were no protrusions. Where a handle had once been (judging from two rusty scroll marks) was a hole, into which Barnabas promptly inserted his finger. He poked around in the inexplicably moist innards of the door. The operation reminded him of gutting a goose. Finally, upon slight pressure, some internal apparatus yielded, and the door opened.

Smoke hung in the air, but not cigarette smoke, as one might think, and Barnabas stood still, so as not to impolitely disperse it.

"Pretty," he murmured, and for a while admired the haze, until he felt it was appropriate to seem to have noticed the Police Chief seated on his milking stool by the window, the curtain of which, half ripped from the rod, draped the Chief's shoulders like a cape. The Chief was burning something in a metal crate.

"I just came from a meeting with the Head Clerk," said the Police Chief. "And then, on a plate, I saw a slice of cheese. I knew I shouldn't have touched it, but . . . and then . . ." The Police Chief looked and sniffed at Barnabas, especially, it seemed, at Barnabas' hand. "Who are you? Disregard, please, my report on cheese. It was not for your ears. I thought you were my Secretary." He gathered the curtain tighter about his neck.

"Barnabas Pierkiel, sir. I've come to report a crime."

"Can't you report it to Yany and Sabas? Can't you come tomorrow?"

"Thank you. I'd be pleased to come tomorrow, too. I like it here."

"Fine. What is the nature of this irregularity?"

"A dangerous madman named Yurek Pierkiel has fled the asylum at Troshku. The army must be called."

"You're telling me there's a dangerous criminal in Odolechka? How many in his gang? How many weapons per head?"

"For now, I think, it's only one. I didn't smell anyone else. But he is cunning. Once, I witnessed him approach an old stump with bark beetles on it. He got them all. Another time, there was a gigantic mouse in our cellar . . ."

"Mouse, is that his partner's pseudonym?"

"It could be."

The smoke began to irritate Barnabas' eyes, which were designed for gazing at flowers, gypsy girls, and clouds. The Police Chief's small and strangely black and glossy eyes apparently remained untroubled.

"Understandably," the Police Chief said. "What is this man's name, again?"

"Yurek Pierkiel. He goes by Yurk."

"I see a trace here, a bridge. I see it as if through fog."

"The fog is a tasteful addition to your ofuce," complimented Barnabas.

"I see it in the very back of the rear of my brain . . . I'd like to bring it to the front." The Police Chief bit the tip of the eraser off his pencil, chewed, and spat it out. "What is on your finger?"

"What?"

"Your finger, young man."

Barnabas regarded the offending digit, coated with a brownish paste. "I'm sorry, sir. I don't . . . ." He brought it to his nose. "It smells like *bigos*, sir."

"And at the crime scene, what, if not *bigos*, did you say you smelled?"

"I didn't smell anyone else, just Yurek the thief. He stole a hat, a gluey ball, and some snuff used by Jesus' wife."

"I know!" said the Police Chief.

"You do?"

"What did you say *your* last name was?"

"Pierkiel."

"You're the one who found the priest. I questioned you outside this very Town Hall not two days ago! It was dark, but it was you."

"It was. I was asleep behind the tavern, *not* out by the windmill. I'm not to tell anyone."

"Yes, behind the tavern. Good. You don't tell anyone. The trace is holding together. Now I have to ask you this: are you sure you are not Yurek Pierkiel, recently escaped from the asylum at Troshku?"

"I am sure," reported Barnabas with 99 percent confidence. "Though I never thought about it before, I admit."

"Taking into consideration the evidence, the chances of it are less than . . . less than that word for a very small number, don't you think?"

"Yes, I agree."

"No, come to think of it, this trace was a false one. But I have another one. Is this man related to you?"

"No." For was this not a *public* official? Admitting relation to Yurek in Town Hall was admitting it *publicly*, was it not? What if the Secretary was, at this moment, eavesdropping at the door, recording everything he and the Police Chief said, compiling an Official Public Record?

"I notice you and the criminal share the same last name," said the Chief.

"It's incidence."

"You mean co?"

"No, I don't mean co," said Barnabas, nervously shuffling and sniffing his finger. "There is nothing co about me and Yurek, *nothing.*"

"It is not coincidence, then?"

"No."

"Then this is a difficult case." The Police Chief bit into the pencil wood, having finished the eraser.

"Yurek stole my presents."

"Where was this?"

"Behind the church, by the horse trough."

"Right, you mentioned Jesus. And is by the horse trough where you saw him last?"

"I didn't see him, thank heavens!"

"You did not?"

"No. I smelled him."

"Smell, young man, no matter how horrendous, is not an acceptable proof of guilt."

Barnabas inhaled the cabbagey aroma of his finger with growing alarm. "Not even boletus mushrooms?"

"No."

"Boiled eggs?"

"No."

"Old kasha?"

"Fraid not!" said the Police Chief. "Come back when you have more evidence. For now I am busy making progress on the Kumashko case. It seems he hanged himself."

"Yes, I know."

"You're a bright boy. Don't tell anyone. I know you won't." The Police Chief shook Barnabas' hand, wiped the transferred *bigos* onto Barnabas' shirt with an apologetic nod, and led Barnabas to the door, propelling him through with a hand on his back.

"Was he *here*?" the Secretary asked the Chief, pointing at Barnabas.

"He was," the Police Chief said and closed the door.

"And was he in there?" asked the Secretary.

"Yes," said Barnabas, "he was."

Barnabas walked to the exit, then hesitated. "Where can I find Yany and Sabas?"

"They're investigating the tavern," she said. "They haven't been out in a month. They're even busier than the Chief, so I wouldn't disturb them. Would I?"

"Would you?" And with a soldierly gait, Barnabas left Town Hall. He was so upset over the loss of the gifts, he felt in his nose a dangerous tingle. Crying *publicly?* Intolerable. But what could bolster Barnabas? No romance he had read included a hero whose gifts for his lady are stolen. Polensky didn't mention gift-theft either. Or, if he did, Barnabas did not remember it. The only axiom Barnabas could think of was: *It's impolite to scratch your head over beverages. (Bouillions are exempted from this rule.)*

Muttering, he fled across the square into the tavern. Inside, Dzaswav the tavernkeeper was spitting on glasses and passing them to Anechka, who polished them with the hem of her slip.

"One moonshine in this one, please." Barnabas pointed to the cleanest glass.

"Oh no, for you, I'll shine it extra." Anechka sprayed the glass through her teeth and buffed it, using not only her hem but the wine-dark lace of her bodice.

"I don't need it extra clean, regular will do," said Barnabas and turned to the room lined with wooden tables and benches. The tavern was empty, except for Kashak sleeping with a beer mug cradled between cheek and neck. Barnabas might have left after a single drink, except that he, mid-moonshine, recalled a particularly poignant Polenskyan axiom: *Only after one's fifth serving of alcohol is it appropriate to slide beneath the table.*

Yany and Sabas were not known for their lack of etiquette.

Placing his moonshine on the best table in the tavern, Barnabas ducked underneath it. Once again, the genius Polensky was right. Yany and Sabas slept in a shallow pool of liquid and other matter, accumulated and coagulated over generations.

"Excuse me, sirs," he addressed them cordially. "Sirs?" There was a snort, and Sabas extended his arm and dropped it into the communal heirloom slime. They wore nearly identical suits that looked as if they had been Sunday bests before this particular bout of bacchanalia. "You are Yany and Sabas."

"No."

"No?"

"We're volunteers."

"I see. I'm sorry to disturb you."

"That's all right. We fell asleep while working."

"What were you working on? Volunteer police work?"

"Working on finding the note that Yany passed me that I dropped under the table."

"I see. I'd never interrupt a man on duty, but if you have a moment," Barnabas said.

"That was the only evidence we had," said Yany, attempting to push Sabas' head off his shoulder.

"Gentlemen, perhaps what I have to report will help you."

"You know where *it* is?"

"I know about thieves," Barnabas said mysteriously. With this philosophical remark, he gained their attention. "A dangerous halfwit named Yurek Pierkiel has fled the asylum at Troshku. You can detect him by his smell."

"Can you describe exactly what he smelled of?" Yany said.

"Boletus mushrooms, boiled eggs, old kasha."

"Sure, I sometimes smell eggs." Sabas managed to keep his head up for a moment, before it flopped back onto Yany's shoulder.

"Sniff around the Solstice Celebration, is my advice . . . if he's to be smelled, you'll smell him there," Yany suggested.

"Except everyone's leg hair singeing in the fire kills all aromas," Sabas blithered into Yany's shoulder.

"Skeptic," Yany said.

"Don't worry. I'm certain I will sniff him out. His smell is unique," Barnabas said, encouraged. "Thanks for your helpfulness. You each deserve a police medal. Or an honorable mention, at the very least." He walked outside, and was about to mount Wilhelm, when he saw something stuck to the tip of his shoe. A small scrap of filthy paper, curled into a moist ball, adorned Barnabas' toe with the adhesive help of the tavern floor's perennial coagulant. He picked up the ball and gently unrolled it. Something was scribbled across it in pencil. Barnabas brought it close to his eyes.

Meet me under the table. I have something to tell you.

CHAPTER XVI

In which Apollonia divulges her "secret"

"YOU'RE GOING TO INJURE YOUR WRIST ONE DAY," APOLLONIA SAID, EMBIT-
tered by Kryshia's superior embroidery, "working like that, on
such a thing. As long as it's not for your Sunday table."

"Why . . . ?" Kryshia reconsidered the tablecloth in her lap.

"Primulas? You'd serve Sunday *pierogi* on primulas? Those
are not even botanically accurate. Primulas are the worst flowers
in south Scalvusia. It's well known they symbolize lechery and
Venus disease in old paintings. You are shameless," Apollonia
whispered and, with a rapturous hiss, jabbed her needle underneath her thumbnail.

"I don't like it when you do that," said the Doctor's Wife. "It
reminds me of my husband."

"It's because you're not a true Christian." Apollonia pushed
the needle with finesse, until a drop of blood appeared. All three
leaned over her stigmatized finger with reverence.

"That's what I call faith." Kryshia crossed herself and looked at her primulas doubtfully.

Apollonia waited for the blood to brim beneath her nail, then raised it in the lamplight, turning it from side to side.

"One day it will be a saint's relic," Kryshia complimented the digit, and the Doctor's Wife looked ill.

"Sometimes I hold it up for hours," Apollonia said, "just like St. Balbina, whose hand dried to dust after fourteen days of waving to the Heavenly Queen."

"But do tell us about the scandal!" said Kryshia, cutting a thread with her teeth and swallowing it ostentatiously.

"Are you trying to impress me? Because shameless displays like that simply do not. Any heathen can do what you just did. Even Mongolian infidels ate their blankets. I know of *one* pilgrim"—Apollonia winked at Kryshia, then glanced at the Doctor's Wife—"who claims to eat rags."

"Oh, no, I was just—" Kryshia tried to clear her throat.

"But what about the scandal?" The Doctor's Wife set down the serviette she was making and leaned toward Apollonia.

"I see your excitement over it is somewhat sinful," said Apollonia.

"What a saying," said the Doctor's Wife. "What a suggestion."

"Oh no? It is sinful, your excitement. Yes it is, yes it is, daughter of Lilith."

"Who? I?"

"She who mated with archangel Samael."

"What a suggestion." The Doctor's Wife, subdued, picked up her serviette.

"Are you ready, then? Incorporeally? Seraphically?"

"Both," said Kryshia.

"I, too, am ready," said the Doctor's Wife.

"How ready?"

"Like Christ was for Magdalen," spouted Kryshia.

"The wounds in his risen body! O, Holy Wound of the Left Foot of my Jesus, I adore Thee! O, Holy Wound of the Right Foot of my Jesus, I adore Thee!" chanted Apollonia, pointing her bloody finger toward the firmament in the window. "Are you as ready as Yehuda Ben-Sholom was, remember the Doctor before your husband, when he performed his auto-appendectomy, Yehuda Ben-Sholom, who died of Mogdagni's hernia, or so *claims* your husband, the Doctor!"

"Just like that!" Kryshia nodded energetically.

"As ready as Yehuda," said the Doctor's Wife.

"Then I will tell you!" Apollonia waved her finger, splattering some blood onto the Doctor's Wife's serviette. Greedily, Kryshia extended her tablecloth, and Apollonia pressed her finger against it, leaving an admirable blot.

"It happened a few days ago. I was dusting my scapular, when a gentleman knocked on my door. On his chest he wore a medallion of St. Dismas!"

"What was his name?" asked the Doctor's Wife.

"Sir Yurk Simeon."

"What a name!"

"Oh, he was quite a prince!" added Kryshia.

Apollonia took a dramatic breath . . . "He bowed, he kissed my hand, and then he said . . ."

Before I go on to relate what Apollonia was about to divulge, I must remind you of the sole exchange these two Christians ever had had on the subject of gypsies, at dusk, in the Mayor's garden:

"Yurk ate with his [Kumashko's] rabbits."

"Oh? Aha? A metaphor? A prophecy perhaps? A clue? Are you my Simeon the Holy Fool, you who extinguish the lights and throw nuts at women?" she cried into his trousers with great piety.

"Tickles." Yurek giggled. *"Gypsies have* black *goat ... brown."* He pointed at Nanushka's leg.

It does, therefore, come as a sad surprise to find that Apollonia's inference from this learned exchange was nothing other than: "the gypsies killed our beloved priest!"

"The gypsies?" Kryshia opened her mouth and left it open. The Doctor's Wife got down on her knees.

"You two darlings seem so surprised. But when I heard it, I was not surprised at all. Not-at-all!" said Apollonia.

"I am not surprised either! My mother always warned me," said the Doctor's Wife. "And even when we passed by them, she always made sure to cover my eyes and pull my coat button, the top button. If you pull the bottom button, then the gypsies know your thoughts. And then she put a curse on my heifer. Ever since she passed by the fence, the cow won't stop mooing and won't give a drop of milk. And when she does give milk, it tastes like cursed bone-marrow extract, the kind you spread on toast, but cursed."

"Your mother put a curse on your heifer?" asked Kryshia.

"The gypsy did, you fool," said the Doctor's Wife.

"On and on about hooves and udders, both of you," said Apollonia. "You ought to be ashamed. Hooves are not proper talk among ladies. But did Kryshia tell you what we saw Yurk Simeon doing behind my shed? If she did—oh *if* you did," she threatened Kryshia, who ignored her.

"It makes sense to me," said Kryshia. "A priest as holy as Kumashko would never have committed the cardinal sin of suicide!"

"It's true!" the Doctor's Wife expectorated. "He was just now reaching the peak of his powers and piety!"

"How did the gypsies do it?"

"They hanged him," said Apollonia. "Hanged him with his own rope. Now that I have divulged this, we're no longer going to Hell. We have atoned."

"Which gypsy? I cannot believe this," said the Doctor's Wife, heavily rising.

"You call me a fool," Kryshia said, "some Doctor's Wife you are. I know *your* secret. I'll tell Apollonia!"

"You tell nothing but lies. What a suggestion."

"Tell us," said Apollonia. "I will be the judge of what is true. Truth is not relative. Truth is to be found on stone tablets. Either one can read, or one cannot. Most Odolechkans cannot read. Grunvald the impoverished schoolteacher barely can read, and what he does read isn't true. He teaches our children to read books about apes that mate with slightly-not-quite-apelike apes, and those half-apes frantically mate with quarter-apes, and you can imagine what happens next."

"Her daughter fell in love with Bolek," Kryshia blurted. "He wouldn't have her, so *she*"—Krushia pointed to the Doctor's Wife—"went to the gypsy."

"He thought he was too good for your Anechka, didn't he! How arrogant!" cried Apollonia. "Poor Doctor's Wife!" She squeezed the Doctor's Wife's hand compassionately, smearing finger blood into her palm. "But to go to the gypsy . . . which gypsy? Before coming to me! I would have whipped Bolek with penitential willow canes. What is Bolek? A myopic cobbler, who, I should add, von Grushka is about to put out of business. Who is he to think he's better than a barmaid, even if she is the Doctor's Daughter, doctors having fallen in stature in society over the last few generations, naturally, as we drift ever farther away from the days of unity between the Church and the colleges of medicine."

A drop of nervous sweat developed on the Doctor's Wife's brow and traveled down her cheek to be absorbed by the pachydermal creases of her neck.

"She went to Tsura Papusha herself. And then!" Kryshia showed her little teeth. "Tsura advised her to find the dirtiest mongrel in the whole village, feed him *chorluk* root for a week, then take a rag and rub the mongrel *hard*. Then put the rag on Bolek's head."

"Your daughter put the rag on Bolek's head?" Apollonia asked the Doctor's Wife, appalled.

"She made a pillow cover out of it," said Kryshia.

"Your poor, poor girl," said Apollonia to the Doctor's Wife. "How sorry I am to hear this. Such a tragedy!"

"What an outburst," said the Doctor's Wife. "You musn't listen to Kryshia Golonska when she exaggerates. What is important now is that the gypsy sisters hanged Kumashko, probably with help from gypsy men who hide in barrels and in woodsheds."

"Did I tell you what Kryshia and I witnessed behind my shed?"

CHAPTER XVII

In which Barnabas considers pigskin,
thallers, rafts, love, and cavalry

BARNABAS REFLECTED ON THE MYSTERIOUS NOTE IN HIS HAND FOR SEVERAL minutes. He looked from the note to the nearby well. A dame named Yolanda had fallen into this well during the Siege, it was reported, in a heroic refusal to be dishonored by a Russian soldier. Barnabas had heard (but never tried it) that whenever a solitary villager turned the crank to draw the well's bucket at exactly midnight, Yolanda wailed. It was dark but not midnight. Nevertheless, the proximity of the well gave Barnabas a creeping, neck-scuttling-insect sensation, not unlike when—

"Young intellectual at work!" cried a voice. "What are you reading?"

Barnabas whirled.

"My underprivileged friend!" von Grushka thundered, coming from Town Hall. "How is life in the pit of our troubled, but far from lost, economy? The small existence in the oubliette of the pork business? Remember, as long as there are sticks at the river bottom, two sticks are better than one stick, and three is a faggot. Plant one stick, you have a stick bush; multiply that by three, you have a faggot bush; multiply that by ten, and you have a raft!"

"I'm sorry, but sticks aren't my specialty," said Barnabas, with quiet indignation.

"Get on that raft. Upward from that pit!" von Grushka cried, clasped our hero with his ringed hands, and placed five over-moist kisses on his cheeks. He took the crumpled note from Barnabas' hand, uncrumpled it, and read it with a puzzled expression, then crumpled it and stuffed it into Barnabas' shirt pocket.

Barnabas stiffened. "I'm sorry, but there are no rivers in Scal-vusia that flow upward. Not with sticks in them, anyway."

"You are absolutely right. The plebe has to struggle against the current, determination and willpower, half-obliterated, nearly drowned, contorted lips yearning for that air bubble, a trembling hand extended for that twig . . . I know your struggle! At the military school, I was once forced to eat a rotten egg . . . This is really quite good, what I'm saying to you." From his breast pocket, he fetched a small pad and a tiny pen.

"What are you writing?" Barnabas asked, torn between hatred and etiquette, etiquette prevailing . . . but what did Polensky say about addressing one's archenemy?

"A note for my forthcoming pamphlet."

"A pamphlet on bootmaking?"

"A pamphlet of sonnets, my boy. Mine is not merely a commercial mind."

"Sonnets about the egg you ate?"

"No, no, sonnets to the air bubble of promise of upward

social mobility, the rewarding pursuit of the raft of accumulated twigs."

"I don't think there are many poems about rotten eggs. I don't think it's a noble subject, definitely not. And I must now go," said Barnabas.

"I hope you're not upset because I several days ago suggested I might buy your horse. I know he's not for sale. I understand the mentality of a peasant who takes pride in what astonishingly little he has."

"It's she."

"What's that?"

"My horse is a woman!" said flustered Barnabas.

"Piss, vinegar, and *benzina*! I see where your eye keeps traveling. Do not be bashful, my friend. If you gather enough twigs, one day you'll be able to afford such a *machina*!" He shoved Barnabas between the shoulder blades in the direction of his Gippopotam, parked by the tavern. "For now, I'll take you on a ride, so that you know what to aspire for."

"I must go," said Barnabas. "I'm in the middle of looking for a dangerous man. A known bandit. I'm working with the volunteer policemen Yany and Sabas."

"Oho, a local bully?"

"Not at all."

"Some friend of yours with whom you argued?"

"I barely know him."

"One of your own, fallen down into the cracks of the national problem? Drunk somewhere in the bushes, I assume? I'd be more than happy to participate in the reeducation of such a man. Remember, as long as the thaller shines brightly, there is hope." He scribbled something on his pad.

"And now I must go, sir."

"Young man. A boy of your lowly position can't afford to refuse my help. When I was a young boy at the Akademy, could I refuse? One time a cavalry officer asked me to shower with his daughter. Did it turn into a wedding? Not your business, but I'll tell you this, she looked so much like her father, to this day I can't say with whom I took that shower. The moral is, does it behoove a swineherd to refuse me, pelt and leather mogul, master of belts and soles? Think about it very hard."

"I guess it doesn't," Barnabas admitted after almost a minute of reflection. It would indeed be impolite not to, he thought. Yet what of the central, insufferable fact that von Grushka was, perhaps every night, usurping Barnabas's place by the side of his inamorata? How did this stand in relation to the problem of a swineherd refusing a leather mogul?

"Get in," von Grushka said, having pulled Barnabas to the automobile while the latter had been ruminating on the complex relationship between items abovementioned in the chapter title.

"Fine," said Barnabas. He walked to the passenger's side. "Do you buy pigs for your leatherworks?" he said, situating himself in the armchair-sized passenger seat.

"A Gippopotam 260394TYDCLS Suprasupra! Four-cylinder engine. 2545 overhead valve!"

After a few rounds of the square, they drove down the bumpy road from the town to the woods. "Does she know when to stop, your machina, I mean?" Barnabas asked, while von Grushka dashed over divots and holes.

"It stops when I tell it to." Von Grushka took a sharp turn, his knobby, potato-like shoulder nudging Barnabas'. "Why don't you tell me about this degenerate bully, drunk in the bushes."

"His name is Yurek."

"How do you know him?"

"I don't know him at all."

"How will you be able to recognize him?"

"By his smell."

"How often *do* the peasants bathe?"

"Never. Sometimes Yurek takes a piece of sandpaper and rubs himself. Also, sir, I don't exactly consider myself a peasant. My great-great-grandfather Barnabas the First was emancipated and developed the family name, if you don't mind me telling you. Also, as a matter of etiquette, I feel I must tell you I am the only Odolechkan who bathes."

"Ah yes, the cruelty of feudalism. Half the time emancipation turned out bitterer than bondage. Then you *do* know this stinking drunk bully who steals from his own people?"

"No, I don't. Who told you I did?

"Does he beat his wife?"

"I'm certain he would, were any woman smelly enough to marry him," said Barnabas, quite unaware that Yurek had recently entered into holy matrimony.

"I do have a free hour! Odolechka is my interest as much as yours, you know. A bandit at large in my bailiwick is a hole in my raft. Any idea where he might be found? What are his interests other than wife beating, drunkenness, banditry, skulking, and whatever all else you do?"

"Scratching his pimples. He likes that very much. I'm not aware of his other hobbies. I don't think he drinks. He does, as you somehow knew, like bushes, or so I've heard . . . from those who know him."

"There! We could start there. Seems like a place secluded enough for your degenerate woman hater, plenty of bushes to explore." He pointed to some poplar trees surrounded by dense shrubbery. "In fact, these are the very bushes you people most often frequent drunk, these ones being so close to town, am I wrong?"

"This is not a bad idea!" said Barnabas, who rather liked bushes himself (except when they contained the corpses of priests, or when his beloved had punched his face and propelled him into the weigelas, or the time he had hidden from Burthold and the other boys at school, only to find out later that his rear end had protruded from the bushes, and that the boys had snuck up on him and had carefully glued to his trouser seat a sign that read PRIVATE PROPERTY: NO HUNTING OR FISHING, nor did he, come to think of it, like von Grushka's parable of stick bushes, nor did he like nettles. But, other than those special cases, bush examination could be, to a certain extent, a pleasurable activity. Maybe this was why Yurek spent so much time in bushes. Maybe there was a germ of the Pierkiel intelligence in Yurek after all), and he looked from the poplars to the gold rings pinching von Grushka's overlarge knuckles. Von Grushka wasn't as bad as Volodek had said. Volodek had often warned Barnabas that von Grushka was "of the subclass of lazy annuitants," whatever that meant.

"We must approach this methodically. You start from one end and I from the other, and then we meet in the middle." Von Grushka indicated the long row of bushes. "And when you find him, yell."

"What do I yell?"

"Yell, 'Found him.'"

"Found him," Barnabas repeated. "There is another problem. How do we know where we meet exactly?"

"There." Von Grushka, with self-conscious symbolism, picked up a stick, thrust it into the middle of the bushy row, and marched to one end, while Barnabas marched to the other. They spent close to twenty minutes peering amid the twigs.

"Make sure to check close by the ground!" cried von Grushka, kneeling, proceeding on all fours. Barnabas followed this example.

"Find him?" von Grushka asked, when, on all fours, they met by the stick, in the shrubbery's deepening shadows.

"Not in my half."

"Not in my half either," said von Grushka. "You did say he was drunk in these bushes, did you not?"

"All I found is a bird's nest. But a bird's nest is not Yurek." Barnabas sighed.

"We did our civic duty," said von Grushka, sitting. From his pockets, he took his pad, which he placed on one knee, and his flask, from which he took a martial swig. He passed it to Barnabas. No Scalvusian with etiquette refused a drop of liquor, no matter the time or locale. Barnabas drank, thinking of all the bushes he and his new ally against Yurek might just have to search before the Solstice Celebration. How many bushes in and around Odolechka? Would he even have time to attend the Solstice? Should he ask von Grushka for some money to purchase new gifts? The man was scribbling something on his pad.

"I am a poet, a man of the people, and master of soles, and yet I am unhappy," von Grushka said, allowing the pad to slide down from his thigh onto the grass. "I say this knowing you won't betray me. Men don't betray each other after they have searched bushes together. It's a matter of honor." He picked up a ladybug and crushed it, scrupulously wiping its entrails into the grass. He drank and passed the flask.

"I'd never," Barnabas agreed. "Is it a problem with your pamphlet?"

"Not my pamphlet but an epic love poem I've been working on for some time."

"I have experience with romances and epics." Barnabas drank. "I'd be happy to help."

"The story is very simple. It involves a charming young aristocratic mogul, who wrestles like Hercules and shoots like Cephalus."

"Hercus and Cephlos are your heroes?"

"No, the charming mogul is."

"What's his name?"

"Tarol. This charming Tarol is in love with a woman."

"What's the woman's name?" said Barnabas, more and more prepared to like this poet, this man of the people.

"Moosha. The story itself is simple, it's the *verse* that delivers the punch to the testicles, if you know your military school culture, if you know what I mean. Tarol gives Moosha a brassiere for her birthday. She vows to never take it off. She wears the brassiere all the time, day and night. At night, he asks her to take it off, and she won't. This bothers him for reasons you are just a year or so too young to understand, but he appreciates how much she loves the gift. Then Tarol, who tries to keep his affair with Moosha secret from everyone in town, brings his trusted friend to meet her."

"What's the friend's name?"

"His name is the Mayor. It's all theoretical, of course. Are you following?" He drank and passed the flask.

"I think so," bubbled Barnabas out of the corner of his flask-plugged mouth.

"Suddenly, two weeks after she is introduced to the Mayor, she changes. She is now not so coy, and that twinkle disappears. Also, the Mayor plays glass *koogel* with the mogul's wife. A sinister character, you see, he has a hand in every pocket."

"What twinkle?"

"Twinkle she had in her eye," von Grushka somewhat slurred, "each time she looked at Tarol."

Barnabas drank. "Like a sty?"

"A love-sty, of sorts, if you like." He picked the pad up from the grass and noted something quickly. "I have my own system of notetaking. Code, you know. Scalvusian cadet code. Don't try to read over my shoulder. It will do you no good. But it gets even more dramatic—one day, the brassiere disappears. She claims it's in the washing. When Moosha isn't looking, Tarol sneaks to check her clothesline, digs in her dirty clothes chest."

"All of this is in the epic?"

"Every line."

Something about this poetic summation distressed our hero, though he couldn't fathom what it was. He drank and passed the flask.

"But there's no sight of the brassiere," von Grushka said, "not even a thread. Not even a hook! Then, one day, hunting muskrats with a 1921 Mannlicher rifle in her garden, Tarol finds something in the bushes. That rifle was discontinued after 1921, you know. The epic hero, Tarol, has the third-to-last one ever made."

"Bushes? What?"

"Yes, bushes. Mere coincidence. It is a handkerchief monogrammed BP."

"And what does it stand for?"

"These are the little-known initials of Tarol's friend, the Mayor."

Barnabas was so affected by this story that he took the flask from von Grushka's extended hand, which weaved in the dark before his face, and swigged rather too ambitiously and reeled with vodka pouring from his nose.

"Careful now, young intellectual."

"Do you borrow much from life?" asked Barnabas, recovering.

"Hardly anything. It's purely Orphic verse, more challenging this way. But here comes my question on the subject of the plot that has tortured me for some time. Are you ready?" Von Grushka clutched a tuft of grass, and, Barnabas noticed, two dark sweat stains had appeared on his shirt, his vest having come unbuttoned.

"Yes." Barnabas leaned forward curiously, so close he could see red bumps on von Grushka's chin.

"Is the Mayor responsible for all this?" Von Grushka drank. "Is he her secret lover? Is he the Judas, the dastardly handkerchief-dropper, the wicked brassiere-snatcher?"

Barnabas reflected, "It seems that, from all the suspects, the Mayor is the most likely," then said with conviction, "I don't believe it could be Cephs or Hercs. Do you know Yany and Sabas?"

"It is the Mayor, then!" Von Grushka tore a grass tuft from the earth. "Is that what your instinct tells you? I like to get the opinion of the lower classes, even for my epic poems. Plebeians operate with prehistoric instincts, which, more often than not, and not often enough, are right."

"I am convinced," said Barnabas, proud to be participating in a work of culture so important. "I am convinced it is the Mayor who snatched the brassiere."

CHAPTER XVIII

In which too much transpires to be summed up

THE TRADITION OF THE ST. JOHN'S CELEBRATION DATED TO WHEN SEMI-mythic Porevit chased Danica around the fire, attempting to tear off her tunic, and Porevit, frenzied by Danica's yelping, fled through the woods in search of the legendary fern egg, the only gift that might make her forgive him, and dug many ditches in hope of finding one and, naturally, failed to, because there is no such thing, and so her brothers killed him with a petrified egg lashed to a horse's legbone. No one remembered what any of this had to do with St. John. Over the centuries, many a Scalvusian had looked for the fern egg, but by the summer of 1939, nobody had the strength or faith for further excavation. A few septuagenarians traditionally searched for clover and coltsfoot that, gathered before the St. John's sunset, was said to cure polyps and gout, but most merely honored the Solstice with mirthful imbibing, speechmaking, wrestling, and wading in rivers.

Before I delve further into these practices as they manifested in the town of Odolechka, I must recount the gathering that took place at von Grushka's residence, which involved the crème de la crème of local society. Indeed, such a privilege it was to be invited that the wife of Celestyn the barber had stabbed her pinky with a pair of shears in hope of befriending the Doctor, thence entering the refined inner circle, but the Doctor, while shakily applying a zigzag stitch, had had to explain that his own wife had had to beg to have had them invited at all.

(Had I had to write *had* one more time in that last sentence, this chronicle surely would have had to be consigned to the Hades—if I may—of manuscripts, for English is a strange and exhausting language, indeed.)

Von Grushka held court from the end of a table heavy with Scalvusian cuisine, including, but not limited to, chops, tenderloins, bowls of *kroopnioks*, and, of course, *bigoses*. His sniffling wife sat on his right. All the dignitaries were present: the Police Chief, the Mayor, the Head Clerk, and, cornered up against a gigantic sideboard, the social-climbing Doctor and his Wife.

Apollonia, with a carefully cultivated attitude of a grand dame, arrived forty fashionable minutes late. The Mayor had been there, and drinking, for an hour. Wrapped in pink chiffon, she crossed the room and, with the zest of an insect pollinating a flower, descended onto a chair between the Head Clerk and the Doctor's Wife.

"You look lighthearted and pretty," said the Doctor's Wife, fidgeting in her chair.

"It's the lambency that only a promise of God's Grace illumes." Apollonia spread her napkin on her lap and waved at von Grushka's manservant Romek, who approached, bearing a tureen of goulash and a wine decanter and, while pouring wine into her glass, poured a tastefully small amount of goulash on the table. Apollonia dabbed at the spill with a finger and tasted it approvingly.

"As long as we have Jesus' water." Apollonia cast a provocative glance at the Police Chief, who, across from her, had just pushed something large into his mouth with a fork. "Doctor's Wife," she said, "why do you keep fidgeting?"

"What a suggestion."

"Yes, you are fidgeting."

"My shoes are too tight, but they're the only ones I have," the Doctor's Wife whispered.

"The meager Doctor's wages, yes, I know," said Apollonia with a bassoonist's lung capacity and volume.

"Yes," whispered the Doctor's Wife, tucking her feet under her chair. She drank a shot of vodka. "Do you think you might say something to your husband? Maybe there could be some civic project. Might we need a hospital for animals?"

"If you had actually *read* the enlightening *Melancholy Labors of the Spleen: An Account of the Surgical Profession, Its Triumphs as Well as Its Best Efforts* I've so many times recommended to you, which Kryshia has finished, you'd know you're not the only ones in the medical profession to be treated no better than schoolteachers. Amyad, that genius who performed the first appendectomy, was discriminated against as well."

"Why?"

"He was a Huguenot," Apollonia said, at the same time extending her leg so that it grazed the Police Chief's.

The Police Chief moved his leg and looked up from his *bigos*, not at Apollonia directly, but somewhere in the proximity of her right ear. She turned to see the Head Clerk devouring a plate of stewed pork knuckles, an action interrupted by suppressed hiccups.

"Head Clerk, do you have a hiccup? You know the cure," said the Doctor, hinting at the well-known remedy of saying a particularly filthy line of verse just as one feels the hiccup coming to the surface.

"Yes," said Apollonia—apropos of what, who can say?— "the road to happiness is often paved with red bloody lace . . . Do you have a pencil?" she asked the Doctor's Wife. "Don't worry, I'll return it. I know Anechka had to debase herself for it in the tavern," and, receiving a stub of charcoal from the Doctor's Wife's bag, scribbled on a napkin:

You have touched me, fornicator.

She reached for a plate of *gowumpki* and stealthily dropped the note onto the Police Chief's plate, just as he was stabbing for a bite of pig's ear. He got the pig's ear on his fork after a few tries and, when he was done masticating the cartilage, noticed the note, attempted to pierce it with his fork, discontinued the futile efforts, reached for it with his fingers, and placed it in his mouth. Finding it distasteful, he spat it out and examined it more carefully.

"Jezebel!" the Police Chief whispered.

Apollonia assumed the attitude of an inappropriately groped relic. Between Apollonia's behavior and that of the Head Clerk, the Police Chief was under a great deal of stress. The Head Clerk had finished the pork knuckles!

"A friend of mine in Kowomunak," the Doctor started, "called on me about some trouble with their hens. All day they would run in circles. I examined the birds, and there was nothing the matter with them whatsoever. I took one egg to my laboratory, cracked it, and I saw it contained a tiny demon, Hippocrates be my witness."

"A demon?" Apollonia addressed the Doctor. "Why would a demon be inside an egg, even if this is the night of St. John? It doesn't seem a natural habitat for their species."

"Must've been the gypsies," said von Grushka's wife, and coughed up a delicate thread of blood onto her napkin. "Don't worry, everyone, it's just croup."

"And what do you intend to do to the gypsies, now that we know they killed the priest?" The Doctor addressed the Mayor.

"Who told you they did?" the Police Chief said.

"My wife," said the Doctor. "The Mayor already knows, if he hasn't told you."

"Who says Kumashko is dead?" said the Mayor.

"Oh never mind that. It's been known for some time," Apollonia said. "Answer his question, *dear*, what shall be done with those strumpet jades?"

"What do I intend to do?" The Mayor wistfully regarded the reflection of his nose in his butterknife. "What do *you* intend to do?" he asked the Police Chief.

"What I?" The Police Chief crumpled Apollonia's note in his lap. "I touched it not!"

"Oho! Who is the Mayor here?" Von Grushka dropped his utensils from eye level onto his plate, producing a terrific set of sounds. "As irresponsible a head of state as ever walked this competitive planet. Your kind"—he pointed to the Mayor—"soon enough, will go extinct, like the Chinese."

"Who?" said the Mayor.

"The Mongols," explained Apollonia with great disdain for her husband's education.

"The Mongols aren't extinct," the Head Clerk hiccupped.

"Was that supposed to be a line of ribald verse?" inquired the Doctor. "Because, if so—"

"What *are* you going to do about the gypsies?" said the Doctor's Wife to the Police Chief, who looked at the Mayor, and then the Head Clerk, who had finished the mutton *bigos* and was reaching for the venison *bigos*.

"I suppose we'll have to take some punitive measure," said the Mayor.

"Nothing too extreme, of course," von Grushka said, glancing at his wife, who thankfully was looking at a sore on her forearm and not listening, "considering we don't have proof or a real court of law in this metropolis."

"We at this table are the court of law in this town," Apollonia said, glaring at the Police Chief, who stared forlornly at the Head Clerk, who had finished the venison *bigos* and was reaching for the marmalade *pizy*. "We are all that stand," she said, "between lechery, drunkenness, gluttony, sloth, and Venus disease in this Devil's town."

"Soft on the gypsies, are you?" said the Doctor to von Grushka, bitter that he had not been invited to this dinner "man to man."

"Oho! Careful what you say, my quack. Just because I am a landlord doesn't mean I'm soft on gypsies. They pay rent, but I admit it, I'm a trifle absentee. I nearly never go there to collect what I am owed."

"A quack, am I? *Who* pays their rent?"

"You want to know who's soft on gypsies? I hear he's been loitering around that place I rent to them." Von Grushka pointed at the Mayor, who immediately choked on his *gowumpki*. "Sniffing their gypsy silks on the clothesline."

"What!" the Mayor spat. "Sniffing their *what*? My grandfather, I will remind you, exiled all the Jews in this town to Lublin! *I* am soft on gypsies? I will have those witches hanged!" He felt the onset of a spell, not unlike what had happened in the church, and so became abruptly meek.

A new note fell onto the Police Chief's plate. He unwrapped it, feeling hungry, nervous, overmatched, and altogether ill:

You hath coveted thy Mayor's wife.

He crumpled it and forced it underneath his belt. The Head Clerk winked at him and finished the last cheese *pierogi*.

"What about Yehuda Ben-Sholom?" the Doctor's Wife challenged the Mayor and, indirectly, his grandfather.

"Whoah, my friends! Who said anything about a hanging?" said von Grushka.

LET US NOW GO TO THE SOLSTICE CELEBRATION IN THE WOODS. BY THE TIME Barnabas reached the event, he was a tad tired from having sniffed for Yurek in approximately one fourth of Odolechka's major bushes. The glade swarmed with Odolechkans young and old, a few courageous ones jumping the bonfire, the rest sitting cross-legged and spread-legged in growing, sweaty numbers, faces ruddy, eyes wild with beer, mead, vodka, schnapps, and moonshine.

Before Barnabas could enter the crowd, Boiko the peddler confronted him, leading a horse.

"Just who I want to see on this night commemorating the exploits of St. John," said Boiko.

"I don't have any more money. Everything I bought from you last time was stolen."

"Here is something even the thief who was crucified beside Our Lord wouldn't steal. A horse that once belonged to that famous Odolechkan, Kumashko. A horse this holy would make any young man nearly a knight templar, were he to ride it."

This rhetoric appealed to Barnabas, as you might imagine, but not only did Barnabas lack capital, his loyalty to Wilhelm made him far more knightly, he reasoned, than this stick-legged stallion ever could.

"I'm sorry, but I have a horse."

"Ah, but this horse is known as Mr. Konskipysk," haggled Boiko.

"No thank you, sir."

As Barnabas strode away into the crowd, Boiko had already turned to Yanko (whose only other appearance in this chronicle, you will remember, involves a rather too-large dose of *chorluk*), and the two of them were merrily debating an installment plan.

Barnabas, the afternoon's alcohol having left his blood, stepped over a few limbs and, through some persistent wriggling, managed to create a square of grass for himself between two substantial lasses. Graciously, he accepted a bucket of what smelled and looked like Kashak's moonshine. Barnabas drank with great seriousness. He savored odors of moonshine, singed hair, Odolechkan dirt, and burning wood. A figure rose vertically out of the crowd, a meter above everyone else, the halo of the bonfire behind him. Barnabas stood to see who it was. It was his mentor and employer, Volodek, atop a crate labeled SURFACTANT. Barnabas returned to his nook between lasses, looking forward to some first-rate oratory.

"People of Odolechka, social animals," Volodek began. "The change of value that occurs in, for example, monkeys intended to be converted into capital, not unlike the monkeys playing a piano in an infinite sequence of public celebrations such as this one, playing for money of course, an infinite number of such monkeys playing forever for an infinite amount of capital, this change of value cannot take place in the monkeys themselves, nor in the barrel out of which they came, since in its function of means of purchase, it does no more than realize the price of the commodity it pays for, that is, public musical enjoyment, possibly even eventually the Fourth Symphony of Popin, as long as enough monkeys have played enough notes on enough pianos at enough public celebrations like this very Solstice, my people.

"The second essential condition to the owner of a monkey finding labor power in the market as a commodity is this: that the monkey, instead of being in the position to be sold, must be obliged to offer for sale his own owner! Thus invalidating the tyranny of man over animal, for what is man but the social animal?

"The question why this free animal sells his owner in the market has no interest for the prerevolutionary owner of monkeys, who regards the labor market as a branch of the general market. Definite historical conditions are necessary that—no, let me change the subject from animals to minerals.

"There is, in the ground, 'something.' Iron perhaps, or gold, or potatoes if you will allow me to consider them a mineral. Such questions as 'Is this a potato or a nugget of gold?' claim our attention only insofar as they affect rates of exchange. But the exchange of marriage vows between those who wear rings of gold and those who wear rings of potato is evidently an act characterized by a total abstraction from use value. Then one use value is just as good as another, provided only it be present in sufficient quantity. Or, as old Barbon the English bourgeois economist says, 'One sort of marriage is as good as another, if the man and woman be equal. There is no difference or distinction between women and men, for I have seen them without their robes.' A hundred pounds' worth of woman or gold is of as great value as one hundred pounds' worth of man or potato. And I, Volodek the Scalvusian prophet of inflationary war, concur."

Some cheered, especially at *potato* and *woman,* but Barnabas' head hurt, as did his hands, from all the bush rummaging, and he understood little of Volodek's speech, aside from the piano-playing monkeys. He had never met a monkey, though, he reflected. This in mind, he would have fallen asleep on the grass, had not Burthold and his flunkies, Matteush and Stashko, arrived to stand over him laughing and grunting.

Until now, I have successfully avoided the unpleasantness of describing this thuggish trio. It can no longer be avoided. Burthold's face drooped, his nose bridge was crooked from beatings, his nostrils were stretched from overzealous picking. From the fleshy lips that fit together in the manner of folded veal cutlet, an errant tooth protruded horizontally. No lack of local dames had enjoyed the grazing of that tooth against their cheeks. The other two hoodlums, Stashko and Matteush, looked like two drops of grubby water, their chief talents being, respectively, smashing flies midflight and drilling holes with a knife in any surface you like.

"Hello, sirs," said Barnabas, resisting an urge to clutch a substantial lass (substantially drunk, heaving with giggles) beside him for protection.

"Where is the thing?" said Matteush.

"Where is the what thing, fellows?"

"I know you took it, my fair bed-fouler, my best chum from school days." Burthold sucked on his tooth with gusto. "Stashko saw you in the bushes by my cabin."

"That's right," Stashko, the able fly smasher, confirmed. "Every day, I wake up, I make myself tea, and every time the lid of the teapot falls into the garbage, every day, I pick it out of the garbage, I wash it in the kitchen bowl, but first I need to go to the well, to fill the bowl with fresh water. I take my bucket and put on my sandals. Every day, there is a problem with my right sandal strap—"

"Proceed, my lengthy-winded whiner, to the part about the thing that is the thing we wish to impress upon our little best friend from schoolhouse days," said Burthold.

"As I walk with my bucket to the well," Stashko continued uncertainly, "my right sandal flapping, the strap pinching me, I bend down to fix it, and I see, as always, Burthold's wheelbarrow in his yard."

"Her was a beauty. With flowers in her belly!" interjected Matteush, whose near-Yurekian intelligence and countenance had terrified Barnabas since childhood.

"And then, I see something in the bushes," continued Stashko. "Something blond that looks like Pierkiel, though I wasn't really looking, focused as I was on my strap."

"What say you to that, my charismatic mattress-besmircher?"

said Burthold, and Matteush clapped his hands in joyful affirmation. "Which is all to say," continued Burthold, "you're a purloiner of wheelbarrows."

"I wouldn't steal your filthy barrow even if I lacked all etiquette!" Barnabas wailed, while Burthold danced above with woodpecker-like thrusting motions of the head and neck, threatening to jab Barnabas with his wayward tooth. "Besides, I wasn't in the bushes in the morning, only in the afternoon."

"You took what is not rightfully yours," said Burthold.

"I did not! Perhaps it was Yurek. I've been looking for him in the bushes."

"Who?" Matteush said.

"You might have heard of him as Yurk, his nom de guerre," said Barnabas, excited to at last employ his single phrase of French, obtained from *The Dead and the Bleak: A Romance of the Gaulish Occupation.* "A dangerous criminal, he is."

"So it *was* you." The tooth was so close to Barnabas' face, he could see its chipped edge and tartar coating. "Yurek Pierkiel, Pierkiel. You think we don't know about your feebleminded brother, you think we don't remember him from schoolish days?"

"I certainly don't have a brother! And I already told you I didn't take your wheelbarrow. What would I do with it?" Barnabas reasoned.

"Don't insult the wheel!" Matteush roared, grabbing the moonshine bucket that had made its round yet again, pouring it over his face.

"When I was fixing my strap, I did feel sad, though I didn't know why," said Stashko. "I thought it was because of my sandal. But I see now it was the loss of the wheelbarrow, that, by rights, was Burthold's, for whose else could it be, when it had always been his, other than when it was Dudrovski's, who sold it to Burthold's father, who left it to Burthold in his last will and testament, and may he, Burthold's father, rest in peace—"

"Shut up, my wet-straw slumberers. The time has come for retribution!" Burthold grabbed Barnabas by the sleeve, and Barnabas, being of a much more meager statue than his opponent, merely suggested, "Be careful with my shirt," and collected himself to a standing position.

"See this coppice there?" Burthold pointed his tooth to the trees at the edge of the glade.

"The birch trees?"

"I want you to weave their roots with your entrails."

"In a bow," added Matteush poetically.

In one novel, Barnabas could not remember which, Rudolf Vasilenko is surrounded by three hulking pirates in the port of Gdańsk: a tattoo-faced ventriloquist Russian, a harpoon-wielding Zulu, and a 180-kilo Turkmenistani.

"This is cowardly, sirs, three against one," Barnabas opined as he was dragged from the crowd to the accompaniment of Volodek's continuing oration:

"In 1630, a wind-sawmill, erected near Krool by a Dutchman, succumbed to the excesses of the populace. They abused it in the following ways: morally, politically, unmentionably, and critically. They wrote many editorials about it, not mentioning it. As late as the beginning of the eighteenth century, sawmills driven by water overcame the editorial, political, critical, and marital disaffection of the people, mentally, mentionably, musically, and onomastically dominated as these social animals were by the Church. No sooner had St. Ignacy in 1758 erected the first wool-shearing machine that was driven by water power, than it was set on fire by one hundred thousand social animals who had been thrown out of approximately forty thousand houses, hovels, tents, and covered ditches by the forces of machinery organized into a system mentionably, approximately, onomastically, and gubernatorially, and the cycle repeats! Have not our neighbors the Czechs already fallen to the German machine?"

"Friends! Volodek! Grandma!" Barnabas cried. "Wilhelm!"

Matteush kicked Barnabas' ankle, then produced a bottle cap and rammed it into his own forehead with a grunt of appreciative pain, such that it stuck there like a diadem.

"Quid pro quo," said Burthold and kicked Barnabas' other ankle. Then he kicked the ankle Matteush had kicked. They were now beyond the firelight, well into the trees. Barnabas, though brave, felt spontaneous urination was not out of the question.

"We aren't actually going to kill you, my little mole-hole-humper from school days of yore. We only intend to kick your ankles for a while." Burthold demonstrated this, and indeed, they took turns kicking Barnabas' ankles for some time, hoping, it seemed, to elicit a counterattack from their quarry, some pretext for beating him in a "fair fight." They were kicking his ankles not terribly hard, it should be said, though they had begun to kick a little harder (and Barnabas was feeling rather terrorized and wondering if his strategy of nonviolence had failed to bore them) when an infernal yowl resounded from the nearby ferns.

"Fern egg?" said Matteush.

"Just fine families celebrating," Burthold said and jabbed Barnabas' ear with his tooth.

"Auuu!" Barnabas clasped his ear.

"What did you say, wheelbarrow kidnapper? Admitting your guilt, are you at last?"

"I'm looking at him, and he's saying nothing," Stashko observed. "Pierkiel, I mean to say, is the one I am talking about, the one who, right now, is saying nothing, even as, you, Burthold, ask him, at close range, what he has said."

"That's witch sounds," Matteush said. The howl came again, not loud, but nearby.

The ferns shuffled and, bizarrely, jingled.

"The Solstice gold." Matteush lumbered toward the jingle.

"If I were you, which I am not, and which, I mean to make it understood, I could not be," said Stashko to Matteush, "such things are, they say, impossible, but on St. John's Night, who knows? And perhaps they say it for the right reasons, but were I you, which I am not, I would not, under no circumstances, go to those ferns by using my feet and then touch the ferns, as you are about to."

But Matteush, ignoring this sensible advice, was already waist-deep, batting at fronds.

"Ahh!" Matteush exclaimed. Something vaguely resembling a womanly form sprang from the ferns and ran out onto the forest path beside them. The figure had twigs in her matted hair and high-boned cheeks warpainted with soil.

"I think I know you. Solstice Fairy?" Matteush said.

"I thought it was a *turlak*!" cried the figure, and, under the nest of hair, Barnabas recognized Tsura. Distressed and relieved to see Tsura, he peered into the dark to see if Roosha was there, too.

"Do you carry a bag of money coins?" Matteush said.

"No, do you?" Tsura looked up at him with interest.

The ferns stirred on the other side of the road, and Roosha emerged, bearing a nosegay of dry *zhebina*. She looked from one man to another and began to dig a small divot in the soil with her bare heel. "What is this gathering about, men's gymnastics?"

"These three bed-saturators know nothing of nocturnal contortions. I, on the other hand, am a master of ceremonies of the mattress, o my agile wet nurse of the night," said Burthold, sucking on his tooth, approaching Roosha.

"Your tooth, I'm afraid, is the only teat that will nourish you tonight, cavalier," responded Roosha. "Hold my *zhebina*, please." She pressed the dry stems into Burthold's arms. "Just don't touch the thorns; they might crawl under your skin, and, before the night's out, you'll be as rigid as my grandmother Tschilaba, when we pushed her dead body down the frozen waterfall in Lesosibirsk."

"I thought she was buried with the rope around her toe, that's what you said before, Miss Roosha Papusha," said Barnabas shyly.

"No, that was when we made a mistake and she was not dead yet. These things are not always apparent; besides, she always had such a pale complexion, almost like a Scalvusian's. You boys don't look in proper health yourselves. Perhaps you shouldn't stay in the woods for too long. Midnight vapors are unhealthy for those who are not accustomed to them."

Matteush poked at Tsura's headdress of twigs. Tsura slapped his hand. He retracted the hand and studied it.

"Miss Roosha, this is not a fitting place for you," said our brave Barnabas. "The midnight vapors are quite pleasing, I admit, but this company—"

"Quiet, rank and dank mole-hole-enthusiast! Think of your ankles." Burthold stepped backward and brushed his hirsute calf against Barnabas' calf. "This is our old friend from the grand old days of school," Burthold explained to Roosha, grinding the nosegay into the top of Barnabas' head. "We shared chalk together. Fed him lots of it in the classroom corners. But now, the old hole-pounder's done a nasty thing and stole my wheelbarrow."

"I witnessed it myself this morning, when I leaned down—" Stashko said.

"Just as I thought," said Roosha. "I've met this swineherd before, when he tried to rob first my garden, then my pipes."

"And he got paid twice for the pig and did not return one thaller," added Tsura.

Barnabas was outraged. Far worse than having one's ankles kicked, to be accused of thievery by one's own inamorata and her family!

"It's convenient you have him right here," Roosha continued, playing with the gold chain (surely purchased by von Grushka) around her neck. "I've been looking for him all over town. I'm here to cast a curse on him, if you'll allow me. The curse I have in mind is one we used on a pork butcher in Tarnopol, who would not sell us even tripe, though our money was money, was it not? It seems fitting to use that curse now on a swineherd."

At this, the threat of urination manifested yet again, but manfully, our hero held his own, as it were.

"Cast a curse on *me*, first," Burthold said, dropping the stems, walking over them, and placing his hands on Roosha's hips.

Stashko closed a hand on Barnabas' wrist. Matteush remained transfixed by his own hand.

"Oh, no, curses are cast only on those who deserve them." Roosha wriggled from his grip. "Though it *was* very ungentlemanly of you to have dropped my *zhebina*. He who walks on *zhebina* goes impotent early in his middle years, around the age of forty, it is well known. It's not a curse, just a fact. I heard it from the best gypsy urologist in Lvov."

Barnabas regarded the trampled flowers of this unfaithful woman, this heart-destroyer who accused him openly of thievery, when it was Yurek who had stolen, Yurek who had ruined his attempt to woo her in a gentlemanly fashion, and yet, despite his outrage, he fought an urge to pick up the *zhebina* for her. This interesting turmoil was disrupted when, on the narrow path between the ferns, at a distance of thirty meters or so, a few men came out of the woods. Two walked toward our assembled conversationalists, hands held out at some distance from their sides so as to graze the ferns, and stopped within earshot, in the branch-cage of a weeping willow. A third man crossed the path, twirling his black hat in his hand, and receded into the trees.

"Are these fellows with you?" Burthold inquired of Roosha.

"Who is with anyone?" Tsura said. "Maybe they're just someone's brothers out for night air. Some get their tan from the sun, some from the moon."

From the direction of the darker trees beyond the three men came the sound of air blown through a gap in teeth, not a whistle exactly.

"Is a gypsy." Matteush pointed into Tsura's hive of hair.

"I will leave you now, o dewy *rushoolka*," Burthold said. "But I will be back for my curse."

Roosha picked up the *zhebina* and caressed a few remaining, crumbling heads. She arranged the flowers in her hand and set off toward the clearing and the bonfire, Tsura behind her. Soon only her silhouette was visible in the distant firelight. She stopped and turned. "Pigboy," she said, beckoning.

"Good night, sirs," Barnabas said, with a modicum of rekindled dignity and aloofness. As he limped away from Burthold and company, he looked back once over his shoulder for the gypsy men. In the woods behind the bullies, a tossed black hat sailed between two trees.

THE CELEBRATION HAD QUIETED. SOME REMAINED ENGAGED IN ODOLECHERY, others slept, a few mumbled tearfully in drunken stupors. Only Volodek remained undiminished atop his crate, approaching, indicated by his modulation and acceleration, the conclusion of his speech. Roosha listened, Barnabas behind her, his face almost touching the back of her head. His face hurt from the fire's heat, and when she moved her head, a coil of her hair brushed his face: Barnabas died, was reborn, died, was reborn, et cetera.

"A man, woman, or monkey of either sex can have a use value without having value." Volodek shook two fingers in the air. "This is the case whenever a man is born of a woman who does not labor. Caesar was one, Christ another, Volodek as well. Also without value but with use value are air, virgins, pastures, and so forth. A man, a pasture, or woman of either sex can be useful and can, in certain cases or barrels, be the product of human labor without being a commodity.

"Take examples from history. The medieval peasant produced quit-rent-corn for his feudal lord and tithe-corn for his parson. His parson produced quit-rent-domination-of-the-laity for his bishop and tithe-domination-of-the-laity for his Pope. The Pope produced quit-rent-excommunications for his Holy Roman Emperor in Speyer and tithe-excommunications for his critics. His critics include economists, gypsies, sodomites of either sex, Jews, astronomers, doctors, doctors' wives, Mohammedans, Mongols, bolsheviks, Lutherans, and prophets of inflationary war! Thank you."

Barnabas (who had closed his eyes while dying, etc.), upon Volodek's mention of gypsies, opened his eyes to look down into Roosha's lovely hair, but she had gone.

CHAPTER XIX

In which two friends become friendlier in a shed

THE POLICE CHIEF PASSED HIS BULK THROUGH THE DOOR. A HORRIBLE STENCH assaulted his nostrils. Tumbled blankets lay on the shed's floor, as did a blackened pipe. Soiled garden tools lay jumbled in an iron bathtub, the bottom of which held tufts of hair and rings of filth. Black pellets littered a pile of hay and the floor's rotting planks.

The Police Chief stooped over a pellet and sniffed. "I see. Why is there goat shit everywhere?"

"Oh? I haven't noticed," said the Mayor from the floor, playing glass *koogel*. "Do you want to play? Moreover, it can't be goat shit. I do not own a goat."

"This is not the right moment for games, if you don't mind. This moment is too momentous."

"I wish Nastya were here," said the Mayor.

"Who's Nastya?"

"Von Grushka's wife. Please make yourself at home." The

Mayor pointed at an inverted wooden bucket and flicked a glass ball with his thumb.

"Dear, dear friend," the Police Chief started, attempting to fit himself onto the bucket. "May I call you brother? Are we at that point yet in our long relationship as caretakers of this troubled town?"

"Mm," said the Mayor, fiddling with his *koogel*.

"Well, then let me say, having heard your strong stance at the Solstice dinner yesterday, I feel as if we are brothers at last. I've spent God knows how many sleepless afternoons on this case. I've thought it through thoroughly, inspected it from every side and angle. This entire time, I knew, I mostly knew, that there was something to be done, but didn't know what. My mind was too small to figure out the solution."

"What solution? What stance?" asked the Mayor sourly, closing one eye and lowering to his hands and knees in the blankets and goat dung, lining up his next shot.

"Also, this is no time for modesty, Mayor." The Police Chief leaned forward and the bucket toppled. To regain his balance, he caught the edge of the bathtub.

"Can you move your foot?" the Mayor asked. "You're in the way."

"I am referring to your plan to hang the gypsies."

"My plan? I think it was von Grushka who suggested it."

"No, I know you are a modest man, but it was you, my friend, the rightful head of this wonderful town of Odolechka, more or less the Pearl of the Outer Wheat Belt."

"No, it wasn't. Besides, punitive measures are not my job, but yours," said the Mayor, and he sent the glass ball rolling across the room, where it ricocheted against an old washing board and embedded itself in a briquette of dung. The Mayor stood, walked to the ball, and examined this troublesome arrangement. "It is strange, indeed. We don't even have a goat." He scratched his pate.

"Underneath the goat shit, do you smell something else, something . . ." The Police Chief's investigative senses activated. He sniffed. "Something *mushroomy* almost?"

The Mayor, abandoning his *koogel* with a shrug, walked to an unsteady shelf by the shed's back door and examined the objects displayed thereupon: a punctured metal bucket, a queer gluey ball, and a shiny canister labeled SNUFF. "To me, it smells like boletus," he said, after some reflection. "Whose things are these?" He pointed at the gluey ball.

"There is also something else." The Police Chief sniffed. "Getting back to our subject. How do you want the gypsy case handled?"

"Whatever you want to do will be fine."

"I am just the hand here, Mayor, metaphorically talking. You're the brain of this organ. Probably only a brain like yours could've . . . well, do you know what I'm talking about?"

"Oh, I don't know," said the Mayor. "It was von Grushka. Do with the gypsies what you please or what someone else pleases. No, it is out of my hands."

"Mayor, sir, I could never take this from you. It would be like the hand ordering the brain."

The Mayor thought about that as he picked up the canister labeled SNUFF. "I've read somewhere that aubergines in Australia do that and they're fine. The hand goes first, the brain second, then the feet, I think. I read this in the *Krool Gazeta*."

"But they are just barbarians." The Police Chief turned the wooden bucket over so that it was no longer inverted, noticing it was wider at the mouth. Perhaps it would be rather more functional as a chair in this arrangement, "Here in Odolechka, the brain goes first, then the hand," but his right buttock sank into the bucket with his left left aloft. He stood and debucketed, breathing heavily. "By my ancestors the Kooza, Mayor, what do you propose we do? You have to talk to me, or what am I, a telepathic?"

"Oh, what do you suggest? It really *is* your job, not mine." The Mayor fiddled with the shiny canister.

"I'll tell you, Mayor. We are a democracy after all, aren't we? Didn't our grandfathers fight for the popular vote. Why don't we organize a town meeting to see what other Odolechkans have to say? We're not Russians, after all. We believe in group decision making, no?"

"The vote?"

The two men stared at each other for several bewildered seconds, trying to recall a single instance of a single Odolechkan voting anywhere, on anything, national or local.

"That's exactly what I propose," said the Mayor. "Let us organize the town for a meeting. I really must go to bed quite soon."

"Mayor, may I call you brother? You are a great man indeed. Ever since the dreadful murder, I've felt as if the entire country were waiting for us, for the solution, as if even the Pope in Spain wants you and me to do something . . . Do you know what I'm trying to say?"

The Mayor grunted in semi-assent, trying and failing to open the canister.

"I'm saying you are defending our land, as you did during the Siege," said the Police Chief, and the Mayor mentally congratulated himself on his little oft-told tale of combat, so persuasive he himself had come to believe it. (In truth, the Mayor, at that time known as the Mayor's Son, had spent the Siege locked in his coal cellar.)

"By your wise decisions," said the Police Chief, "you're saving both me and the town from the greatest humiliation this century has seen. You're my dearest friend, you know, and if you asked me never to see the Head Clerk again, I would renounce him!"

The Mayor bent and from the hay gathered a stashed bottle of vodka, mysteriously half-consumed. Now *who* could have stolen his vodka? Apollonia never drank vodka. "A glass for each leg to celebrate whatever you're talking about," he said, and they both drank from the bottle that, the Police Chief noticed, rather distinctly possessed the anomalous smell.

"And now a glass for each hand," said the Mayor.

The Police Chief's face was patchy with emotion. "My God! If only your grandfather Anatol could see!" He gave the Mayor's cheek a vodka kiss. "I may not be the holiest man, but I think Heaven could be possibly full of Mayors and Chiefs," said the Police Chief, pointing to the shed's A-framed ceiling. "And Anatol is drinking one for his hands and one for his legs for you right now. I don't claim to know if angels have vodka, but if they do, Anatol is toasting you, his truest heir, for bringing back the days of glory for Odolechka."

They drank again in silence: an impromptu vigil for Anatol.

The Mayor finally broke this reverend quietus: "I think we should again have a glass for each leg, not to feel unsteady, but I do feel certain that *something* will happen. We may not have to do anything at all! This town will prosper. I do feel certain of that."

They finished the bottle, and singing an old coal miner's ballad, the Police Chief went home.

WHEN APOLLONIA ENTERED THE SHED, SHE FOUND THE MAYOR ON HIS KNEES, extracting a *koogel* ball from a piece of goat dung with a pair of tongs.

"Why is there so much goat dung?" asked the Mayor.

"Always asking questions, aren't you? I know I am the Alpha and Omega, but really, is there no end to this?" Apollonia buttoned and unbuttoned the collar of Mshchiswava's dress. "I've been in the house for hours improving myself. I use books, I use physical exercise, I use nutrition, I use spiritual methods so advanced that a heathen like you would be struck dead to hear them. What do *you* do? I find you in here picking at whatever that is you are picking at. I'm only thankful we didn't have children. I'm thankful Jesus chose to curse you with impotence. Was the Police Chief here?"

"Is this yours?" The Mayor showed her the canister.

"Perhaps it's the Police Chief's. I know he was here, I heard his drunken giggles. As your wife and one of the town's dignitaries, I feel obliged to tell you that this man should be demoted. He is lascivious and incompetent." Affectionately, she picked up one of the filthy blankets and pressed it to her athletic breasts.

The Mayor hunched over the canister and attempted again to open it, this time with success.

"Are you listening?" said Apollonia, reading the lid of the canister. "You shouldn't use snuff, you're too sensitive for it."

"He's a friend, you know, the Chief," the Mayor mumbled, taking a pinch. "I'm not impotent, you know." He snorted lustily. With a noise like an elephant dying in childbirth, he lurched backward, doubled over, and crashed onto the washing board, expelling from several facial orifices a slurry of mucus and powdered fish.

CHAPTER XX

In which the People are heard

ON THE EVENING OF JUNE 25, 1939, KAROL VON GRUSHKA, LEATHER MOGUL, landlord, lieutenant of the Sixth Scalvusian Cavalry (retired), and gypsy sympathizer (for apolitical reasons with which the reader is familiar), drove his Gippopotam at high speed along the Viluga River, past some dozen fords and bridges of rope and wood, fourteen kilometers north, across a dangerously creaking bridge of wood and stone intended for horse- and ox-drawn carts, and then fourteen kilometers south to Odolechka, to the square, and parked directly in front of Town Hall. He leaped out and jogged up the front stairs and into the Hall, then up the internal stairs. Halfway up these stairs, a cloud of dust and paper bits collided with his face. He stopped and looked up at Grigor the janitor, who looked back at him expressionlessly and swept another stockpiled pile of civic dust down into the vicinity of von Grushka's head.

"I understand," von Grushka said and jogged up the remaining steps, pulled back his bulky arm, and drove his ringed fist into Grigor's face, which, before impact, rather resembled that of a stoat and, after impact, that of a stoat that's been punched in the face.

Von Grushka stepped over the semiconscious, bloody janitor, and past the Secretary, who did not look up from her beverage, and past the pantry and official ofuce, to a second staircase, leading back down to the back of the first floor, and descended it in time to be the first citizen, other than the Mayor and the Police Chief, to arrive at the Town Meeting on the Subject of the Gypsies and Decency, posters of which, designed and penned by Apollonia, had hung for several days on the well, the door of the tavern, the door of Town Hall, and either side of the Police Chief's horse (which he could no longer ride, so why not?) tied by a very long rope to the back fence of the empty church.

"I'm here to keep things sane and, well, *decent*," said von Grushka, striding through a disorder of chairs and crates and boxes to the front of the auditorium, which had not been used in years, as was evidenced by the preponderance of cobwebs on the walls and fixtures. Floor dust, however, von Grushka noted, was in conspicuously short supply. He brushed off his shoulders and mustache and said, "Did you two hear what I said?"

The Mayor and the Police Chief looked up from behind the podium, where they had been examining something in the Mayor's hand. The Mayor returned to his pocket a small metal canister of some kind and said, "We're nothing but glad you have come, Karol. After all, it was you who demanded this meeting."

"Now listen, Mayor, I like to see things done in the right way. I come from a cavalry background, as you know, and I like to see the basic rights upheld, as they say. You might think I am here to protect an investment," said von Grushka, cleverly, he thought, "and perhaps I do have a monetary interest in two of my best renters not being hanged, but also there is the question of a proper trial, with evidence and what all else one needs. There is a court in Kowomunak, after all."

"I didn't want to have anything to do with this," the Mayor whined. "You forced me into this. I *hate* large groups. I hate when Apollonia invites even two other women over. I go into my shed. I'm a man who likes games in which both players win and whatnot. You *forced* me into this. Are you saying we don't have to have a meeting at all?"

"Now Mayor," said the Police Chief, "certain motions are in motion, if you—"

"No," von Grushka interrupted, "no, we do not have to have a meeting, not without the law of the land, as they say, the basic rights."

"Oh, good," said the Mayor.

"What about the glory?" said the Police Chief in a soft and piteous voice.

The ceiling began to rumble.

"Glad we got that settled," said von Grushka to the Mayor, "now another thing, why would you, of all Judas sneaks, want to punish the gypsies, hmm? You can tell me, old friend. Did someone, I need not say who, finally spurn you after all?"

"What!" But the rest of the Mayor's indignant reply was drowned by all the villagers of Odolechka, pouring en masse into the auditorium and taking chairs and crates and fighting over the former and kicking the latter and singing and thumping the backs of crying infants and one, Achym the unemployed, playing unintentional atonal modernism on a ram's horn bugle. Nearly everyone had come (except Roosha and Tsura, naturally, but also Barnabas, who was nursing his ankles and mating his pigs at a pig farm in Kowomunak, and Burthold, Matteush, and Stashko, who were "watching the tavern" for Dzaswav, and Yurek, who was honeymooning, and von Grushka's wife, Nastya, who was ill), and nearly everyone who would come had arrived at once, for reasons beyond my understanding, but then, the dynamics of mobs is a science in its infancy. Who can say why we, in groups of two or three, make love and conversation, and in groups of forty and above, make misery, religion, war, and manufactured goods.

Apollonia vaulted onto the meter-high stage and took the podium, stiffening an arm to full length to push the Police Chief aside. "People of my village!" she screamed. "We are here gathered, though we are damned, most of us, not to make Jesus weep anymore, but to take upon ourselves the duty of removing from this land the murderous, the Devil-worshipping witches who have too long festered like a *blue* gangrene and a *cryptic* gangrene, respectively, in the bowel of our Odolechka!"

She paused while a few arguments over chairs resolved more or less peacefully. Her husband stood behind her to one side, holding his palms against the sides of his face. Von Grushka had already slipped from the stage and taken a chair in the front, having little interest in appearing too *involved* in this riotous conclave of the plebs.

"I now present to you my husband, who, we may all admit, has not always been the most pious or effective civil servant, nor has he shown us much of an appreciation of righteousness thus far, however! This, his most recent and decisive enterprise, this meeting and the information he will reveal to you here tonight, will surely redeem his family name. I present to you—the Mayor!"

She stood aside. Someone in the audience simulated a post-digestional function. The Police Chief grinned at the Mayor, then frowned at Apollonia, then grinned at the Mayor, and the Mayor removed his hands from his face and shuffled to the podium.

"Odolechkans . . . ," started the Mayor. A wave of phlegm, produced by his nervously overstimulated membranes, rolled up his throat like a *grushik* noodle. "Citizens . . ." He cleared his throat.

The Police Chief hovered behind the podium, careful to stoop a little so as not to appear too much taller than his friend. The Mayor turned to the Police Chief and put his hand on his shoulder, seemingly in fraternal affirmation, and the Police Chief also clasped the Mayor's shoulder, and there ensued a brief struggle (masked by doltish grins) in which the Mayor attempted to pull the Police Chief in front of him to the podium.

"Listen to this Slavic Cicero!" exclaimed the Police Chief, finding himself somewhat to the front of the Mayor. He pointed to the Mayor with faux gallantry, saying, "Let him speak!"

The Mayor bowed and resumed his position.

"Odolechkans!" the Mayor started again, and though his throat was now clear, his voice had a strident, unnatural tone that surprised him, so that he doubted himself and stopped at once.

A hiss came from the left back corner of the room, and a raucous voice exclaimed, "Horchensky stole my gate wire!" It was Barnabas' grandmother, waving a stocking above the gathered heads like a banner.

"No, he did not!" Horchensky supplied from the right back corner, waving his greasy cap at her in return.

"Yes he did!" She swung the stocking lassolike. "It was hanging off my gate for fifteen years, then Horchensky came and stole it!"

"The antithesis between *lack of property* and *property*, so long as it is not comprehended as the antithesis of thesis and synthesis, still remains antithetical to the thesis synthesized, not unlike rubbers, vinyls, surfactants, consolidants, and lining adhesives," began Volodek, rising from his chair and stepping onto his box labeled SURFACTANT.

"Gypsies are the subject here, not rubbers!" the Police Chief yelled over the Mayor's shoulder, such that the Mayor jumped in fright and cringed.

"It was the gypsies stole it, not Horchensky!" Horchensky offered and removed his shoe and put it in his cap and swung the makeshift sling around his head and launched both cap and shoe at Barnabas' grandmother, over the gaping Odolechkans, but she dodged, and the missile struck Celestyn the barber in the front row. (Hereforth, when I say *row*, I am referring to a loose grouping of chairs or boxes that, in a genuine auditorium, would be aligned.)

"Lice, I don't doubt!" Celestyn kicked the capped shoe with disgust, and it slid against the polished amber leather of von Grushka's boots.

"Keep the plebeian disputes out of this!" von Grushka refereed. "Besides, this meeting is adjourned!"

"Let us not forget it's murder we're talking about," said Apollonia, extending her arms toward the podium, like a vestal hailing her fire pit.

"Let us not divert from the subject at hand," agreed the Mayor.

"I have a subject to raise." Basia the spinster raised three fingers. "There are three bricks missing from the well. When I went by it in the morning, I took a good look, and it seems someone's started picking on the fourth one. Yolanda died in the well. The corner of the brick was chipped." She curtsied.

"This meeting is about the gypsies, not the well bricks!" The Mayor looked as if he might collapse.

Daria the spinster raised her hand.

"You"—the Mayor pointed at her—"in the middle, in the helmet-looking thing. As long as it is not about the bricks."

"No. It's about the gypsies," said Daria and curtsied. "It's about what happened in my barn on Tuesday afternoon, if I may." She smiled. "On Tuesday afternoon, I tapped a chicken's neck with a chisel, and the next thing I see, if I may, the head is off on the ground, clucking and squirting blood. I barely touched it. I lean to grab it, and it moves away. It rolls and clucks, and I run after it down the street, in my house slippers, as it runs toward the town square like a Beelzebub chasing an atheist . . ."

Kryshia: "There was an atheist in *your* barn? Because in Apollonia's shed—"

Apollonia: "Silence!"

"I saw the rolling head, too! I was leaving Guzik Incorporated, where I bought strings for my wife's bonnet, and the head rolled over, clucking. I bent down to pet it, and it nipped me," said Kashak the moonshiner.

"This meeting is about—" began the Mayor, but Kowalchyk the tailor stood up.

"A similar thing happened to me last week. A letter came. Yoosef read it aloud to me. It happens that my sister gave birth to a three-headed ram," Kowalchyk announced with a mixture of embarrassment and pride. "It wasn't in this town, but it concerns this town, does it not? She *is* my sister, and I'll fight the man who denies it! She married an Orthodox shepherd."

"The Orthodox are gypsies!" yelled Horchensky.

"I wasn't there," confirmed the Doctor, waving his stethoscope.

"The answer is simple, brothers and sisters of Jerusalem! It shines clear like the star that led the darling Herod to the babe, as bright as the frankincense he lit by the Messiah's cradle. The gypsy harlots are poisoning our well with their cursed gypsy harlotry!" Apollonia announced.

"I don't see how the gypsies are to be blamed for a herdsman fathering a ram," said von Grushka grumpily, throwing one impressive leg over another. "Such things are to be expected with the plebs. The most efficient solution to this minor power struggle is to penalize the gypsies with a ticket. Perhaps issuing a reprimand."

"If you're saying Sister's my brother"—Kowalchyk's voice shook with offended honor—"or if you're saying Sister's a herdsman father, I'll fight you right here, not caring how many fancy guns you own!"

Apollonia: "Mere reprimand for murder?!"

Volodek: "Punishment is the *right* of the criminal. It is an act of her own will. The violation of a herdsman has been proclaimed criminal. The sister's crime is the negation of right. Punishment is the negation of this negation. The gypsies must become productive members of society. They live off the fruits of a factory baron!" He pointed at von Grushka.

Von Grushka: "Not true. They pay rent."

"*Do* they? Or do they not?" The Doctor bounced up and down on his seat.

"A ticket? A reprimand? As the brain of this organ and Anatol's descendant, I say these measures are enough." The Mayor had mustered the courage to deliver this breathless sentence.

"'Not enough,' my husband says, for those of you who are partially deaf!" Apollonia screamed.

"As the hand of the same organ, of which the Mayor is the fertile brain, I approve! Not enough. Hear the wise Mayor!" the Police Chief cheered.

"Organism, you mean organism!" said Grunvald the impoverished schoolteacher, who taught the children about half-apes mating.

"Was Anatol also an undergarment sniffer?" snapped von Grushka at the Mayor. "Did Anatol lurk around certain women not his own?"

The Mayor: "What!"

"Garments are my trade," Kowalchyk yelled, "and I'll fight the man who tries to put me out of business with a factory, just like Bolek's out of business!"

"I think a reprimand is a punishment good enough. I can deliver it," said Yoosef the postman, making a crude spanking gesture. "What I want to know is, who stole my scale?"

"You, *deliver* it?" Volodek said defensively. "You don't ever deliver anything! Why don't I ever get any mail?"

Bolek: "I'm not out of business!"

Yoosef to Volodek: "Nobody sends you mail, you warlock."

"Are you telling me you *never* received any mail of mine from Krasnoyarsk and Odessa? You are hiding it, you slave of the bourgeois authorities." Volodek kicked his SURFACTANT box in a genuine rage.

Over the Mayor's right shoulder, the Police Chief said, "The mail is not the subject today, the subject is—"

Volodek: "Oh it is, it *is* the mail that is a most crucial organ of communication between the social human and his brother!"

Kowalchyk: "I will fight the man who calls my sister Father!"

"I have something to say." A man in a long green sweater raised his hand.

"Who are you?" barked the Police Chief over the Mayor's left shoulder.

"Gavazyl Andryoshka."

"Are you a citizen of this town?"

"I've lived here for forty years." Andryoshka bit his sleeve. "Recently I had a chance to observe there have been some new displeasing developments. On the wall surrounding the church, there seems to be an excess of pigeon droppings. I had an unpleasant experience of leaning against it as I stopped to think about how life passes faster than you think when you are a boy of eight, off mother's milk at last—"

"Piss!" von Grushka said, jabbing a finger into his orange-tufted ear, "vinegar and *benzina*, we're not here to discuss pigeons! Let the strongest take charge of this squadron."

Andryoshka wiped his nose and muttered something into his sleeve.

"I am the one presiding over this gathering," said the Mayor to von Grushka.

"Then gather your troops and charge, instead of whimpering like a beggarly hireling!" Von Grushka brandished his fist.

"Ha! Look who says that, the most disreputated gypsy sympathizer Odolechka's ever seen! Oh, I will charge. I will charge!" the Mayor screamed, half flinging himself back to the podium, away from which he had been inching. This outburst, though electrifying, depleted the last of the Mayor's public capacity.

A gurgle came from the rearmost row. It was one of the two

village elders, until now nodding by the wall, awakened by the Mayor.

"Let the wise men speak!" said Apollonia. Everyone turned, and the elder opened and closed his mouth, with no further vocal emission. Elder number two also opened his eyes, enough to show his yellowed eye whites, and dramatically (and possibly with greater meaning than anything thus far said in this meeting) shoved out his dentures, a terrible, locally manufactured contraption that cut more tongues than Lechoswava the sausage rope maker, wife of Yerzy the butcher.

"The elders agree the punishment must be severe!" interpreted Apollonia.

"When will we have paved roads?" demanded Lechoswava. "In England, they have women's rights!"

"Where did you read that?" snapped Apollonia. "Such ideas are an abomination!"

"I don't have a wife!" yelled Guzik of Guzik Incorporated. "Where's my women's rights?"

"I do not read," Lechoswava said with pride. "I heard it from Zhmiya the spinster."

Police Chief: "Women's rights are not the subject!"

"I have a wife," announced Yerzy the butcher, in defense of his wife, and then, seeing the village expected of him something more: "Someone rode by me in the night, and just as he rides by he drops his trousers, and I never saw who it was."

"I have something to add," said Artur the greengrocer.

Grandmother Pierkiel: "You add nothing! You don't stock them limes or lemons!"

The Doctor: "It's true, Kumashko had scurvy. We all will soon if nothing is done."

"The gypsies are to blame, not scurvy." The Police Chief pounded the podium with a weighty fist, the Mayor leaning weakly against him.

Apollonia: "The gypsy sisters murdered Kumashko, Martyr of the Outer Wheat Belt!"

Twelve or more voices in staggered chorus: "Kumashko is dead!?"

Only the top of the Mayor's head was now visible above the podium, supported as he was between the Police Chief and his wife.

Dzaswav: "He's not dead. He's in the church."

Bolek: "The church is locked. He can't be dead."

The Police Chief's Secretary: "The church is locked because it is Sunday."

"He's officially dead. I have his death certificate." The Police Chief waved a piece of paper.

Grandmother Pierkiel waved her stocking.

Ludvik the gravedigger/notary: "So *that's* what I notarized?"

Anechka the barmaid: "Kumashko was short for a priest!"

Basia the spinster: "He's not dead. He just came to my house for tea last week!"

The Doctor: "Kumashko's been dead for just a bit less than a week. I tapped his knees myself. His neck was broken and one ear pierced."

"I've seen worse!" cried Kazhimiezh the shepherd and stood up. "In 1899, I saw a man put on his sister's underwear!" This made an impression, and the crowd grew silent.

"Liar!" screamed Grandmother Pierkiel. "My son would never!"

"He died like a man," Kazhimiezh admitted. "Olek saw it."

Apollonia: "The priest is dead. The subject is, do we hang his murderesses by the neck? A neck for a neck."

Kowalchyk: "A sorry from von Grushka for my sister!"

Dzaswav: "A beer for 90,000 thallers!"

Volodek: "In the free market, A may be clever enough to take advantage of B or C without their being able to retaliate. A sells beer worth 90,000 thallers to B, and obtains from him in exchange corn to the value of 550,000 thallers."

Grandmother Pierkiel: "Horchensky stole my wire!"

Kryshia: "But you heard Horchensky, gypsies stole your wire."

Horchensky: "Horchenskys don't lie!"

"I am old, and I say, arrest them!" screamed Grandmother Pierkiel. "Let no one get away with taking other people's wires!"

"They rob and they murder," screamed Zhmiya the spinster.

Kazhimiezh: "I've seen worse!"

"I've seen even worse than your worse," drunken Yayechko yelled. "The gypsies took the Jesus out my curd!"

This final evidence of gypsy criminality eclipsed all else. Yelling and arm-flailing became widespread.

Artur the greengrocer: "There's a toad in my yard that's Tsura's familiar!"

Dudrovski the farmer: "The gypsies are Russians and communists!"

Celestyn the barber: "Punish the uncoiffed archfiends!"

"I believe they are from Austrohungary!" Von Grushka climbed onto the stage and attempted to calm the populace with "Hear me now!" and "Peasants of Odolechka!"

But Apollonia muffled him with her shrill cries: "Arrest them!" She waved her arms like a deranged conductor. "Bring them to judgment!"

Ludvik: "If we hang them, do I notarize it?"

"What!" screamed Grandmother Pierkiel into his ear.

Ludvik: "Do gypsies have death certificates?"

Von Grushka: "Peasants of this town!"

Grigor the janitor staggered into the auditorium with a swollen bloody eye.

The Mayor to himself: "The whole voivodeship, the whole voivodeship."

Von Grushka: "Hear me, plebs!"

Bolek to Kowalchyk: "Let's beat von Grushka and take his boots!"

Grigor to Bolek: "I don't recommend it."

Dzaswav: "A free stein of mead for the first ten to get to the tavern!"

This adjourned the Town Meeting on the Subject of the Gypsies and Decency and catalyzed immediate near-total exodus. Chairs and crates were kicked and toppled. Zhmiya was knocked to the floor with a wail. Kowalchyk, at this point in good position to be first to the tavern, perceived a new insult to his family honor, this time from Yayechko, who was in position to be second to the tavern if not first, depending on how much he planned to save for the final sprint, and the two began a bout of pugilism in the exit of the auditorium, until the second wave of running villagers collided with them.

Then there was general quiet, other than the whimpering of Zhmiya and Basia cooing over her (Daria, the ablest spinster, had abandoned her housemate and bosom friend for a chance at a stein of mead), and von Grushka found himself on the stage beside his Judas of a Mayor and Apollonia and the Police Chief, with only the Head Clerk (who was eating something from a satchel and appeared in a very cheerful mood), and Grigor the janitor for an audience.

"So," said Apollonia to the Police Chief, "you incompetent apostate, are you going to arrest those Babylonians or not?"

"I believe they come from India," the Mayor offered, clinging to the Police Chief's jacket.

Yany and Sabas stumbled into the auditorium.

The Police Chief: "I suppose the—"

Grigor the janitor, bleeding: "Migdawovynos the convict escaped from our jail in one night."

"Make him do something!" Apollonia, who had screamed and stomped herself into a frenzy that had not as yet subsided, shook the Mayor by his shirt, who, being shaken, shook the Police Chief by the jacket.

"*Please* arrest the gypsies," said the Mayor to the Police Chief.

Von Grushka: "Dignitaries of Odolechka, hear what I must say—"

Police Chief: "Yany and Sabas, arrest the gypsy sisters."

Zhmiya the spinster, weeping: "The Russian Orthodoxes trampled me . . ."

CHAPTER XXI

To the previous chapter, a slender adjunct,
in which our volunteers, having been volunteered,
return to the tavern semi-involuntarily

YANY AND SABAS FELT OFFENDED AT BEING ORDERED TO MAKE AN ARREST. They had never before made any such thing. Far drunker than sober and soberer than usual, they had traipsed from the tavern to the carriage house they shared, removed the Sunday bests they'd worn continuously since last Sunday, donned their Saturday second-bests, and traipsed to the Town Hall, for what event, they couldn't recall. To find whatever was occurring adjourned within moments of arrival, and themselves immediately ordered to arrest a pair of dangerous midwives or some such, had put our volunteers into a state of frustrated confusion.

They decided to alleviate this state at Dzaswav's tavern, which, to their surprise, though never desolate on Sunday nights, tonight was filled to overcapacity. Not only that—a screaming altercation was under way at the bar, with some twenty villagers demanding gratis mead (as the reader might have guessed, Dzaswav himself had not been among the first ten to arrive and thus had been in no position to confirm who had), and further complicating Yany and Sabas' frustration, Kowalchyk and Guzik appeared to be wrestling and punching each other in the slime pool underneath Yany and Sabas' customary table.

"Do you have any money?" said Yany.

"I think mead is free tonight," Sabas said. "Let's get in line and yell."

"I don't think there's a line. I think it's who yells loudest."

"My throat hurts, though."

"Yes," said Yany sadly, "mine as well."

"Let's borrow money from Yayechko."

"Yayechko," said Yany. "Give us 700,000 thallers."

"Why?" Yayechko belched.

"Because we're borrowing it," Sabas said.

"It's worthless anyway," said Yany, "just ask Volodek."

"It's fiat," Volodek confirmed, leaning in from the yelling crowd at the bar.

"Here's 600,000," said Yayechko, warily, "but it better not be worth things after all."

"That was simpler than Matteush. We should always borrow. What else can we borrow?" Sabas said.

"What I'd like to borrow is a pair of dangerous arrests," said Yany.

"You can't borrow arrests. Speak of the wolf, there is the Matteush boy. Meet me under the table."

"The undertable's occupied. Your memory is like a rotten leek."

"How can a memory be like a leek?"

"Yours is rotten."

So Yany and Sabas stood for a while in a mental lacuna, then ordered eight vodkas and sat on stools. It was after a vodka each that Sabas had the cleverest idea in Odolechka since Kumashko had determined that if Jesus killed the fig tree, he (Kumashko, not Jesus) should kill himself:

"What if we *borrow* an arrest by giving vodka bought by money *borrowed* from Yayechko the curd eater to Matteush the simpleton in return for him, who is a huge boy, bringing to Town Hall the midwives?"

"Meet me at Matteush's table," Yany said.

CHAPTER XXII

In which Barnabas returns to Odolechka and sees (and feels)
a thing or two (or three) he's never seen (or felt) before

ON THE MORNING OF JUNE 26, THE PRINCESSES KUNEGUNDA AND PELAGIA
were still virginal and disinclined toward the dubious charms of
Hektor, farmer Charek's scrofulous *krskopolje* boar. Every time the
boar attempted to approach either of the royal rears, the ladies
curled their tails and dove into the mud. When no amount of Barnabas' lullabying and Charek's tackling resulted in a procreative
union, they were forced to use a Yashchuk box, a contraption that
encouraged porcine intimacy by significantly reducing personal
space. As Barnabas sat by the box, from which all sorts of puzzling
noises came, he felt an unexplainable urge to visit Roosha.

Thus with two pregnant princesses and two still-sore ankles,
Barnabas rode, over the dried mud tracks of von Grushka's Gippopotam, some sixteen kilometers south along the river back
from Kowomunak, dropped the confused and tired royals off at
Chateau Pierkiel, spent approximately twenty minutes examin-

ing his face in a pan of water, and then approximately thirty minutes engaged in his anti-pen-odor ablutions (with which we have become familiar) from that pan, and mounted his mare and galloped to Roosha's house.

He had not yet had time to take one of his usual clandestine positions by her fence when he heard her call out: "Bring the evening mail in here."

Barnabas stopped and reflected, for he had no evening mail, he was more or less certain of that. He tied Wilhelm to a tree and was about to squat behind the fence, when she called again: "In here, hurry up."

Shyly, he assumed he had been seen or heard and walked in through the gate. Roosha lay in a hammock stretched between a locust and a fence beam, purple skirts billowing, silver chains around both ankles. In the lap of her skirts lay a box of bonbons.

"If you're not Yoosef, you better be bringing the evening mail like he does, or you have no business here." She licked the inside of her palm and each one of her fingers. Barnabas stopped half a meter away from the hammock. He noticed some chocolate on the corner of her lip. This agitated him intensely, and his agitation was compounded when she added impatiently, "Lothario, where's my mail?"

Barnabas searched his pockets. Where could the mail be? Had he somehow had some mail for her and forgotten it? In his shirt's breast pocket, he found a crumpled note. He began to unfold it to see if it might be mail, but Roosha snatched it from his hand.

"'Meet me under the table. I have something to tell you?'" Roosha read the note out loud. "Under the table, pigboy?"

Barnabas, entering a state of mild shock, felt *something* was expected of him, so he nodded. He eyed the bonbons cradled in her lap and tried to sample one. She slapped his hand, picked a bonbon herself, placed it in her mouth, and closed the box.

"Wait here, and in a minute or so, come into the house. Up the stairs and the second door on your left. Only don't make a mistake and enter the first door. Entering that first room will almost certainly make you go blind in a fortnight. In some rare cases, you might also sprout parsley from your eyebrows," she said, chewing, and, pressing the candy box to her breast, she swung out of the hammock. "The first door, remember!" she whispered.

"The first door," he repeated.

"Don't make a mistake, the second door," she said, entering the house.

Barnabas waited by the hammock. He looked at Roosha's tulip beds, wherein the albino peacock stood pecking at a twig.

"Hello, Roosha's pet," Barnabas said, but the narrow-minded bird snubbed him. Barnabas sniffed disdainfully at the bird's poor etiquette and started after Roosha.

Inside, he inhaled a heavy herbal aroma. He coughed to announce himself and climbed the stairs. "Which door was it? She said the first door. The second?" He hesitated in front of two identical doors.

"The first door!" he decided and entered. Someone was at the table, not underneath it: clearly he had picked the wrong door. Shame and fear assaulted his intestines. At the table was Tsura, her hair looking, Barnabas imagined, like Brom Pierkiel's must have, at the moment he had been struck by that lightning, shortly after having impregnated Genovefa the scullion. In this ancestral frame of mind, Barnabas took a moment to wonder whether humans had ever used anything like a Yashchuk box, and, if so, whether the box had been filled with silk and flowers instead of muck.

"I'm sincerely sorry," Barnabas said, blinking his suddenly unfocused eyes and touching his eyebrows for signs of rapid thickening.

"Oh, no, this one you won't have!" said Tsura, looking at an object in her hand. Barnabas stepped forward and saw she held a mushroom on which someone had painted a face. "This time you won't steal it from me, even though I know you like it."

Barnabas looked at the mushroom's two round eyes and wide malevolent smile.

"I do like it, I admit. Especially how it smiles at me. But I have no intention to steal it, not at all. I came in here by accident. I was on my way to meet someone under the table. I am in the wrong room." He backed toward the door and placed his hand on the handle. "Please, tell me. Does it really mean that, because I picked the wrong room, I will go blind within a fortnight and grow parsley on my brows? Between the two, I think I'd choose the first one. Big eyebrows would not harmonize, not really, with my nose and other parts." Barnabas waited for a response. He waited one minute, two.

Tsura said absentmindedly, "If planted during the waning gibbous, it should sprout two yellow gardenias in the chancellor's beer bottle and two in his concubine."

"I see," said Barnabas. "A riddle. I like those." He left the first room and entered the second one.

"What took you so long, pigboy?" Roosha said from underneath a table, the tablecloth so long it brushed the floor.

"I was trying to decide which door to enter," he lied. "I was also going to ask you, what is the purpose of meeting under the table? I know the mail said that, it was the police case, though, with Yany and Sabas, you know, by the way, have you read Polensky, the author of the *Guide to Etiquette*? He advocates meeting *at* a table, at the very first, at least, not *underneath* it."

"Be quiet and come down here," she said.

The tablecloth tremored, and a beckoning bare foot extended from beneath it.

"But what for?" he inquired.

"I have to convince you? Because you're the new evening postman. Because I'll show you something you've never seen before, and that is *what for*."

"All right," said Barnabas, approaching the table. "I like to see new things, especially if I haven't seen them before. Five minutes ago, for example, I saw a mushroom with a face on it."

"Are you coming or not?"

"Only if we don't have anything to do with curses."

"I will cast a curse on you if you don't come down here right now."

He bent to dive beneath the table, gripping a table leg that came off in his hand, and the table collapsed to one side.

"What are you doing now, breaking my table?" She crawled from under it.

"I didn't break it, the leg was just in my hand. It must have been cursed. You probably cursed it one time when you weren't looking?" Helplessly, Barnabas showed her the table leg.

Then something struck the window with considerable force.

"It must be that nasty Doctor coming back to rob my *chorluk* to sell it on the black market." She stood and sashayed to the window.

Barnabas followed and was scandalized to witness Burthold, Matteush, and Stashko pushing through the garden gate, with red-faced Apollonia stomping in the lane. Roosha opened the window.

"Pigeon?" Matteush asked (or possibly threatened) the peacock.

"More curses? Is that what you came for? But Burthold is already impotent. Do you other two want to end like your zoo-keeper Burthold? We just cursed him yesterday. We had forgotten about it until a pickled short gourd fell from the kitchen shelf and broke in half and reminded us," said Roosha through the window. "Another thing is this is 'private property,' and the man who likes to remind everyone of that is due before long. I called your local huntsman Karol von Grushka here to guard us from any and all devil dogs that might have been awoken from the boneyards by your noisy little town meeting, and it looks like I was an intelligent fox to have done so. Which reminds me"—she turned from the window and said to Barnabas—"it's time you fled out the back like a little blond rat. They have blond rats in Nagykaposi, you know."

"The wet wet nurse!" Burthold bellowed, bowing. "And do I see, too, the top o' the head of our long-missed friend from the wood, our best school days friend, the faithful nursed babe and wetter of the straw! What a reunion!"

"Only try walking through that front door," Roosha yelled at Burthold, "and I'll put a curse on you and your family, so that the next time they unite, it will be at the boneyard! Each of you will find your death beside a kitchen stove. The next time you stand by it, a gust of wind will change the flame's direction and set your hair on fire. A lunar eclipse will occur then, and your heads will burn so brightly that Cossacks in Yeniseysk will show the strange new stars to their children and cheer!"

"Silence, coven!" Apollonia decreed. "We've come to execute the law of Odolechka. Yany and Sabas have deputized these three in the sight of men and priests!"

"The priest is dead," said Stashko in confusion, "not that I am disagreeing with the true fact that we were deputized, as surely it is so we were, but how can it have happened in the sight of men and priests if all the priests in Odolechka, all being one in this case but not in all cases, are no longer living, and how can the dead see? If the dead can see, I wouldn't like to be a deputy at all, but rather I would like to be a priest, for then the world is an eviler place than I knew. But if the dead *can't* see, how can I be a deputy? And if the dead *can* see, how can I be?" he concluded, one of the finer examples of Odolechkan logic in this chronicle.

"Silence, deputy, and silence, murderesses! Your curses are impotent in my presence! No Christian head burns brighter than Moses' bush!" cried Apollonia, tugging at Mshchiswava's dress's collar such that its button snapped, exposing her anserine neck. "I see your stricken face when I say burning bush, you're thinking of von Grushka's ear hair! Poor Nastya von Grushka is *ill*, I say *ill*. Is she not ill with a Venus contracted from you? All know your guilt. Fornicator!"

At this, Matteush butted the front door, and the deputies entered the house.

Barnabas looked at his arm and saw he held the table's leg. "Don't worry, I'm armed!"

Roosha screamed something to Tsura in Romani, then ran onto the balcony. "Follow me, pigboy!" She climbed over the railing (a thunder of loutish boots approaching up the stairs within) and hung from the base of the railing's bars, her skirts' hems brushing the sunflowers' heads. She swayed back and forth and dropped to the ground.

"Stop!" Apollonia screamed. "Stopstop!" leaping up and down in the lane.

Barnabas followed Roosha's acrobatics with lesser grace. From within came the noise of a lout decapitating a stained glass lamp, for having found no obvious human victims in the house, our deputies were violently arresting furniture.

"Run for my horse!" Barnabas battle-cried as his feet touched the ground, and he ran toward the gate, but Roosha clasped him by the wrist as he ran past and pulled him against her. Her cheeks were flushed and her eyes peculiarly watery.

"Come here," she said, "feel this. I run faster than horses on water and camels on sand." She pressed his hand against her upper outer thigh. "Feel," she commanded.

A strange sensation crashed over our hero like a blood-red wave full of water-logged trombones and broken short gourds (not quite translatable from Scalvusian, but one of my best turns of phrase, if the reader will go on trust), in which wave, he had to admit, there was something of the urgency of farmer Charek's scrofulous *krskopolje* boar.

"Polensky says a gentleman must kiss the lips before he— *palpates* is the word he uses—before he *palpates* the thigh," said Barnabas, palpating her supple limb with vim.

Roosha licked Barnabas's neck from cerulean collar to ear, and as she did, a roaring filled his head (it was all quite over-whelming, for though Kunegunda and Pelagia now were women of the world, our young Barnabas was, as yet, *of* nothing but the

Outer Wheat Belt), as if of pistons slamming into piston shafts and an automobile horn blaring and wheels spinning in dirt and a car door slamming open and shut, and a man demanding: "Vinegar! What's this? What do I see transpiring on my own property?"

Barnabas and Roosha disengaged and saw von Grushka struggling with the gate, half tearing it from its hinges, running toward them.

"The burning bush!" Apollonia croaked from the lane in a cloud of dust beside the diagonally parked Gippopotam.

"Go down and punish the mattress-felons and other bedroom delinquents," Burthold ordered Stashko and Matteush on the balcony above the garden; however, none of them moved, blessed as they realized they were with box seating for the confrontation between Roosha's rival suitors.

"Kill those ruffians who broke into your house," said Roosha to von Grushka, pointing at the louts on the balcony, but von Grushka thrust an arm out into Barnabas' chest (Barnabas, in his confusion, had forgotten to let go the aforementioned quadriceps that ostensibly outran horses on water and camels on sand) and sent the boy staggering backward four meters into the weigelas, which by now seem to have been bred and cultivated for the purpose of receiving Pierkiels.

"Fine!" she snarled. "They all came after me, the swineherd with them. I did all I could but preferred his swinehugger's hug to the loss of my only life."

"That is not true! I'd never hurt her or hug her of my own will. I was protecting her from Burthold." Barnabas brandished the table leg, picking himself up out of the weigelas. "Yes, I love her, but only with etiquette. First, she lured me under the table, to show me something, but the table collapsed. Then Burthold and Stashko and Matteush broke into your house and chased us off the balcony, but she insisted!" Barnabas delivered in one breath.

"Quiet, you offal! Quiet, you gypsy whore! Collapsing tables with the swineherd?! I don't want to hear about your filthy misadventures in the offal!" Von Grushka ran to his Gippopotam, from the trunk of which he gathered his 1921 Mannlicher rifle.

The louts, who had been hired for six shots of vodka and thus had little loyalty to their mission, disappeared from the balcony and could be heard thudding down the inner stairs.

"Don't shoot him!" Roosha ran after von Grushka and pulled at the back of his jacket and—

Let me interrupt the narration here to apologize for the operatic, maudlin turn events have taken. In this, Scalvusia was like nearly all nations, that is, rife with melodramas, all without even an iota of concern for the dignity of future historians.

—and von Grushka violently shrugged, but she wrapped her arms around him and clung to his back. Dragging her behind him, he approached the gate and brought the rifle to his shoulder.

"Further murders! Further murders!" Apollonia screamed in delight in the lane. "The earth has opened up! This town is flying down the sinkhole toward the Exterior Darkness!"

Von Grushka shoved Roosha aside with ungentlemanly force, sprang into the garden, and lined up his sights on Barnabas' chest. Barnabas, now on his feet, still wielding the table leg, was backing over lettuces toward the far end of the garden fence. Meanwhile, our deputized trio had fled, as had the albino peacock, to the other far end of the fence (as they ran through the rear of the yard, spontaneous unspoken unanimous sentiment dictated they demolish the outhouse with boots and shoulders) and were boosting each other over the fence in preparation for flight into an adjacent wheat field.

Now Roosha yelled something rather too maudlin for history, and, ignoring it, von Grushka pulled the trigger, but (of course, for how could this end here, when you clearly see how many pages yet remain) the rifle did not fire.

"No wonder the Austrohungarians discontinued these!" he spouted, while Barnabas sprinted toward the fence. Von Grushka opened his rifle, spat into it, and prepared to shoot again.

"You are arrested for the hanging of Kumashko!" Apollonia jumped up and down in front of Roosha, who was picking herself up from the dust of the lane. "You won't be saved by fornicator number two! For the Lamb has jammed his gun. You are arrested! No bullet shall touch us, for our skins, like Uriel's wings, are impregnated with the Divine Will of the Maker!"

"*You're* impregnated," said Roosha, putting her feet beneath her, headbutting the wailing zealot in the stomach.

"Piss!" von Grushka roared. He ran, holding the 1921 Mannlicher like a club, toward Barnabas, who was climbing the back fence.

Tsura lurched out of the house, the smiling mushroom in one hand, dragging a tremendous sausage-shaped sackcloth bag in the other.

Apollonia, divine wind knocked from her, crabwalked to the Gippopotam and leaned against it, wheezing like a teapot.

Roosha, alternately ululating in no language and screaming

in Romani, ran after Tsura and picked up the dragging back half of the bag.

Barnabas found himself over the fence before von Grushka, not as fast as in his Sixth Cavalry days, reached the lettuce patch. Barnabas ran back around the outside of the fence to where he had tied Wilhelm. Wilhelm was gone.

CHAPTER XXIII

In which the first drop of the storm of
History descends on Odolechka

EARLY ON JUNE 27, AN ODD DOT APPEARED IN THE SKY. IT PROCEEDED IN A
steady downward zigzag, growing bigger, influenced by the wind
so that it hovered interchangeably above the church and the square.
There was no one to witness this atmospheric discharge (soon
enough, it landed in a flurry of flapping appendages, missing the
opening of Yolanda's well by less than ten meters) other than
Grigor the janitor, who, for this miraculous visitation and little
else, was willing to interrupt his sweeping. He stood on the Town
Hall's outer stairs, swollen-faced and gaping.

After an inspiring show of parachute cloth billowing and
heaving, a man in a wrinkled London drape suit emerged. This
man, Boguswav Bobek (or so he called himself on this mission,
and no other name remains in any archive I could access), removed
a crumpled homburg from the lower compartment of his pack
and placed it on his undersized head, where it immediately slid

into an unintentionally avant-garde position. Cursing the Luft-
waffe for dropping him not at all in the wheat fields as planned,
he attempted to fold his parachute and, after several futile trials,
managed to force it half into his pack. Beside him were the
medieval-looking stocks. He granted these an approbatory murmur, then smartly strode toward the only building in the square
not in a state of advanced decomposition.

Grigor the janitor, judging correctly Boguswav's approach
and intention, ran inside Town Hall.

There is not much of interest to be said about Boguswav's
face, only that it was ruddy, that peculiar and distinctive ruddiness of the alpine, lager-quaffing nations. There is, however, much
to be explored within the tragically miseducated brain behind
that face, and so, dear reader, with apologies, we plunge into a
rather darker point of view than this innocent history has yet contained:

As Boguswav walked, his shoes, above which his argyled
ankles flashed (his pants were a trifle too short, and his superiors had demanded he wear hideously un-Teutonic socks, socks
like the Duke of Windsor wore, to charm the Scalvusian subhu-
mans), gleamed like arguments against the dilapidation that surrounded him.

He passed a statue of some barbarous dignitary that exhibited the total moral and gnathic degeneration of the Slavs and
climbed the outer stairs. Within, he looked up the very clean (he
noticed) inner stairs at a menial, who, cementing the impression
the degenerate statue had begun, looked like nothing so much as
a stoat that had been punched in the face. Boguswav's own face
drained of its ruddiness, and he started up the staircase. When
he had reached the middle stair, the menial, with a stroke of

his broom, expertly beclouded Boguswav in dust and perished flies.

"*Du Hurensohn, du Arschgeige!*" Boguswav screamed and leaped up the remaining stairs, grabbed the menial's broom and broke it in half, then beat the creature with the top half of the stick. He beat the degenerate until it was sufficiently subdued and threw the broken pieces onto it. (Poor Grigor, who was a man of only one compulsion and desire, collapsed, drooling blood and mumbling something about his mother and something else about laundry.) Boguswav adjusted his homburg and proceeded to the Secretary's desk.

He was not at all surprised that this Secretary had neither protested nor even spoken during the beating of the *Arschgeige*. These people had no sense of racial solidarity, and thus it would be straightforward to annex them. Boguswav nodded to one of the abhorrent swellings on the Secretary's face. This face looked as if it might, at any moment, fall apart if it hadn't been strapped into place by a soiled handkerchief tied around the woman's head. Apparently, some foul disease of the face was afoot.

"Good morning, handsome Frau," he said.

She grunted in response and offered him a look into her cup of coffee dregs.

Boguswav peered in, his homburg's angle shifting from avant-garde to Weimar burlesque. "This is handsome *Kunst*, yes," he complimented the dregs, imagining her gesture to be some rural Scalvusian greeting his briefing had not mentioned, and the Secretary's swellings blushed.

"Are these the *Kommissariat* and Bürgermeister's *Büro*?" he inquired.

Her only answer was to move the cup up and down, as if the answer were contained therein.

He looked into the dregs again. "Yes, good, and I will let *mich* in," he said, glancing at the two doors. He knew none of the three words painted on the two doors, but the door with one word on it seemed the more declarative. He hesitated, muttering, and finally tapped on the door marked PANTRY. When no response obtained, he pressed the handle, looked back at the Secretary, and walked within.

The room was small, with shelves to the high ceiling crowded with barrel-shaped jars of thick glass, jars filled with revolting pulps and chunky semisolids. He picked up and examined each jar: gelatinous balls, tumbling brown mush, warty cylinders resembling brick-red pickles, some strange intestinal-looking blend. These abortive people apparently subsisted on a diet that would kill a stray Potsdam cur after no more than a week. Nevertheless, calories were calories, and math was math, and invasions were equations, *und so weiter*.

Boguswav was shaking vigorously a jar containing yellow spongy ovals when what must have been a booby trap detonated in the jar. He fell onto the floor, fumbling for his revolver. A fetid smell filled the room. A lump fell from his head onto his neck, and something wet and sour slid down from his cheek onto his lip. Unimpressed, he stood up very straight and coughed.

He picked up a sack and felt its bottom, then opened it and closely examined the peas therein. He checked each shelf, taking notes in a small black leather booklet with a pen chained to it, making sure not to touch any more jars. Reaching into a cobweb at the far end of a shelf, he pulled at the end of a long dark shape that turned out to be a pellet gun. He examined this last item with extravagant attention, adding to his notes some points in a very small, unclear hand, then smearing what he'd written with his left hand's heel. He removed and shook his shoe, for one of the dubious legumes had violently decreased the *Lebensraum* around his toes. He left the pantry and knocked on the door on which were painted *two* words.

"Come back tomorrow," said a bass voice.

Boguswav knocked again.

"Tomorrow!"

Boguswav knocked again.

The door flew inward and an ogre of a Slav stuck out his many-chinned head and said, "Who are you?"

"Good morning," Boguswav said, adjusting his hat. "I am—"

"A visitor from out of town?" The man seemed to rejoice at this and opened the door wide enough for his entire dreadful mass to be observed. "Please come in," he said.

Boguswav squeezed himself, with some trouble, past the ogre, into a chamber with a smoky odor. The chamber contained a milking stool, a dingy sofa, a desk, and some cabinets with mangled papers hanging out of them. A second man, also unconscionably obese, was pouring what appeared to be some kind of homemade distilled liquor into a potted rhododendron, which looked as if this was the first drop of liquid it had received in days.

"Are you from Krool?" the small fat man asked and plodded toward Boguswav, examining him rudely, admiring first his parachute pack, then the Duke of Windsor atrocities upon his ankles.

"He must be," said the large fat man, admiring Boguswav's offensive London suit.

"I am from Krool," Boguswav confirmed. "I am a functionary, *ja?* In your government in Krool. I come to see that Odolechka has what things it needs."

"How sophisticated your speech is, sir," the smaller fat man fawned.

"You are the Kommissar and Bürgermeister?" Boguswav demanded with increasing impatience and dust in his hair and yellow slurry on his suit and mustache.

"Did you have any difficulty jumping off the train?" the small one asked. "We've been trying to devise the most effective technique for the sake of public safety measures. We have been corresponding with the Locomotion Agency—you did say you're with the government? The Locomotion Agency by any chance?—to ask them if, if they won't build a train station beyond the edge of Dudrovski's farm, then might they not provide detailed instructions by the train's doors on how one must jump? Of course, it takes some practice to jump from locomotives, though you'd be surprised how quickly the citizens learn."

"Jump, yes. You are the Kommissar and Bürgermeister?" Boguswav repeated, hoping that his briefing had been accurate when it had maintained that these words were the same in German and Scalvusian.

These *Schwachköpfe* stared at him with curious confusion. Boguswav began to wonder whether his superiors had either played a brutal joke on him or considered Odolechka far too unimportant to demand a proper briefing. Wasn't this to be the corridor through which the Panzer Divisions would proceed to Krool?

"I am the Mayor, and he is the Police Chief," said the small one.

"I am the Police Chief, and he is the Mayor," said the revoltingly obese one, almost at the same time.

"Ah," said Boguswav, grinning with difficulty. "You"—he pointed at the small one—"take the criminals and put them in the prison, yes?"

This man appeared embarrassed and flattered. "No no," he said, "*he* does that," pointing at the vast one, who was now precariously sitting on the milking stool. "I don't like to touch people."

"You are the Bürgermeister, then."

"I am the Mayor. He's the Police Chief."

"Yes. In Krool we use the words the *Bürgermeister* and the *Kommissar*. You don't?"

"We do . . . *sometimes*." The Kommissar was clearly bluffing, but to what end? Had they figured Boguswav already for a spy?

"My personal technique, which I consider to be the best one," said the Bürgermeister, "is to jump legs first. I also like to wrap my head in my jacket, just in case."

"I, on the other hand, find it best not to try to land on my feet, but to attempt a very basic style, face forward, with a rolling ending, in the soft wheat," said the Kommissar. "You did find the wheat soft enough, I hope?"

The Abwehr masterminds had at least prepared for him a lie about his trip by train, though no one at the briefing had informed him that there was no station! Also, there had been no mention of how to reply when asked about the softness of the wheat, though wheat in general was central to the mission.

He had soundly beaten the sole obvious witness of his landing, but that menial certainly wasn't dead. It would not serve to lie, especially as one half of a parachute trailed from his pack.

So Boguswav said warily, "The government in Krool sent me by airplane."

"I *thought* that was a parachute!" the Bürgermeister cried in a very unmanly fashion and even clapped his little hands. "What a glorious day for Odolechka."

"Does this mean we'll get a station?" said the Kommissar.

"Perhaps, perhaps," said Boguswav.

"You must be quite a personage. No operator's ever stopped a train out by Dudrovski's farm, not since the railway came in 1910," the Bürgermeister said. "Not even when the Bishop came to town to sanctify the cheese. But yes, of course, the government in Krool knows this. It all makes sense. There is no pilot who will land in Odolechka, not even for the government, and so you jump. We jump from the train, you jump from the plane. We understand. We do not take offense. We are honored you have come. Just like the Bishop, with the cheese, that is."

"No, *danke*," said Boguswav politely, refusing what he took to be an offer of cheese; then, realizing he might be slipping into German too much, he smiled at them as foolishly as he could, as it seemed these Odolechkans comforted each other by smiling foolishly. Indeed, at this moment, the Bürgermeister and the Kommissar were smiling very foolishly at each other, and both appeared quite comfortable. Boguswav removed his parachute pack and placed it by his feet. The exotic sight of this pack on the floor, with its entrails hanging out, seemed to increase the foolishness of their grinning to a level Boguswav was certain he had never before had the displeasure to witness in grown men.

"May I take your valise?" asked the Bürgermeister and reached for the pack, but Boguswav swept it out of his reach with one foot.

"The pack it stays with *mir*."

"Perhaps *I* could take it," said the Kommissar. "The Mayor is too busy with important matters to be taking care of rucksacks."

Boguswav picked the pack back up and held it closely to his chest. "This rucksack pack is very important, *die Zukunft* depends on it. I say, rather, the government in Krool depends, yes?"

The Bürgermeister and the Kommissar nodded and grinned. They did not seem suspicious.

"And so I come to help you with your town needs, no? So I must ask the questions."

"Wonderful!" The Bürgermeister clapped. "And what, sir, is your name?"

"Boguswav Bobek, of the Bobeks of Krool."

"Yes, the Bobeks of Krool."

"Yes," said Boguswav uncertainly.

"Yes," said the Bürgermeister, more uncertainly.

In the pause that followed, Boguswav felt nervous and blurted: "*Und* where is the garrison?"

"So you're a man of military interest? Glorious and fine!" The Kommissar slumped back onto his stool. "Wait till you see the Odolechkan barracks."

"Yes." The Bürgermeister scratched his pate. "We must take Mr. Bobek to the barracks—yes, that is the place to tell him, proper atmosphere, you know—and we will tell him there the story of how we fought and defeated the Russians during the Siege!"

"You're meeting a war hero, Mr. Bobek, sir. The Mayor fought for our Fatherland during the Great War," said the Kommissar with quiet awe. "You may have heard that conscripts in this voivodeship fought for Austrohungary, but in truth, we fought the Russians in our own defense of our own Scalvusian land."

"*Russen?*" Boguswav sniffed. "And when they did defeat you, did they left a garrison? There is the *Russen* in this town?"

"What?" the Kommissar exclaimed with deep incomprehension.

"*Rus—*"

"Of course, there's more than the barracks. You must see our haylofts!" the Bürgermeister continued.

"Don't forget the straw stacks," said the Kommissar.

"And the windmill." The Bürgermeister looked into his empty glass.

"And the abandoned string factory," the Kommissar said.

"And did you notice the well? And the scarecrow in the corn field by the wheat field by the edge of town? And our split oak tree, where Kashak crashed his bicycle? And—and the scorched bootlegging barn, the property of Kashak the Older, God protect his soul in the heavens!" the Bürgermeister cried, suddenly frenzied with some sickening excuse for patriotic feeling.

"Then there are cabbage fields," added the Kommissar.

"How many tons per year the cabbage?" Boguswav snapped, producing his black booklet.

"Hectares and hectares of cabbage. Wherever you look. There is much to see in Odolechka for an eye that is hungry." The Kommissar tapped his stomach, while the Bürgermeister filled his own glass, then the Kommissar's, and looking about and finding nothing but an empty flower pot, filled this pot with vodka to the brim and pressed it into Boguswav's hand, saying, "Drink, my new friend, drink!"

"*Zum Wohl!*" Boguswav took a sip and coughed. He kept forgetting not to speak in German, but these Slavs had, over many generations, so devolved in terms of cranial capacity that a slip or two could not compromise his mission.

"Kashak's tub distillery is a fine one," boasted the Bürgermeister. "It's one of the sights of Odolechka. It, of course, is nothing like Kashak the Older's place, but that exploded when Kashak was a boy and wanted to become a circus juggler, baby goats and knives and torches, all into the air at once, you see, because our youths have aspirations to expand into the world, to travel, maybe university . . . Alas, when I myself went to the university for one year, I became afflicted with, you know, the sleepy book disease, such that whenever I opened a book, I started yawning uncontrollably and tears obscured my vision, so I could not read. Then, right behind the burned-down barn, there are some picket fences we could show you, made entirely of wood," the Bürgermeister prated, picking up the vodka bottle and finding it empty, covetously looking first at Boguswav's flower pot, then at the rhododendron's moistened soil.

Boguswav had meanwhile seated himself on the sofa and was writing in his booklet on top of the parachute pack he had balanced on his lap.

"Are you writing down what I just said? Sincerely?" The Bürgermeister leaned over Boguswav and tried to read the writing upside down. "Is it for an article in the *Krool Gazeta*?"

Boguswav pulled the booklet to his chest, filled as it was with as-yet-unsmeared German.

"The well he mentioned is missing four bricks, though," said the Kommissar. "Please make a note of that."

"Now, why would you point out something like this? To dishonor Odolechka?" demanded the Bürgermeister, incensed, it seemed, by having run out of alcohol. He rifled through the file cabinet. "What happened to the schnapps?"

The Kommissar appeared overwhelmed with shame. What curiously demented children these Scalvusians were.

"Can you read it back to us?" the Bürgermeister asked, having slipped behind the sofa.

"*Was?*" said Boguswav, looking up and back at him.

"What you wrote there." The Bürgermeister pointed at the booklet, which Boguswav promptly closed. "I'd like to hear myself quoted. I have never heard myself quoted."

"Mayor," said the Kommissar, "I'd like to say, just as a matter of us treating facts as facts, that I have sometimes quoted you, both when you aren't around and when you are."

"You have not."

"Yes, I have."

"Name one."

"Well, I can't think of one immediately, but I—what about when Mr. Bobek first came in, and you said 'I am the Mayor, and he is the Police Chief' and I quoted you immediately?"

"No, you didn't! You said 'I am the Police Chief, and *he* is the Mayor,'" said the Bürgermeister, pointing to himself.

"I have questions for you to *beantworten*!" A subtle madness had begun to bubble up in Boguswav. These people were infecting him with mental devolution. He had had to thrash the very first one he'd encountered, then he'd been besmirched with yellow filth, and now, his mind, his mind, what were they pouring into it?

"Anything you want to know!" the Bürgermeister said, flattered.

"*Bantiworten*? Is that what they say in Krool nowadays?" inquired the Kommissar.

"*Ja! Beantworten!*"

"*Ja*," the Bürgermeister imitated, finding, to his delight, a half-filled bottle of schnapps amid some piles of unopened, dusty mail.

"New friend, Mr. Bobek, now I didn't want to say, but I can barely understand you. It's like you are from a different country altogether, with your fashionable jargon. I am slowly recognizing we don't know a thing here, in our poor, lost Odolechka. We're a carrot sliver in a vast tureen of cabbage soup!" The Kommissar bit the edge of his empty glass.

"Calm yourself, Police Chief. It's the strain of the last few days." The Bürgermeister, hiding the schnapps behind his back, patted the Kommissar indecently. He turned to Boguswav. "As a matter of fact, you've picked a fine moment to visit and report our strengths to Krool. We've just completed a most difficult operation, placing us, I'd say, in a position to be well thought of. The whole country should know, as we have just dealt with two gypsies, murderers, thieves, and well-poisoners," confided the Bürgermeister with pride.

"Gypsies?" Boguswav awoke from deep within a spiral of bewildered misery. "How many? Are there *noch* any left??"

"*Noch*? What is *noch*?" whined the Kommissar. "We don't know your city jargon. Pity us, but please, talk in plain words."

"And gypsies? They are killed by you?"

"There *are* no gypsies. Exiled. The village is saved!" The Bürgermeister nearly danced.

"Jews?" said Boguswav.

"No, not since my grandfather Anatol the Mayor banished them to Lublin in 1897 and again in 1899!" The Bürgermeister raised his glass and, noticing it was empty yet again, refilled it with the last few centimeters of the schnapps.

"What about Yehuda Ben-Sholom?" said the Kommissar.

Boguswav's pen proceeded speedily across the page. "*Und* homosexuals?"

"Good God!" thundered the Kommissar. "This village is entirely men who only share a bed with other men when they are too poor to afford a second bed, and always in this case with wool pajamas. Underline *pajamas* if you're writing what I'm saying."

"*Intellektuellen?*"

"Who?"

"You know," the Bürgermeister said, "intellectuals, the people who put *ist* or *ian* on the back of dead or not-quite-dead-yet people's names, and then the different *ists* and *ians* argue. You have surely read about them in the *Krool Gazeta*. They are terribly upset about something."

"Ah," said the Kommissar.

"The answer is . . . I don't think so. We don't have those."

"There is someone," said the Kommissar. "Dudrovski the farmer, the very man whose field you did not jump into out of the train. He said something about politics, I think, during the town meeting."

Boguswav wrote *Dudrovski*, then a little crossbones sigil.

"What *are* they so upset about? Do you know, Mr. Bobek, being from the capital?" The Bürgermeister stuck his tongue into the bottle, tilted back his head, and shook the bottle and his head.

"And do you have a newspaper or radio tower near?" said Boguswav.

"It's really kind of you to be so interested in our small community. There are some who'd rather snigger at it. There are some who'd rather go to Kowomunak," said the Kommissar, with what looked like a tear in his right eye.

"Why should they go to Kowomunak?" snapped the Bürgermeister, smacking his lips to absorb the last few drops of schnapps.

"And no garrison protects your citizens?"

"There's just the defunct barracks," the Kommissar whimpered. "I suppose I protect the citizens. Yany and Sabas, as well."

"Soldiers?"

"Volunteers."

"*Und* you will spell *Yanyandsabas?*"

The Kommissar explained, with suspicious uncertainty, as if he doubted the truth of what he said or possibly was lying, that these were two men, and he spelled their names.

Boguswav wrote "*Der Kommissar und Yany, Sabas, Freiwilligen-Regiment*," and then the crossbones. "But you have no radio tower? Do you have the radio or telephone or telegraph?"

"I am ashamed to say we lack these modern pleasures, though if those in Krool who read your report should bless us with a few machines, we would be very grateful. We would like electricity on the east side of the river, if that can be arranged. Now shall we see the picket fences? We will take you there right now. We haven't anything we cannot cancel this afternoon." The Bürgermeister nodded at the Kommissar, who nodded back. "And later we can luncheon in my house. Where are you staying?"

"No hotel," said Boguswav, placing his booklet in his pocket. "You will have an inn?"

"You will be my houseguest," said the Bürgermeister. "Do you like to play glass *koogel*?"

CHAPTER XXIV

In which Anechka attempts to sell her chastity
to start an animal hospital

"WHEN I WAS A CADET, THE BOYS WERE NOT ASHAMED OF EACH OTHER. NOT
in the dining hall, not in the showers, and not in the field," said
von Grushka. "Sometimes a boy forgot to put his pants on altogether. It didn't matter. Men were men, or boys were men, or—"

"But I'm a virgin," piped Anechka from beneath the bed.

"What does that have to do with the fact that we all need
physical exercise? I'm merely saying, do not be ashamed, and do
not change the subject, girl." Von Grushka disposed of his jacket
(thus he was entirely nude) and lowered to his knees. He reached
beneath the bed and gripped Anechka's kicking ankle. With a
series of gentlemanly (not too hard, that is) yanks, he managed
to produce her legs up to the knees before he felt much opposi-
tion. It seemed Anechka was holding on to the bed's frame. "Think
about it," he said. "Your father is a man of science. Is it a sin for
him to see his patients naked?"

"I think not." She giggled.

"And why is that?"

"I don't know." The legs continued kicking in a slower tempo. Von Grushka used this moment to secure his clutch.

"Perhaps it is because he is a man of science and of education, and so am I. As I am sure you know, I went to the Akademy. I graduated with honors, like your father did from his own school, I'm sure. God likes that, honors in school, no? How could he not? He's the landlord."

"Is being the Doctor the same as being a military man?"

"With certainty. They both deal with blood, but in a different way. One rips what the other repairs! What a lieutenant wounds with his bayonet, a medic fixes with a scalpel. One couldn't exist without the other. In a way, a medic and a lieutenant are almost the same person, really."

Her kicking halted, and von Grushka admired her dirty curled-up toes.

There was a moment of confused silence under the bed. "You and my father are the same person?"

"You could say so." Lustily, he examined a pink plump round of calf revealed by a hole in her stocking.

"It doesn't seem right." Her leg began its pendulous movement again.

"How old is your father?" Von Grushka's arms moved up and down with Anechka's legs. This, he mused, was not unlike riding, though these reins were rather thick.

"Fifty-two."

"I am fifty-three. I will be fifty-four in August. How old is your father's brother?"

"My father doesn't have a brother."

"You're so simple sometimes. Not what you would expect from the Doctor's Daughter." Von Grushka feigned a sigh of disappointment and loosened his grip on her ankles. "Let me rephrase. You agree he could have had a brother?"

"I guess," she said.

Von Grushka artfully inserted his finger into her stocking's hole.

"And how old could this brother be? Remember, we're not talking about a real brother here. Could he be fifty-four in August, for example?"

"Yes, he could," she said, following the indefatigable Odolechkan logic.

"Just like myself. Isn't that a coincidence? I am old enough to be your uncle." Von Grushka delivered his conclusion. "Therefore all we do together is familial and natural. Your father agrees with me."

"He does?" A relaxation of the calf muscles indicated to von Grushka's sharp instinct that now was the proper moment for the Cavalry's next maneuver. He firmly grabbed Anechka's legs and pulled. She slid across Dzaswav's greasy floor from beneath the bed, and von Grushka's gold-ringed fingers closed on her waist and turned her over, revealing a very Odolechkan face, a stringy mud-brown mane, and an ample bodice with a crumpled banknote in the cleavage.

"You are tall for a factory owner. And for my father's brother," she said, biting her knuckle reflectively.

"I'm even taller with shoes and a hat on." Salivating, von Grushka picked at the bodice's elaborate lacing. "This bodice is probably as old as what's underneath it."

"You mean it's *sixteen*?"

With a sensation just shy of nausea, von Grushka regarded the yellowed laces in his hands. He thought about his ex-mistress, whose continual refusal to remove her brassiere (before it was pilfered by that turncoat, the Mayor) seemed, in retrospect, somewhat ungrateful, if not prudish. He would not allow such a development this time. "Bodices are meant to fly off, fly back on, off and on, you know, with great frequency. That's their natural function, and there's nothing sinful about it, I assure you."

"Oh, it flies off. Sometimes, at work, when I'm polishing glasses, I don't even realize when." She raised her head and regarded her bodice's enigma. "I wish I had a better one. I wish I had nice things and clothes. I heard some people say in the village that it was 'beery,' my bodice was."

"So they did? They might be right. We had better remove it," said von Grushka, all ten fingers engaged in the laces.

"My father's poor."

"A shame."

"There aren't enough sick people in the village."

"A shame."

"I've noticed there are lots of sick animals around," said Anechka, submitting to his machinations with a resigned flutter of lashes.

"Sick animals? They should be all shot dead and promptly. A sick animal is better dead. You don't want the disease to spread into the human population. When I was nine, before I could ride a horse, but only one year before, one year I tell you, a—"

Anechka shrieked. "You mean a sick little dachshund puppy should be shot?"

"Is your dachshund sick?" von Grushka asked, at last having succeeded in unlacing the bodice's upper half.

"I don't have a puppy. I never liked them," she said. This confused von Grushka. He decided from now on he liked his women simple, simpler than Roosha certainly; even Anechka was apparently complicated. He had come to the tavern straight from the scene of catastrophe at Roosha's house, determined to alleviate his mind and loins, and had no interest in further misfortune from the female quarter.

"What's the problem, then?" he said. "A quick bullet into the head does not hurt much; it's a scientific fact I learned at the Akademy."

This elicited some whimpering. He hesitated for a moment, and Anechka managed, with a swift combined maneuver of her legs and her stein-lifting biceps, to partially return beneath the bed.

"I meant to say one should never kill puppies." His hands slid down to her hips and rested there in an avuncular embrace.

"One should save them. Every single one of them. Think what Odolechka could be if we had more puppies, also cows and goats. If every sheep that breaks its leg in a pasture could be restored to health . . . how happy our village would become," Anechka said to the underside of Dzaswav's mattress. "Also then my family wouldn't be so poor, and I could have a better bodice, and then maybe you could lace it and unlace it sometimes?"

"An infernal menagerie! Even on the Right Bank, there is so much mooing and bleating, I can hardly go to sleep, and often not without stuffing my ears with cotton."

"You can fit cotton into those ears?" asked Anechka, peaking from beneath the bed.

"Come, I'll show you. There are some who'd give a kingdom to touch one of my tufts," he coaxed. "We can also discuss dachshunds until your face is blue and so is my—come now, let go of the post. I think I'm changing my mind about animals. Why should we shoot them? Why not make them citizens?"

"You will no longer say cruel things about shooting the animals?"

"I won't say another word. You'll speak."

She wriggled out, and von Grushka hungrily pressed his face into her cleavage, wherein he enjoyed not only a tactile experience but also an invigorating olfactory one, which made him crave the froth atop an icy beer.

"I used to love Bolek," Anechka said, "but now I just love animals."

"Bolek?! That myopic? I don't know why anyone still buys his fourteenth-century shoes."

"I don't care about him anymore. I do think I know someone who could help the animals," she said, as von Grushka bit the last lace in his teeth. She reached to his ear and lazily fondled his fiery tuft. "I'm thinking Papa could have an animal hospital. You said yourself you are like his brother."

"What a progressive idea. The best one I've heard since this nation declared independence. We'll cure all, rabbits, hamsters, and snails," he said.

"You think that's something we could do together?" she asked, loosening her clutch on her skirts, which she had been pinning to the floor.

"Of course! We'll get to work on that at dawn tomorrow, with your papa." Now the vanguard was in position. Any moment he would sound the charge. He lifted her skirts and eyed her gray bloomers.

"We could make little beds for the puppies and goat babies

and sheep babies with canopies of pink and white crinoline. I could get a new bodice and give them injections and mint drops," she fantasized in a suffocated whisper, bearing the weight of the entire Sixth Scalvusian Cavalry (retired).

The door opened.

"Dzaswav, how often . . ." said von Grushka, cocking his head.

"Oh, pardon me. I am from Krool," a stranger in an over-sized hat said from the door. "I thought it was *Herrentoilette*."

"It's funny you say that," said imperturbable von Grushka, getting up and putting on his pants. "Is German now to Krool what French once was to the Russian upper classes in the better days before the bolsheviks?!" He donned his shirt and buttoned up his vest and extended his hand to the stranger. "Karol von Grushka, the sole and boot mogul!"

"Boguswav Bobek, government functionary of Krool, the Bobeks of Krool, also nature walker and *frisch* air hobbyist." The man nodded stiffly.

"The Bobeks of Krool. Why not? And here we just were having a committee meeting about nature." He gestured at Anechka, who had nearly finished her laborious relacing.

"We're building a hospital for animals," said Anechka, the final tightening producing a violent upward motion in her décolletage, which interested both men.

Boguswav produced and opened his booklet and wrote.

"What's that? Cadet code?" asked von Grushka, tapping the booklet with his signet ring. "I'm class of 1909. What year were you?"

"1900," said Boguswav absentmindedly, adjusting his hat.

"Impossible! You look remarkably young. Many tell me I look young, too. So, for both of us, it must've been those runs across the snowy fields with boxes on our heads that toughened us. Or the breakfasts, weevils in the milk. Or the weekly spankings with birch twigs. Oh, those were something, those hardened the will!"

"*Ja.*"

"What? Yes, fellow cadet," said von Grushka. The government man seemed confused, but then, he was genuinely old if he was Class of 1900, possibly a trifle senile, even if he looked so young. "Now let us go downstairs. It's not as atmospheric as the dining hall. Do you remember the drafty floors? The iron chairs?" He winked at Boguswav. "Anechka, here's one of the famous boys I've told you about. Now he's all grown. Run down and pour us eight fingerglasses of schnapps for the old memory's sake!" Von Grushka patted her rear as she passed him and ran down the stairs. The only pastime he could think of better at this moment than deflowering Anechka was a drink with a fellow alumnus of the Akademy.

Gallantly, von Grushka led his guest downstairs to the tavern, and across the gluey floorboards to a table by the wood-stove.

"The peasants have *gekämpft*?" said Boguswav, pointing at the shattered chairs still piled in a corner, remnants of the aftermath of Dzaswav's recent first-ten-to-the-tavern contest, after that ruinous fiasco of a town meeting von Grushka had failed to stop.

"Now lately I've been drinking schnapps," von Grushka said.

Boguswav pointed at the chairs yet again and punched the air.

"Oh? You'd like a bout of pugilism to reignite the memory?"
Von Grushka then noticed Boguswav's socks. The man's suit was
a beauty, too, so finely made that the smears of food all over it
were more or less excusable. "I guess you have a boxing club in
Krool? Perhaps after more schnapps. My form is not what it used
to be at the Akademy," said von Grushka, tipping his schnapps
straight into his throat.

Boguswav examined his glass and raised it to the oil lamp in
the center of the table. "The Akademy. You studied *was*?"

"How charming your inflection is. I tell you, it has been too
long since I was sociable in Krool. I studied pugilism, yes, a bit."

"And tell me, do you have, in Odolechka, ditches?"

"We have an admirable number of them."

"Barns. Crops."

"Once a practical man, always a practical man. That's what I
admire about the upbringing they gave us. Yes, the local economy depends mainly on crops, and it is a challenged economy, but
what can one do about that? Only so much. Last year our crops
were eaten by a potato beetle. We produced mainly cabbage and
turnip. It's the church that owns the greatest stretch of turnip
land. Their justification is something about St. Francis. If you
only knew what goes on here, it's such a relief to meet a civilized
man," von Grushka said.

"Yes, and it was my liking to have met you and good-bye,"
said the government man, "as I must go to dinner at the Bürgermeister Mayor's house." He rose and smiled forcedly down at a
stunned von Grushka.

How impossible, the cad has snubbed me, thought von
Grushka.

"Anechka!" he boomed as the cad exited the tavern, "bring these extra schnappses on your tray. It's back upstairs for you, you mint drop."

To be snubbed was impossible enough, but for a man of the Akademy to prefer the company of that Judas, the Mayor?!

CHAPTER XXV

In which one rider on two horses is two riders on one horse

BARNABAS FLED THROUGH THE WOODS, FEELING VERY MUCH LIKE GRAND-father Borivoi, who, it was said, with both ankles twisted during the carnage of Muzhiko, had wriggled to safety through a full kilometer of briars. Barnabas breathed heavily, his side ached, and yet he sprinted, occasionally flinging himself against trees for brief rests, at one point dropping to the ground, whereupon he ripped and scattered handfuls of grass. After an hour and a half of feverish flight, he sat on a patch of moss, fell asleep, and, early the next morning, woke up with his hair tangled in milk thistle flowers.

Dragging his aching legs, he plodded through some birches, scraping them with a stick, then through a cluster of reeds, and dazedly sat by the river, splashing his face and flicking thistle heads out of his hair into the water, where they eddied before leaving on the current.

If you've never been shot at, don't judge Barnabas too unsympathetically for skulking the whole next day in the reeds. The poor boy spent the day fasting, drinking river water, and debating whether or not it might be safe to sneak back to his home, and whether his grandmother, if von Grushka came armed, could protect him. Thus, in deep dejection, hungry, but at least not cold in his wool suit in the mild summer night, Barnabas spent his second night bedless and fireless in the woods.

He awoke and drank more river water and then spent some intimate and thoughtful time with his reflection. This reflection on the state of his reflection soon was interrupted by the sound of not too distant pounding hooves. What mad lancer was it this time? Who would try to kill him next? His life had become romantic at last. His imagination had collapsed onto his boredom like a one-ton unicorn onto a pygmy pig. Barnabas squatted behind a stump and watched the forest path through the gap between two birches. A rider in opulent reds and purples, trailing an enormous hurricane of hair, came galloping along the path. In fact, he saw, it was two riders on one horse. The hurricane of hair was that of two women intermingled. And judging by the stumpy legs and piebald coat, what horse could this be but his own Wilhelm?

"Miss Roosha Papusha! Miss Tsura Papusha!" our hero yelled, dusting off his abused but still quite pretty shirt, and ran after them onto the path.

"Prrrr," said Roosha, and the horse stopped and, after some confused stomping and a spin or two, returned at a canter in Barnabas' direction. "Pigboy, shall we be surprised to see you? No," said Roosha, licking her lips as if she had just sampled one of her bonbons.

Tsura's face, inexplicably covered with something like violet paint, peered over Roosha's shoulder.

"Miss Roosha Papusha! How happy I am to see nothing villainous has happened to you. And to you too, Miss Tsura."

"Why should something *villainous* have happened to us? Aren't you a cruel boy to hope so?" Roosha asked, winding the reins around her wrist.

"I didn't hope so! Last time I saw you, you were ramming the Mayor's Wife's chest with your head. I was worried you might hurt yourself," he said.

"Oh, no, it was her stomach, and I often do that. It restores the flow of blood to my head," Roosha explained. "You can't think without at least a little blood inside your head, you know. Have you considered having some poured in through your ear?"

"I have some extra in my bag," said Tsura.

"But what about Burthold and von Grushka? Von Grushka *shot* at me."

"Von Grushka and I? We always wrestle," Roosha said. "That's how we became friends in the first place, in a muddy wrestling pit. Secondly, he didn't shoot at you. His gun misfired or wasn't loaded properly, and that's a problem he's had for a while and will be having more and more. And Burthold, this boy doesn't know what's coming to him after dusk."

"I'm so glad to see you both," said Barnabas. "Of course, I would've never left you if I'd had a rifle of my own, or a sword at least, or even a hayfork like when peasants fight their barons in the better paperbacks, even though my great-great-grandfather Barnabas the First was emancipated, so I'm not a peasant anymore exactly, but I thought you would survive, with all the curses you can use to protect yourself. Thank you so much for bringing Wilhelm to me," Barnabas said, patting the horse's head.

"Who?"

"My horse."

"I don't know what a nest of gibberish you're telling us. First of all, this is a female horse. Second of all, her name is Lyubitshka." Roosha petted the mare's mane.

"But this is Wilhelm. I can prove it. I left her tied to a tree outside your house, and when I came outside, she was gone. If that's not proof, what is?" Barnabas raised his hand to Wilhelm's nose, but Tsura whipped it with the long leather string hair of a queer faceless doll in her hand.

"This couldn't be Wilhelm. This is a female horse," repeated Roosha. "It's impossible Wilhelm could be Lyubitshka. Think about it."

"I admit it doesn't sound right, but it's one of these . . . paradoxes of overproduction, as Volodek calls them, I think that is right. No, it doesn't seem to be Wilhelm, and yet, I am quite sure it is."

"In any case," said Roosha, "we ought to at least provide you with a ride. I was interrupted just when I was about to show you what I intended to show you earlier under the table."

"Yes, and when I think about it now, I realize it was not the best place for us to look at things," Barnabas responded gallantly. "Are either of you hungry?"

"There are places we could take you to, you know. Caves, earth dwells, secret cabins, out where no one bothers anyone, and there, if you think you could behave and not speak gibberish, I just might show you *all*."

He didn't know what *all* could mean, but certainly it sounded like a lot, and how could all of that fit in a cabin or a dwell . . . and what was a dwell? "Couldn't we perhaps go sit somewhere sunny? With more light, so I could see properly? There's a nice meadow nearby." He cleared his throat.

"You're looking tanned," said Tsura. "Have you been out in the moon? You look almost like a gypsy."

"Do I truly?" Barnabas smiled. "I haven't been out much at night, not at all, in fact"—determined still to tell no one it had been he who'd found Kumashko and embarrassed by the last two nights of hiding in the woods—"but I'm glad I look almost like a gypsy."

"You don't want to look like that in Odolechka anymore," said Roosha. "You Scalvusians eat too much Jesus wafer . . . goes to the liver and clots. Don't you know about the resolution of your town's town meeting?"

"No?" said Barnabas. "I was mating in Kowomunak, my pigs I was, that is, mating."

"Quite disgusting," Roosha said, "but evidence of general good health in a young man. Your townsfolk have decided gypsies are no longer queens to be bowed to, just queens to be guillotined."

Barnabas' deep confusion deepened. Wilhelm extended her muzzle and nibbled at Barnabas' sleeve.

"Lyubitshka likes you," Roosha said. "I usually trust her taste. If she likes a man, I like him too."

"Miss Roosha, I haven't had a moment yet to tell you because of all the not very nice situations with guns and maybe guillotines and people yelling recently, but I do think, after our, ah, palpating, that your legs are the strongest I've ever felt. I'm convinced they are the strongest legs in the whole of Odolechka."

"They have to be. I am about to climb Mount Elbrus," she said, lifting her skirts and flexing her calf.

"Where's that?" said Barnabas.

"The Caucasus," said Tsura, and Barnabas noticed the smiling mushroom tucked into her belt. The mushroom looked out at the world as if on tiptoes peering over a leather wall. Barnabas still liked the mushroom, he decided, though it was somehow slightly ominous to see it out here in the woods. Despite his considerable hunger, this particular mushroom seemed no longer edible.

"You may touch me here." Roosha pointed to the inner bend of her knee.

"Here?" Barnabas jabbed his finger into the moist ravine. He swallowed and felt himself unable to quell an insurrection in his trousers, and immediately wondered if he had fallen a victim to some new gypsy curse. Nevertheless, he did not withdraw his finger.

"You might go to the Caucasus with us," said Roosha, "if you don't have other lands in mind."

"I don't, I mean, what would I do there, once we get there? What would be my profession there? Because it's true that pigs are beautiful and flavorful, but I would like to change my profession to something more to your liking, Miss Roosha, once we are married, because whenever you call me pigboy, I think, I guess she doesn't like them, pigs. Maybe a horse breeder or factory owner or a revolutionary?"

"*Factory* owner?" Roosha said with one eyebrow very high.

"Revolutionary," Barnabas amended.

"Married?"

"Only after I court you for four or five years, of course. I plan to court you in the most polite way you have ever been, Miss Roosha."

"First, we're going to catch some Caucasus parsley frogs,"

said Tsura, smiling first at Roosha, then at Barnabas, and in a much less friendly way, it seemed to Barnabas, than her pet mushroom smiled at him.

"Parsley?" He touched his eyebrows.

"You could help us hunt for them," said Roosha, "though you don't seem like you would be good at it. I don't think parsley frog hunter will be your new profession."

"Horse breeder, then?" said Barnabas. "I could breed fast horses for revolutionaries to ride."

"The revolution's over in the Caucasus already."

"Not for me," said Tsura. "I throw needles at the frogs and pin them to the ground. It's easy. The frogs are factory owners."

"She inherited that skill from Tschilaba, who once picked all the teeth out of a living alligator in the Rio Negro." Roosha pressed his finger tight behind her knee.

He felt his vocal cords rebel. The trouser insurrection seemed to be becoming violent, too. Perhaps it was this talk about the revolution in the Caucasus . . . but that revolution was over already. What would Volodek advise? Volodek never gave advice about the female half of Odolechka. This must have had something to do with the fact that he didn't believe in his wife. He croaked, "The alligator did not bite her?"

"Of course it didn't. The alligator only smiled."

"The alligator smiled?" Barnabas wiggled his finger, quite without intending to. Why had he done this? What was Polensky's position on an act like this at this phase of the courtship?

"Why, does that surprise you?" Roosha said. "It's because you didn't know her. Everything smiled at her; once I even saw a hedgehog chuckle at her, just before she threw it in a pot. Men, also smiling, notoriously cast themselves off cliffs, just for one sight of her elbow. Her elbows were her almost-most-beautiful feature, only second to her ears and third to her shoulder blades. Tschilaba's Peaks, they called those blades, and the best gypsy singers from Malta and Lebanon wrote ballads about them. Finally, there was a woman from Pompeii who challenged her to an elbow contest. A hundred and one wise men and women, mostly blind, some epileptic, judged the four elbows against each other. The wise men had been charmed and the women cursed, of course, by the Pompeii woman, and Tschilaba lost, unfairly, and was thrown into the Caspian, a stove tied to her ankle. She did not die, though. She was saved by a drum maker's terrier. That was her end. She got an itch from the terrier, and that killed her."

"She died from an itch!"

"She did, unfortunately." Roosha nodded down at him.

"Dying of an itch is much worse than dying of a bullet in the head," said Tsura.

Barnabas gazed confusedly from one sister to the other.

"Bullets in the head," said Roosha, in a strange tone that made Barnabas nervous, as if there were parts of Roosha as far off and as unknown as all the cities she was always mentioning, but how could this be true if he loved her?

"Not I," said Tsura in an even stranger tone, stroking with her middle finger the mushroom's bald head. "Roosha, hold my doll. I need both hands."

Roosha took the faceless doll, and Tsura redoubled her attention to the mushroom.

"Is von Grushka going to hunt for me?" said Barnabas.

"Von Grushka's a fool. Don't tell me you're scared of him?"

"Scared? Of course not."

"His old rifle almost never fires."

"I saw it fire just once," said Tsura, "and it made a tiny hole between this poor man's eyes, so small you couldn't even see it, but somehow his whole brain matter flew out, like a puff of dusty straw."

"What happened to him?" Barnabas' trouser insurrection instantaneously collapsed.

"Oh, nothing much. After we swept the brainstraws off the floor, we buried him in the cellar, under a bag of beans," said Tsura.

"Beans? Who was it?" Barnabas felt weak, so weak that, had his finger not been firmly held in place behind a knee atop a horse, he'd likely have collapsed.

"Oh, just someone who came in to examine carpets," Roosha said vaguely, "Do you think Lyubitshka's strong enough to carry three?" She patted her thigh, as if she wanted him to climb onto her lap, but Barnabas was, by now, too fraught with frightful visions of his own demise to pay attention to her charms. His own brain flying out between his eyes? Von Grushka was a murderer already! This man, with whom Barnabas had spent a happy drunken hour searching bushes and debating poetry, turned out to be a monstrous murderer of harmless carpet examiners. Barnabas imagined himself dead, contorted in a pile of radishes beside a fence, his soul escaping through his blasted nose and hovering above his head like a misty question mark. (Why radishes? We only can surmise this had something to do with Pierkiel family history.)

"You may take your finger out now, thank you." Roosha indicated her knee with her chin, and Barnabas promptly extracted his sweaty finger and held it suspended in the air.

"I am coming to Caucasus with you!"

"So you are." Roosha nodded at a mere handsbreadth of saddle between her and Tsura.

"Yes, but Wilhelm isn't strong enough. You just said so yourself."

"What are you gibbering again? Lyubitshka's carried ten men at a time, back and forth, across the Siberian steppes."

"I'd rather walk by Wilhelm's side." He took the reins from Roosha's hand. "But could we go say good-bye to my grandmother and my pigs? I'm sure they'd be excited to be told about our journey and our courtship. They might give us some food, too. Are you hungry? I admit I am."

"If you like. Lyubitshka can outrun von Grushka's ugly old black machina, in case we're chased, don't you agree?" said Roosha.

"Of course," said Tsura. "You remember she outran an omnibus in Heidelberg. That was the night the moon was blacked out by a black gypsy moon that passes between the Earth and moon every 29,317 years."

"Perhaps we don't have time, now that I think about it," said Barnabas on the forest path. "Which way to the Caucasus?"

CHAPTER XXVI

In which Boguswav the spy wins one skirmish and loses two

AFTER A STRENUOUS DAY INSPECTING THE ABANDONED BARRACKS AND THE wheat silos, which, Boguswav noted (with what the French call a *frisson*, except that not one of the four Frenchmen I've known, nor the one Frenchwoman I once rather more than knew, would ever permit me to use such a word on such a man), were more than 80 percent full, this agent of the Reich returned upon the horse he'd borrowed from the Kommissar (who, you will recall, had become too portly to ride) to the house of the Bürgermeister for dinner.

Dinner was an austere event, boiled eggs and lean beef, quite edible and proper, cooked by the Bürgermeister's degenerate perhaps but somehow unobjectionable Frau, a woman with a cup or two of Prussian blood inside her, Boguswav supposed. The Bürgermeister himself appeared unsatisfied with the spartan fare but was so lacking in virility that he never once considered complaining or slapping his Frau, not that Boguswav would ever slap his own Frau in Potsdam, but, he ruminated, the idea of slapping this Apollonia had a certain *erotisch* appeal.

In fact, did not this Slavic slattern stare at him continuously while he cut and ate his beef and eggs? The Bürgermeister blithered helpfully about the coming Odolechkan harvest and the wider harvest of what he called "the whole voivodeship," and helpfully about the garrison in a town twenty kilometers north, but also unhelpfully about some game in which it seemed you put either bullets or that *kugel* pudding pie the *Juden* eat into a glass and throw it all at a wall. What better thing to do with *jüdisch* food, but where, Boguswav wondered, did these Catholic savages obtain the *kugel*?

"And where, and most importantly from whom, Bürgermeister, did you purchase *kugel*?" Boguswav asked craftily.

This the Bürgermeister was overjoyed to answer: "I got my set from a merchant in Kowomunak; however, there comes to town sometimes a peddler named Boiko, and he sometimes has, if not a set, a *koogel* or three. Yes yes, it is the game I love more than any other. A man plays this game with his hands and his heart. How is it that in Krool you do not know of it?" The Bürgermeister smiled and wagged his head at Boguswav, who had not understood enough to answer, but was repulsed enough by the Bürgermeister's tone and face to feel that silence was reply enough. "Yes," said the Bürgermeister, "but how ignorant of me to ask. I can't assume the game is quite as socially acceptable in Krool as it once was. You are a younger man than I, of course."

"And you say the peddlers of this *kugel*, they are socially acceptable?"

Maybe he had said too much, because the Bürgermeister and his Frau were both quite silent now. Boguswav looked from one to the other. The Bürgermeister looked embarrassed and confused. The Frau provocatively chewed a shred of beef with burning eyes that did not look away.

The Bürgermeister said, "I see you've eaten all your beef and eggs, and now why don't you join me in my shed for a game of glass *koogel*. That should settle all of your questions, and I'd dearly like to play myself."

Throw a pudding pie against a wall inside a shed after just having eaten a passable meal in a passably tidy house? These Scalvusians devastated their digestive processes without a thought. Boguswav glanced about the room for some escape. In the adjoining sitting room stood a table with an ornate Russian-looking chessboard set up on it.

"Ach, no *kugel* for me at this hour. Let's play an after-dinner strong game, yes?" Boguswav pointed at the board.

The Bürgermeister looked pained and frightened and said, "A strong game, yes."

"Yes, play with a man for once," snapped the Frau. This interested Boguswav. He made a mental note to make an actual note (when it would not look strange to pull a booklet from his jacket) that these Odolechkans, if not all Scalvusians, were either matriarchal or the men lacked any warlike soul.

"But that's a *decorative* chessboard," whined the Bürgermeister to his Frau. "I don't *like* games in which someone ends up feeling superior to me."

The Frau's foot had, without a doubt, just brushed against

Boguswav's knee. "Come," he said, rising from the table, "come show me how you *rochieren* in Odolechka, early in the game or late?"

The Bürgermeister laughed unhappily and stood, bumping the table with his grotesque paunch, and went and sat at the board in the adjoining room. The Frau mouthed several silent words at Boguswav. His Scalvusian not nearly good enough for reading lips, the only word he thought he recognized the shape of was their word for *Gott*. He gave the Frau his best maniacal, icy gaze. She seemed to like it rather well.

"Some port you have?" Boguswav asked.

"It *is* a disgrace," the Bürgermeister said. "I know. We have no wine, just schnapps or vodka."

"Schnapps!" barked Boguswav, but then, not wishing to appear too German, "*nein*, vodka!"

THE FRAU RETURNED WITH SCHNAPPS AND VODKA. THE GAME WAS STARTING well. Boguswav thought himself an able sportsman and three times the mathematician the Bürgermeister was. Therefore it came as a traumatic shock when this Bürgermeister, this degenerate overripe pervert who preferred to throw pudding at walls to the company of red-blooded men, defeated Boguswav in sixteen moves.

(Whether this was a merry accident, a premonition of events to come, or evidence of the Mayor's underrated intellect, who knows? But I must say, discovering this datum in the archive gave me a certain hollow pleasure. Boguswav's balls are covered in dust!)

The Bürgermeister reeled triumphantly, spilling vodka down the front of his waistcoat. Boguswav himself was somewhat drunk, but not so much that he might give himself away.

"Frau!" he shouted. "Bring your husband the king of Odolechka one more, *ja*?"

The Frau came back and stood behind her husband, pouring vodka, mouthing words. Boguswav assumed they were lascivious entreaties, but didn't he see her shape the Scalvusian word for *Himmel*? Probably she was explaining how for him it could be *Himmel* to be tangled in her too-thin, ludicrously lengthy legs.

"And when the Russian artillery broke up the southwest corner of the wall," the Bürgermeister continued, uselessly, as this was evidently a historic battle he was narrating, and nothing of the data in it could be thought of as intelligence, "the Odolechkan group threw bricks from the broken wall at the Russians! I was out of bullets. We had only bricks, and hoo hoo, doesn't chess make one remember battle?"

"He was in the coal cellar the whole time, hiding," said the Frau.

"Hoo, what lies you tell, my dearest woman," said the Bürgermeister, pouring himself a double schnapps.

"And the road to Krool from here. It carries many trucks, yes?"

"Karol von Grushka has a splendid car," the Bürgermeister slobbered.

"Karol von Grushka I have met. And he is of the Akademy, yes? He is an intellectual?"

"You've seen the road from Krool yourself, have you not?" the sharp-tongued Frau demanded.

Boguswav allowed her once again to contemplate his icy eyeballs. Once again, she seemed entirely pleased. He recognized what Odolechkans possibly had not: that, in this woman, struggle was the same as pleasure, and strife was a kind of relish to be spread atop the struggle.

"No, he came by *parachute*! By *parachute*! How lovely. Parachuting should be national," the Bürgermeister slurred.

"And you desire to nationalize *was*?"

"Von Grushka certainly is *not* an intellectual. He hasn't even read *The Melancholy Labors of the Spleen: An Account of the Surgical Profession, Its Triumphs as Well as Its Best Efforts*," said the Frau. "Now as for the Akademy, I suppose he does maintain a slight connection to the military, Mr. Bobek. He is *not* a pious man. Are you?"

"The military Akademy, yes, I see. I have not left the Church," said Boguswav, "and I do not refuse to pay my church taxes, but there is—how do you say?—a cultural struggle, yes?"

The Bürgermeister was on all fours now atop a shabby brown divan. He lightly punched a series of small pillows and arranged them.

"There are church taxes in Krool?!" This idea evidently pleased and worried her.

Boguswav reprimanded himself sternly for his carelessness. "Yes, in Krool, they sometimes have a church tax. And Karol von Grushka, he is not a pious man?"

"He is a fornicator with the gypsy murderesses, both of them at once!"

What warlike soul this Frau possessed! Boguswav made a mental note to make an actual note that swift neutralization of this von Grushka, this gypsy miscegenist with military ties, was to be the first directive on the mission list when they transformed this town into a steppingstone to Krool.

The revolting Bürgermeister now reclined at length across the careful structure of pillows he had engineered on the divan. He closed his eyes and sang in a small, childlike, unintelligible voice.

"A fornicator, *ja*? And may I, madame, see the country stars, not killed by city light, from an upstairs window? The honorable Bürgermeister is *meditieren*, yes, and I, when I drink vodka, like to see the stars."

She eyed him piously for several moments and from several angles. Then she said, "The stars are best observed from—come and I will show you, after all, you pay your church tax," and she led him up the stairs and into the windowless room at the top of the stairs and closed the door with a militant bang that Boguswav admired and that did not disturb the slumbering Bürgermeister. And because it would in no way advance the telling of this chronicle, I will not speculate upon the details of what occurred behind this door.

Suffice to say, Apollonia dishonored herself.

I *WILL* RELATE ONE FURTHER DETAIL OF THIS NIGHT. BOGUSWAV CREPT DOWN the stairs in his undergarment and out the front door into the starlit yard and, not seeing an obvious outhouse, walked around the back side of a small shed to relieve himself against its outer wall.

An eerie gibbering, as of a flock of turkeys in a nightmare, emanated from the shadows. He turned toward the noise. A clod of muck struck his shoulder.

"*Was ist los!*"

Another struck his chin.

"*Arschgeige, Hurensohn!*" He charged into the dark in the direction of the missiles' origin, rebuttoning his undergarment. He stopped and squinted in the gloom beneath a pair of locust trees. The hooligan had fled! This was the second time he had been fouled with unclassifiable organic matter in this miscarried fetus of a town. "*Du Hurensohn!*" he screamed into the night. The only living creature underneath the locusts was a nanny-goat, placidly consuming what appeared to be a pile of muddy documents.

CHAPTER XXVII

In which Grunvald the impoverished schoolteacher is charged with corrupting the youth

APOLLONIA, HOLDING ALOFT THE WARRANT SHE HAD FORCED THE MAYOR TO force the Police Chief to sign, with her redeputized louts not far behind, produced a hammer from her dress, plucked the nail from between her teeth, and nailed the warrant to the school-house door, with a righteousness not unlike that of Martin Luther, even if he was a demonic homosexual Jewish intellectual who had nearly ruined the Church in the sixteenth century.

And yet, over the last few days, she had been less and less concerned with Christianity. She still considered it a fundamental pillar of her being, but just as, in the wake of the Kumashko crisis, Christianity had eclipsed the history of surgery as her primary source of self-definition, now, with the arrival of her white knight Boguswav Bobek of Krool, a profound new dogma had pushed Christianity somewhat to the side.

Matteush kicked the door of the schoolhouse. Children within could be heard laughing and crying.

"I hear children," Stashko said. "I heard them when I was one, when I heard myself, and then, for a long time, I didn't hear myself as one, because I wasn't one. But finally, it was now, because how could it be then if then always ends, and hearing children now makes me nostalgic, and nostalgia makes me sad because I'm no longer a child, but some of the children are laughing, and that's good, because I wouldn't want to live in a world without children who laugh, even if they laugh at me, which they sometimes do, but when they do, I chase them and catch them and I hold them by the hair and rub manure in their faces, because no matter where children laugh at me in Odolechka, just look at the ground, and you will see manure."

The door opened, and there stood Grunvald the impoverished schoolteacher, thin and sickly in his paint- and tea-stained shirt, upon his narrow face an expression of infinite boredom and finite patience. Behind him, the children of Odolechka, of all ages, watched expectantly.

"Apollonia," said Grunvald without inflection.

"By the laws of this town, as Mayor's Wife and in the name of all citizens of proper moral and racial purity, I charge you with perversion, an offense punishable by public humiliation!"

"Oh," said Grunvald. "It's all public, it's all humiliation." His sallow balding head drooped.

"You are charged with teaching children about fornicating quarter-apes! This is punishable by humiliation if not death!"

"It's all fornicating, it's all death, eventually," said Grunvald with expert slowness and dullness, while the children stared at

Apollonia's hammer, quite excited, it appeared, to see if she had come to strike the schoolteacher.

Perhaps I shall, she thought—*someone* has to teach these children something.

"You must be talking about Darwin's theory of selection," Grunvald said. "But it's a very boring theory, anyway. I haven't taught it for a while. I don't suppose I will again. Maybe I will, but to what end?"

"Humans did not originate in the gangrenous uteruses of apes!" screamed Apollonia. "Humans originated in the Himalayas, as any sound thinker who is not an *intellectual* can tell by looking at the shape of human skulls, especially the ratio of the distance from the middle of the basion to the nasofrontal suture, to the distance to the basion from the upper jaw! And so I say, arrest this advocate of the dilution of bloodlines!"

"That's fine. Arrest me. Why not, when it's all a waste? Do I care? What is *care*? Nobody pities me. I pity me when I'm not too bored to forget to pity me."

"Quiet, old schoolteacher from schoolish years," said Burthold, gripping Grunvald by the frail forearm.

CHAPTER XXVIII

In which Barnabas pays homage to the queen
within the thicket

"THE SCHOOLTEACHER'S IN THE STOCKS IN THE SQUARE," REPORTED TSURA,
who had just returned from a last expedition to town to secure
supplies for their journey. She presented Barnabas with a large
wheel of cheese.

Their camp was in Umarlu Grove. Odolechkans avoided the
place, believing it to be haunted by gypsies. What better place to
hide with hunted gypsies, Barnabas supposed. If Odolechkans
avoid this place, they won't hunt gypsies here.

"In the stocks!? Why's Grunvald in the stocks?" Barnabas held
the cheese importantly. "Do the stocks have locks? Do they work?"

"It looks like someone had Olek the carpenter fix them. They
have some new pieces."

"Why is Grunvald—"

"For telling children their mothers are monkeys, is what

I heard one of the brainless telling another out behind the locked-up church," Tsura explained, opening her sack to present the rest of her loot: a long chain of sausages, one half schnitzel, two bread rolls, an onion, a pocket knife, a half spool of yarn, a laundry clip, two apples, three fiddle strings, and a handle from a magnifying glass.

"I hope," said Barnabas with touching concern, "they don't arrest Volodek next. He also teaches about monkeys."

"Our great-great-great-great-grandmother Gaftona was a gibbon," Roosha said, patting Wilhelm/Lyubitshka, an action that filled Barnabas with an anxious proprietary feeling, and so he patted the horse as well.

They made a fire and roasted sausages. The gypsies ate off sticks, while Barnabas held his sausage in his fist, trying to remember what he'd read in Polensky about elegant consumption.

"Even with us sleeping in the woods, you gypsies are so much more civilized than Scalvusians, especially Odolechkans. I don't think I'll mind the wandering life at all. I might even like it," said Barnabas, taking a dainty nip of his sausage.

Roosha turned to him and emitted a belch that put Yurek to shame.

"Oh!" said Barnabas. "Have you heard of Borys Polensky? He wrote a famous book on etiquette called *The Guide to Etiquette*."

"No. Have you read *The Book That Only Those Who Do Not Read Read*?" countered Roosha.

"That's what it's called?"

"Yes." She licked and sucked her thumb and passed her sausage skin to Tsura, who consumed it.

"Who wrote this book?" said Barnabas.

"Djordi Bo Zimionce Pettulengro."

"I've never heard of it. Where can I read it?" Barnabas said with interest. "I don't think they have it at the library."

"No, not at the library. You can't get it in one of those."

"I can't?"

"It exists, but it's not in a book."

"Loose-leaf," said Tsura, devouring a small onion whole.

"Who has the pages?" Barnabas said.

"Everyone has a page," said Roosha. "Everyone who knows, that is."

"I see," said Barnabas, a convoluted urge developing inside him, an urge that had nothing to do with books or etiquette, he was more or less certain of that. He decided he must be tired. Then he decided he was not. Tingling currents of an arcane nature invaded his torso and hips, and he shuffled back and forth, away from and toward the flames.

Then he understood. It had returned, the insurrection in his trousers. He glanced at Roosha, who, having wiped her hands on her skirts, was busy with a study of her foot (devastatingly exquisite, albeit black with filth). He glanced at Tsura, who was brewing mugwort in a small copper bowl in the fire. She spat into her brew and stirred it with a spoon, and something about her procedures inspired in Barnabas a moment of introspective lucidity such as rarely come to Pierkiels (for instance, one had come to Brom Pierkiel only once, while he was navel-gazing in his field, and, though we can only guess at what it concerned, we do know that this lightning stroke of insight was, in a profound coincidence, immediately followed by an actual stroke of static build-up in the atmosphere): Barnabas decided that what bothered him, what was at the root, if you'll forgive me, of these insurrections, was whatever she had planned to show him under the table. Denied this discovery, he had no desire to live.

Inconspicuously, he tried to shift closer to Roosha, to create an environment conducive to *showing*, even if there were no tables in the woods. Alas, each time, when, with feigned yawning and stretching and discreetest wiggling, he managed to progress a centimeter, Tsura, on his other side, moved closer to him, too, splashing mugwort water with her spoon and muttering in Romani, so that, in the end, the three of them sat pressed against each other, and he felt that, though he'd never felt so much of Roosha with so much of him before, he was farther from discovery than ever.

Barnabas at last decided to employ rhetorical measures; that's what Volodek would recommend, whether or not the old man had advice on women in particular. "It is a fact," orated Barnabas, "that we are journeying to Caucasus together. We haven't gone far, that is a fact, but we have started."

"It *is* a long way to Caucasus, even longer for those who walk on their hands," agreed Tsura.

"And is there someone with us," Barnabas inquired, forgetting he was wooing via rhetoric, "who will walk there on his hands? That might take too much time."

"Not I," said Roosha, on his right.

"Not I," agreed Tsura, even closer, on his left. "Why?"

"Didn't you just say someone was going to walk there on his hands?"

"The last time," Roosha said, "I saw a man do that, it was my cousin Kirstur in Montenegro. He did all that was done with hands with his feet and all that was done with feet with his hands, and all that was done with both hands and feet, he didn't do at all. He ended badly."

"Very true. At the end of his life, no gypsy would shake his foot, but everyone stepped on his hands every night," Tsura said.

"I don't know what to say to that," said Barnabas enthusiastically, "but if I did, I'd say it right now."

Roosha stood. "I'm going to do some flower picking."

"In the dark?"

"It's easier to find *zhebina* in the dark. You might come meet me in the meadow behind those trees, see there. Only don't get up before this branch turns to ashes," Roosha warned, pointing at a gnarled bit of bracken in the fire pit.

"Not before it turns to ashes," Barnabas repeated.

Roosha brushed her skirts, arranged her hair, and left the fire.

"With a bit of luck, the ostrich feather will sweep the mantelpiece in the parliament's parlor," Tsura said.

"You are involved in politics?" Barnabas asked, vigilantly observing the burning bit.

Tsura nodded. "I dabble in it only on leap years, and only then when I'm not too tired from leaping over dead sheep sleeping people failed to count. That's why they died."

"Of course."

"Five years ago, though, I was so tired, I slept sixteen nights."

"For sixteen nights? You must've worked all day to be so tired, I mean all sixteen days, or, if you see what I mean," blithered Barnabas courteously to his future sister-in-law. "I don't think I was ever that tired. I admit I was a little tired after mating the pigs inside the Yashchuk box the morning of the day von Grushka tried to kill us. Not sheep, of course, but pigs, and I make sure they don't die. I hope Grandmother takes care of them properly. Yes, it's good to know how long you one time slept. I think it's time we knew more about each other."

"I slept under a linden so long, I had magpies winding nests in my hair. Every day, Roosha poured linden leaves' tea through a gap in my teeth. One night, some villagers built a heap of soil on my belly and filled the heap with boxthorn seeds. They put copper rings on my eyelids."

"And what did you do?" asked Barnabas, casting half-impatient, half-fearful glances at the trees and sky (for, though he was a curious and brave lad, he preferred to navigate Umarlu Grove in the light) and then back at the burning bit.

"I woke up. I placed one of them under my tongue, where I keep it still today. The second one I buried. Look"—she leaned close to the fire and opened her mouth, a reddish sparkle of perhaps a ring beneath her tongue.

"Very pretty. My grandmother, though old, sometimes puts a golden bracelet on her wrist that Grandpa Borivoi plundered in the Great War. Are you not afraid you'll swallow it?"

"Only when a finger's in it."

"Yes, of course, I would be, too."

The bit of bracken in the fire, though blazing, was not nearly ash.

"Now you know," she said and closed her eyes.

"Thank you for showing me your ring," said Barnabas, taking this opportunity to poke the bit into a few small pieces, indistinguishable from other embers. "Excuse me, it's time for me to meet Miss Roosha for some flower picking." Barnabas stood and bowed.

"Pick carefully. I've heard of men whose minds turned into Chinese fingertraps while picking *flowers*. Also men who lost their fingers in nepenthe pitcher plants."

"Thank you, Miss Tsura."

With outstretched arms, Barnabas waded through the dark toward the meadow.

"Miss Roosha?" he whispered loudly.

He stepped out of the trees. Beyond the meadow, guarded by granite formations that looked vaguely human, the Viluga River continued southward toward the faraway Black Sea. *Zhebina* grew in sparse tufts, taller than the meadowgrass.

"Miss Roosha, here I come! My eyes are ready, if you'd still like to show me something, though it is dark!" He ran into the meadow.

Near the middle of it, realizing Roosha hadn't given him specific directions, he decided further running was potentially poor etiquette. He waited for a minute or more . . . There was a dry crack somewhere in the dark. An owl or owl imitator hooted.

Finally: "Pigboy!" from the thicket on the meadow's southern side.

He opened his mouth to respond. A small light blinked in the night—a cigarette end, an animal's eye? He strained his eyes in that direction. Something sailed into the air—a black hat, spinning—then disappeared behind one of the granite forms. Barnabas searched the sky above the granite and the river for more hats. The stars reminded him of burdock bracts randomly caught in a sweater's sleeve.

He advanced across the meadow.

"Pigboy."

"Is it you there, Miss Roosha?"

"Hurry up."

"I was waiting for that piece to burn," he said, stopping at the meadow's edge. "Miss Roosha, are you there? And do you own a hat? If so, you shouldn't toss it in the dark if it is black."

"I left my hatbox at von Grushka's," Roosha said.

He walked toward her voice.

"Remember how I said I'd show you something underneath the table?"

He had stopped before a thicket. Had she somehow climbed into it? Her voice felt very close.

"I was *just* thinking about that," he said, "and since we are on this journey to the Caucasus, and, even if we use our feet, it's still a long—"

"Remember how I told you earlier about the gibbon princess?" she continued hoarsely. "Get onto your knees. Crawl to me."

"Princess? Do you mean you have some royal blood?"

"All gypsies do. Get on your knees before the Queen of *Zhebina*."

He did and saw before him, less than a meter high, a sort of entrance to the thicket. Inside, it was darker than the bottom of Yolanda's well.

"But I can't see!" he protested and flailed his hands in front of him, until his fingers brushed something smooth and long and slim.

"Is that a polished stick?"

"Follow it to the bottom with your hand," she said.

He did, and when his hand slid off the stick or stem, it fell onto bare flesh. He died and was reborn so many times that it was all one feeling—at least, it was until, at the end of a canyon between two heavenly hills, his hand was gripped in her hand and pressed against a knobby, bony end of sorts.

"Miss Roosha Papusha, is it a tiny tail?" he rasped.

"Just the last little bone of a tail that I lost."

"And might I, if you don't mind, check some other parts?"

CHAPTER XXIX

What happened after midnight at Umarlu Grove

WHILE GRUNVALD SLEPT WITH PROFOUND ACCEPTANCE IN THE TOWN SQUARE, and Apollonia slept the satisfied sleep of one who has fulfilled her civic duty, and while, at the foot of her bed, the Mayor snored, dreaming he was a *koogel*-headed pawn about to crash diagonally into a cruel glass queen, and in the room above them, Boguswav, head on his folded parachute, slept in preparation for his rendezvous with the Waffen-SS in the woods, and while the Police Chief's vast bulk wheezed atop his sofa, and Yayechko the curd eater, Bolek the cobbler, Horchensky the thief, Kowalchyk the tailor, and Kashak the moonshiner slept with their heads on their arms around Kashak's table, and while Yany and Sabas slept in their carriage house, and Volodek slept in his bunker, and, in the house that had been Roosha's, von Grushka slept atop Anechka, who slept holding her new white bodice, and while Kazhimiezh the shepherd slept with his sheep, and the three spinsters slept in one small bed, and Mr. Andryoshka slept in obscurity, and Tsura slept with her mushroom propped upright beside her on guard, and Roosha and Barnabas slept interwined, one Odolechkan was awake.

I could describe him simply, purply, sundry ways, but one image more precise than all the others must return: the Scalvusian national fruit, the celebrated *groshkikrazny* melon; his sparsely furred head looked like nothing so much as one of these. It is impossible to say what Yurek was doing up so early in the woods, where his wife was at this moment, and how he knew that Barnabas had camped in the Umarlu Grove en route to the Caucasus. Nevertheless, here Yurek was, expressing his familial love as he knew how, that is, by shaking his spherical splotchy head above his slumbering cousin's, meanwhile slobbering and growling very quietly.

There was, however, a tinge of uncertainty in Yurek's affections, a guttural aftergrowl. It was a matter of aesthetics. Though Yurek was happy for his cousin, Barnabas' nannygoat was not to Yurek's taste. To express this, Yurek's groans turned musical, he tugged at his belt (this had, in fact, once been the Mayor's belt, a gift to Yurek from Apollonia; his socks and undergarment, too, had once been Mayoral property) and hopped in place on his right leg.

When Yurek was done expressing all he had to express on the subject of Barnabas' choice of wife, he loped over to Tsura and profusely slobbered on her hair. He admired her mushroom more than I can say. Far more than he felt toward Barnabas, he felt a kinship toward this mushroom. It, alas, was not much of a sentinel (and yet, by the end of this chronicle, a careful reader may suspect this mushroom, indirectly but significantly, awoke its human keepers to a menace unbelievably more terrible than Yurek Pierkiel); the sisters and Barnabas slept and slept.

Yes, Yurek liked the mushroom, but as nothing held our friend's attention for too long, he plodded to the fire pit and examined a bowl with some mugwort dregs in it. He sniffed the sticks they'd used for roasting sausages and, under a pile of pine needles, found Tsura's sack. Yurek was one of those rarest Scalvusians, one who had become well versed in the beautifully perverse, and *reverse*, art of pilfering from gypsies. He rummaged inside the sack, producing a wheel of cheese, some sausages, a schnitzel half, a half spool of yarn, a laundry clip (this item he liked the most, checking its functionality first on his tongue, then his earlobe), three fiddle strings, an apple, and the handle from a magnifying glass.

He placed these items in his pockets (except the wheel of cheese, which he tucked beneath his arm) and was filling the emptied sack with pine needles and a stone or two when he heard the soft whinny of Wilhelm/Lyubitshka, who was breakfasting on dewy grass behind a birch. Yurek ran to her, kissed her side, and, placing his cheese on the ground, lowered himself to all fours and also nibbled at some grass. Soon, he switched from the grass to the cheese.

When Yurek was sated, he stood, untied the mare, and led her off into the darkness of the grove. Perhaps you pity Barnabas for having his horse stolen twice in three days. And yet, what finer irony than this—that only through this theft did Wilhelm live out the rest of her days, if few, in the possession of her rightful owners, the Pierkiels.

CHAPTER XXX

In which Barnabas encounters Satan

BARNABAS WOKE AROUND DAWN AND PREPARED TO PROPOSE, HIS PLAN TO court Roosha for four or five years obliterated by the night's delectations. He felt beneath him and removed a stone jabbing his hipbone, then turned to his betrothed. She was not present. He rolled onto his other side. Here was an old blanket and some stacked pine branches and what looked like the skin of a sausage, but not a lass in sight. He sat up with considerable anxiety.

At the edge of the camp lay Tsura's sack. This was a good sign. Blissfully, he plodded over to it to obtain some cheese. The sisters were undoubtedly preening themselves in the trees, or at least Roosha was, as it did not seem that Tsura cared for hygiene. Approaching the sack, he remembered that the birch directly to his left was the one to which Tsura had tied Wilhelm. His anxiety returned with reinforcements. Wilhelm was not there at all. No amount of staring at the tree and its environs caused Wilhelm to materialize. Had Wilhelm managed to untie herself and flee? Why would Wilhelm, always so docile before, rebel, especially now, on their way to the Caucasus? A good pet would not do that.

After a few more minutes of tree-staring, Barnabas became suspicious—could Roosha and Tsura have stolen his horse and deserted him? He scolded himself for these thoughts. It was not good for a man to suspect his wife. He had learned this much from Volodek. You can't suspect your wife when she is simply not there.

Reassured, Barnabas decided they must have gone down through the meadow to perhaps pick more *zhebina* or to bathe in the river (Roosha, that is, as Tsura did not bathe), and they had taken the horse with them, for horses, too, must drink. He examined the ground and, indeed, saw prints of horseshoes, approximately in the direction of Odolechka, but the prints soon disappeared into the undergrowth. So Barnabas strolled toward the meadow with the casual air of a trusting husband.

With complete serenity, looking down from the rise, he acknowledged the sisters' absence in the meadow. Where, then, had they gone?

As he strolled back to their camp, he concluded Volodek's advice was pointless, possibly because of the differing natures of their wives, Volodek's being imaginary, his being a gypsy (although, he sensed, there was perhaps a link between the two he lacked the depth to fathom at this moment). With his shoe, he nudged Tsura's sack. It appeared to be almost empty. Could it be they had gone back to town one last time for more cheese and half schnitzels?

He pondered this in a final frantic bout of self-deception.

Finally, he understood. He did what he supposed abandoned husbands did in such situations, which was vigorously stomping in the fire pit, then punching the air while cursing. The latter, he felt, lacked proper drama, as he knew only two curses, one of which (the vile *shastoyavskaya*) he was too meek to use.

Misery was a foul-smelling wind that blew at Barnabas from all the chasms in the present, past, and future of his disappointing existence. He contemplated whether such an existence might be terminated with a sack and in what manner could that be achieved? Might he make it into a rope or somehow jam it into his brain through a nostril or ear? How did one go about smothering oneself?

In the midst of these contemplations, he grew hungry and stooped to examine the sack for purposes other than suicide. All of the precious foodstuffs were gone. At the bottom, atop some pine needles, he found a small gray paper package on which Tsura or Roosha had written: THE TURLAK. Unwrapping this, he found a folded leaf in which was a dried muddy paste of what looked to be mushrooms and berries.

At least they had the courtesy to leave me breakfast, he thought, feeling very slightly better about not going to the Caucasus. Perhaps that was too far from Odolechka, after all. He sniffed the paste. It had a faint boletus odor. He was normally not fond of boletus for familial reasons familiar to the reader, but marital strife had increased his appetite. He sampled a small bite and was surprised. It was delicious. Tsura was a brilliant cook. The more he ate, the more he liked it. He licked the last bits off the leaf.

He looked about the campsite and began to feel as good as he had the night before, or even better. Flapping his hands with delight, he picked up a sharp black-tipped sausage-roasting stick and stroked it without a single suicidal thought.

"Pretty," Barnabas said to the end of the stick. Now he knew what the gypsies had meant about smiling alligators and chuckling hedgehogs and other animals. These things did happen. The stick was an animal, and it was smiling. *Everything* was smiling, wasn't it? Barnabas chuckled at length, then, losing interest in the stick, observed a smoked red herring levitating just above the cold ashes of the fire pit.

"Miss Roosha, not before the morning salvation," Barnabas scolded, trying to kiss the herring's lips that were also Roosha's, though the rest of her was shadowy and swinging back and forth behind the herring. No, that was as false as Grandmother's teeth. There was no herring. It all made proper sense: the frogs were factory owners and the not-there herring's mouth was Tsura's copper ring, but *really* it was her berry-eating mushroom, smiling evilly and talking, not now, but in the past, about a wet mattress. Yes, it all made sense.

"I did *not* wet it," Barnabas said to an acorn by his shoe and, feeling queasy, fell onto his knees and began to crawl between the bushes, drooling from both sides of his mouth. He was crawling uphill, feeling his back legs stiffening and maybe growing wet? Von Grushka could be anywhere, loading his rifle with acorns and wedding rings. This time the rifle would not misfire.

"The gentleman requires," Barnabas gurgled, half choking and pressing his face against the cold earth, "to wipe your finger."

Nausea rose and fell inside him, and he felt his legs contorting and his head turned upside down, as if he were tumbling underwater in a river rapid. Voices . . . yes, it all was very reasonable. There were voices coming from the other side of the ferns, and Barnabas' sole task in life was to position himself as close to these voices as possible. If he at least could place an ear or two of his, or even three, if that was what it took, just close enough to hear the words, his father and mother would be there, yes, back from the dead, like everyone else. What did this mean? He couldn't say. He crawled into a tunnel of green peacock tails and albino ferns, and looking through the other end . . .

Who could it be but Satan? It spoke calmly in a terrifying language to two lesser devils dressed in black with little metal skulls embedded in their hats. (I find it tempting here to speculate that had not Barnabas been ill from eating paste, he'd likely have been shot, but as he was crawling and stunned into stillness, he was not noticed.) Yes, it had to be the Devil, because it had potato pancakes where a man ought to have cheeks and, on its head, three horns, and, *natürlich*, it had a tail.

Natürlich? thought Barnabas.

"Diestadiston vertittigung . . . baldangreiffen . . . ," Satan explained to the lesser devils, who, it seemed, were somehow soldiers, and the terrifying language sounded very much like German. It was German, Barnabas decided. This was what they spoke in Hell? How curious. He always had imagined it would be Scalvusian.

Shaking his cheek-pancakes, Satan accepted from one of his soldiers a large metal box with knobs and dials. The three of them leaned around the box and spoke to it in German. Barnabas was overjoyed (at first) when, intermixed but certainly discernible, he heard a new voice, high and eerie, speaking in Scalvusian. Was it the box? No, the box spoke German. Then he saw that Satan's arm, the one holding the box, was raised, and understood that Satan's Armpit was addressing him.

"Why is your grandmother in the stocks?" the Armpit demanded.

"Is she?" Barnabas responded telepathically.

"Is your grandmother's name not Grunvald?"

"No," Barnabas thought about this for a while, then added, "but my horse may be named Lyubitshka."

"Then you see my point," the Armpit continued, "for if you hadn't named Lyubitshka Lyubitshka, you wouldn't have lost Wilhelm."

"But I didn't name Lyubitshka Lyubitshka. Roosha did."

"Therefore you understand my argument, for if you hadn't treated her with bad etiquette inside the thicket, then she wouldn't have left you and gone to Germany."

"Yes, but she didn't go to Germany, but to the Caucasus."

"And yet is not the Caucasus in Germany?" the Armpit argued.

"If the Caucasus is in Germany, why were we going east?"

"If west is east, then why did you hang the priest?" the Armpit snapped, at which point Barnabas quietly vomited.

The Armpit seemed impatient, but our hero had no answer.

"Why is Umarlu Grove haunted this morning?" Barnabas whimpered telepathically. "I thought it was dangerous only at night." He wiped his mouth.

"All of this is in the epic," said the Armpit. "If you'd given her the hat you bought for her, she'd have had something to draw water with."

"But it was punctured."

"Then why did you puncture it?"

"But I didn't. I think maybe Boiko the peddler did."

The box spoke German loudly, and the lesser devils looked about the woods as if afraid. What did devils fear but angels?

Barnabas considered this. If angels were about, and herrings levitated over fires without smoke, what did this have to do with Roosha and his parents?

But the Armpit interrupted these considerations: "If you'd given her the snuff, she might have married you like Jesus did."

"How could I marry Jesus?"

"By becoming a nun, of course," the Armpit said. "If you had given her the gluey ball, von Grushka wouldn't have shot off her tail."

Now this was very odd, even if encountering Satan was not: when the Armpit had just said 'von Grushka,' Satan, speaking German, had said 'von Grushka' to the lesser devils at the *same time*. So von Grushka was one of them, plainly.

"Don't listen to them," said the Armpit, and, just as you can't avoid imagining a schnitzel if I ask you not to (I am asking you not to), Barnabas immediately listened to the Devil and his soldiers, but what good was this? Barnabas knew no German . . . and yet, it sounded like they might be using one or two Scalvusian words; *house slippers*, for example, seemed to surface from the Babel many times. The only words he absolutely understood were *Krool* and *Odolechka*.

The lesser devils looked about again in fear. If not of angels, what? Then Barnabas knew. It was the only possibility: Rudolf Vasilenko. They smelled Vasilenko! They were terrified.

"Von Grushka never shot her tail off. It just fell off by itself," said Barnabas courageously, returning his attention to the Armpit.

"If she had had the gluey ball, she would at least have been able to glue it back," the Armpit said.

"I didn't think of that." Barnabas felt his courage leak out through his mouth in the form of postregurgitative drip.

"And did you *think* when you didn't go to the town meeting to save the gypsies?"

"I couldn't go. I was mating my pigs."

"Is *that* what you were doing in the thicket?"

"What?"

"I said, if west is east, then why did you hang the priest?"

"I didn't hang the priest," said Barnabas, wiping his mouth.

"Of course you did, you found him."

"Finding isn't killing."

"Isn't it? Didn't you find Roosha in the thicket?"

"Yes, but I didn't kill her."

"Where is she, then?" the Armpit asked, and Barnabas lay down, defeated, in a fetal curl, and did not move until long after Satan and his entourage were gone.

CHAPTER XXXI

In which Barnabas unintentionally instigates a confrontation between the local advocates of planned and free market economics, who, arguably, are also Barnabas' father figures

BARNABAS STAGGERED FROM THE WOODS AND VOMITED THE LAST, HE hoped, of Tsura's vile paste into a roadside ditch, then staggered past the windmill to the outskirts of town and vomited again, this time with lesser volume, into the horse trough behind the church. He had noticed a suspicious yet familiar situation in his trousers. Perhaps the paste contained a small amount of *chorluk*?

He dragged himself to Volodek's cottage, in the yard of which Volodek's wife, who was not there, was beating a blanket to death. The blanket gave out strangely human cries, but Barnabas could not protect it. He was here to ask for help and to report to Volodek. He fit his foot into the trapdoor-boot, failed to tie it, tripped, dry-heaved, and hauled the boot with both hands, such that daylight invaded the bunker, and Volodek screamed, "Shall it be dawn at midnight!?"

"Sir!" screamed Barnabas, hanging his torso down the shaft, "you *are* a prophet of inflatulary war!"

"That much is well-known," said Volodek. "Have you come to return that twenty million thallers you extorted, have you come to see the cruelty and the mechanistic debasement of those who labor in the underground?"

"I saw the Devil talking to two German soldiers in the woods."

A dreadfully sober look manifested in Volodek's tree-knot of a face. "*German* soldiers?"

"And the Devil. And his Armpit."

"What did he tell them to do?"

"I don't know. It was German. I'm sick!"

"As much I have said many times in the past, but who has a handle on realpolitik in Odolechka? Certainly not the Mayor. Only beer steins have a handle here, and they're a German import. This is all a necessary consequence, a modern doctrine. Germans, merchants, tax farmers, and private manufacturers, speaking of which, take this." He passed up to Barnabas a length of pipe.

"What's goes in here?" said Barnabas, looking down into the pipe's hallucinatory depths. Far out in the sea at the other end, he thought he saw lost Roosha paddling in a boat made out of aquamarine roses.

"Nothing goes in, nothing comes out. You hold the weapon of the potential victim of colonial usury." Volodek armed himself with a bust of himself he had had made at considerable cost some years ago. He climbed from the bunker. "The only private manufacturer in this town who maintains a shamelessly open connection to the Scalvusian military is Karol von Grushka the enslaver of lower appendages, for what is the boot if not an expression of prison and an abstraction of use value?"

"He tried to shoot me," Barnabas said. "Also, Satan said his name, von Grushka's name."

"Bakunin, too, was a Satanist!"

THUS, THE VERY FIRST PARTISANS OF THE SCALVUSIAN RESISTANCE MADE their way across the river to the von Grushka residence on the Right Bank, Barnabas pausing along the way to dry-heave from the bridge and then to wonder at a dim vision of Yurek kicking a knish against a wall that was also the river's surface.

"Open the gates, you bootstrap annuitant," Volodek yelled, his mouth wetly pressed to the carved oak door. "With two boots two men can be clothed, with one boot only one man."

"Two men are at the door; they appear armed and hostile, sir," yelled a voice from within. A window beside the door was open.

"Open these gates, or I'll throw the first stone," screamed Volodek into the door.

Von Grushka's very real and very ill wife screamed something multisyllabic and inarticulate from a third-floor window. Barnabas slid to his knees on the granite steps, supporting himself with the length of pipe. An internal pounding, as of stairs being sprinted down three at a time, grew louder and louder. The door flew inward, and Volodek raised the bust of himself before his face, interposing it between von Grushka's tooled revolver and his own prophetic pia mater.

"Twenty yards of linen equals twenty yards of linen is no expression of value," Volodek yammered in fear.

"So, have you come here to fight me or not, disgusting runt? What is that little baton in your hand? Why are you on your knees already? Don't you want me to knock you into that position, or have you come to beg my pardon?" Von Grushka aimed the revolver down at Barnabas, who drooled a berry-colored slime.

"The Devil gave your name to German soldiers in the woods," said Volodek calmly, now that the gun was on Barnabas.

"I'll shoot *you* for Roosha and *you* for your nonsense," von Grushka said. "What are you doing on my doorstep? This, not just this, but all this"—he gesticulated with the gun, indicating the whole Right Bank—"is PRIVATE PROPERTY, as you would know if my signs weren't stolen constantly for years."

"I rest my case on my bust of himself, Volodek!" screamed Volodek at Romek the manservant, who nervously stood behind von Grushka in the foyer.

"Satan talks to Germans," mumbled Barnabas.

"The Devil take your Germans," roared von Grushka. "The last one of you two off my stairs I shoot. At the Akademy, they beat us with a martinet! No discipline. Get off your knees. Romek, go and bring the Police Chief. Ivo will take you in the machina."

Romek made as if to step around von Grushka in the door, but Volodek brandished himself, and Romek retreated.

"I will count to six! Then I shoot. The Police Chief will understand. Invasion of one's property is cause! Invasion of one's property is cause!" Von Grushka had become red-faced and overwrought.

"A commodity appears, at first sight, a very trivial thing, and easily understood!" Volodek ventriloquized, holding the bust against his face as the revolver once again was aimed at him.

"One!" Von Grushka countered.

"A, for instance, cannot be 'your majesty' to B!" the bust rebutted.

"Two!"

"The law of gravity thus asserts itself when a house falls about our ears!"

"Three!"

"Your delusion, as well as that of the mercantilists and their recent revivers, Ferrier, Ganilh, and others!"

"Four," said Von Grushka grimly, aiming the revolver at Barnabas, who by now was the only one on the steps, Volodek having retreated to the landing.

"You're going to shoot me," Barnabas screeched, "like you shot the man who came to Roosha's house to look at carpets!"

"What? How do you know about that? I didn't shoot a man, I shot a *mazhona*. Those girls like their jokes. They should be made to eat soap flakes!"

(For my non-Scalvusian readers, *mazhonas* were straw effigies we threw into the river in celebration of the end of winter. We are not allowed to do this anymore.)

"The Devil's Germans wear all black. Their hats have skulls. They said, they said, they said *diestadiston vertittigung*," said Barnabas to a crack in the granite, the crystal veins around which swirled and hummed.

"Oho," said von Grushka, "shall it be nonsense then from both of you? German soldiers come to gossip about me like village women. How, tell me, does a peasant swineherd know what German uniforms look like?"

"They talked to the Devil in those clothes. Volodek said beer steins have a handle."

Volodek himself had become bizarrely still and quiet, squinting from behind his bust, below the bottom step.

The revolver drooped in von Grushka's hand. "The early dawn of an idea is forming, not unlike when I write poetry, when the next line is *just* out of reach. Are you two trying to tell me that you have come here not to invade my peace, harass me with bolshevik claptrap, and cause me to commit two executions in self-defense and defense of property, but as ambassadors of the lower classes, here to prevail upon me, your only hope of protection, for some action to be taken against *actual* German soldiers in the woods?"

"She left me," wept Barnabas.

Von Grushka regarded Barnabas with a mixture of sympathy and disgust. He lowered the revolver to his side. "You there, hiding there behind yourself. Can you give me the facts? This one"—he nodded at Barnabas—"is drunk or the victim of some traumatic prank, not unlike what once went on at the Akademy in Krool. These days, I imagine the Akademy pranks have gone soft. They probably do no more than pour bleach onto each other's meager chest hair in the night. The men of our generation were harder."

Volodek remained in his inscrutable position.

"Facts, you dirty fellow, give me facts. Are there German soldiers in the woods?"

"The real facts," said the bust, "which are travestied by the optimism of economists, are as follows."

Von Grushka waited for these promised facts, but Volodek remained immobile behind himself and said no more, inspired, one might guess, by the open-ended rhetorical flourish Kumashko (who, until his death, had been Volodek's only genuine rival in the art of Odolechkan oratory) had used to end his final sermon. The call of an owl drifted from the vicinity of the river.

"I said, I said, I said they wore black shirts and pants and skull-and-crossbone hats and lightning bolts. I've never seen such lovely pants. If only I had sold my soul for pants like that, maybe she wouldn't have left me. She even took Wilhelm!" Barnabas wailed.

Von Grushka by this time was composed and alert. "Crossbone badges, you say, do you, young troublemaker? Romek, where is Ivo? Get these drunks into the Gippopotam."

"Ivo is drunk, sir," said Romek.

"Get these drunks into the Gippopotam. I'll drive them there myself."

CHAPTER XXXII

In which *the will* is tested

AS BARNABAS, HIS FOREHEAD VERY RED FROM CONTACT WITH THE REAR LEFT window of von Grushka's Gippopotam for hours without surcease, approached for the first time in his short life the capital of Scalvusia (the metropolis of Krool, alas, did not survive the year; by November 1939, it boasted only shattered promenades, smoking museums, and rats and refugees), two sensations warred within him: one was his amazement at the landscape and the towers of the city, amplified in beauty by remnants of narcotic in his blood; the other was his overwhelming urge to drain his bladder, something he had failed to do since sometime in the prior night.

It now was early evening, and the towers of Krool grew larger, as did Barnabas' bladder.

Volodek, too, had begun to complain: "A bladder has a use; it can be only *un*used for so much time."

"What you both lack is will," von Grushka said, swerving around inferior vehicles. "How do you, Volodek, pretend to be a revolutionary when you don't even have *the will*? How do you, Pierkiel, expect to enroll in the Akademy, assuming I go through with my idea from earlier, if you don't have the simple *will*?"

"The will to what?" asked Volodek warily.

"The will to save Scalvusia. Do we have time to urinate when there are Germans in the woods?"

This certainly was argument enough for Barnabas, though Volodek debated with von Grushka the abstracter aspects of this *will* for the remaining twenty minutes of the trip. At last, the Gippopotam was parked before the second-largest building Barnabas had ever seen. The largest was across the street.

Von Grushka trotted up the purple marble stairs, between the pillars, and into the Cornerless Castle, the newly built (and soon to be bombed into brickbats), cylindrical (it looked like a can of smoked herring, but with marble pillars) headquarters of the military. Barnabas and Volodek ran after him. Within, von Grushka discoursed at some length with several sentries, while Barnabas and Volodek danced foot to foot beneath the vaulted ceiling hung with heraldry and streamers.

Before too long (but not before the pressure inside Barnabas had metamorphosed, deepened, and complexified to a new, shall we say *spiritual*, level, a sort of monkish plane of thought that, if not *the will*, then Barnabas did not believe in *will*), our Odolech-kan lads were led into a richly furnished chamber with men in uniform lined up in chairs against each wall and a trio of chairs in the center facing a huge polished desk. Behind this desk sat an impossibility. Barnabas gaped; he had never considered, consummate daydreamer that he was notwithstanding, that there might be in the world, much less within Scalvusia itself, a man whose girth surpassed that of the Police Chief.

This man bade them sit before his desk and said to von Grushka, in a tone that Barnabas assumed was friendly military banter, "So, Grushka, we're all sad to see you. What a shock to see you back within these walls. We all slept better knowing you were out there in the wheat, sewing boots, or kicking wheat, or whatever it is you have succeeded at so devilishly in your civilian life, out there where no one pours glue in your boots at night, where no one spits in your kasha or puts weevils in your fresh milk."

"Ha ha, General Aksamit. You've been told I'm sure the gist already of the plot I have uncovered, but I've brought the boy himself." Von Grushka looked around the room, addressing this next bit to all: "I like to think of my life in the Outer Wheat Belt as somewhere between civilian and military. I keep my eyes as open as a pair of hard-boiled eggs. My factory is very near the German border. Some of you younger men should come down to my hunting house next summer, as long as all goes well, and see what a heaven of wild boar we have."

"Address yourself to *me*, Grushka," Aksamit said.

"I will. It's my suspicion that the Germans are about to try to annex us, and that they plan to do so starting in the area of Odolechka. However, as I've always said, the Cavalry, with proper reconnaissance, prevails, the Sixth especially. So here I am to provide that reconnaissance, sirs."

"The Sixth is no more," Aksamit said. "The budget this year is for Cavalries First through Fifth. But tell me, why do you believe you know the Germans will invade?"

Von Grushka, stricken, sat in silence in his chair. This man tried to kill me, Barnabas thought, also I *really* have to find an outhouse or, if they don't have outhouses in this castle, then a flower pot, at least.

"Tell them," said von Grushka, with a martial tear in one eye's corner, "what you told me in the machina, about the Panzers."

"The Devil in the woods spoke to the Germans about house slippers," said Barnabas, his hands pressed to his abdomen, his legs crossed with great force. "House slippers, Odolechka, Krool, it said. House slippers, Odolechka, Krool." The men all looked at Barnabas, admiringly, it seemed to him. Perhaps he *should* enroll as a cadet. These uniforms were nothing to be scoffed at, winged badges, epaulets . . .

"The boy speaks no German," said von Grushka with a false laugh. "He means Panzers, not house slippers."

(For my non-Scalvusian readers: this slip of Barnabas' was understandable and minorly amusing in Scalvusia, where slippers were *pantsefle*.)

"Is this some kind of Wheat Belt joke!" demanded General Aksamit. "You expect us to believe a peasant and a bootmaker about a house slipper invasion? Is this all a ploy to get a tasty military contract for your boots again? You're branching into other types of footwear, eh? It didn't work with General Zharoovko, and it will not work with me. We don't wear slippers in the army, Grushka!"

"General," von Grushka said, "I find I am no longer in the mood for the show you presume to put on for these men at my expense, not when I have just learned of the disbandment of the Sixth. Not when I've driven many hours to bring you word in time. There are not many things I love, but what I love, I love with vinegar and *benzina*. I've lost my mistress, the economy is poor for manufacturers, my wife is ill, and now I learn the Sixth is finished? I love Scalvusia. To lose Scalvusia itself would be too much. So, if you would, send a detachment and learn for yourself. I don't say that I know there will be Panzers and invasion, but I do say with some certainty that this boy spied on Germans in our woods, Germans in uniform. This boy has never been more than thirty kilometers from Odolechka. How could he know what the new German uniforms look like?"

This was (whether or not I have become too jaded to be moved, and whether you, in your distant lands of plenty, find von Grushka's patriotism quaint or sad or both) to Barnabas, an extraordinarily moving speech. It was like something from the final pages of *The Dead and the Bleak: A Romance of the Gaulish Occupation*. Approximately at "lost my mistress," Barnabas felt himself forgive von Grushka for whatever unimaginable acts he had subjected Roosha to, apparently with her approval. At "I love Scalvusia," Barnabas forgave him for attempted murder.

The General appeared nonplussed, and, to Barnabas, a strange immediacy filled the room. He felt the men along the walls regarding him with deepening esteem. Perhaps they knew about this *will* and knew from looking at him that he had it, that indeed he was, this very moment, in the act of having it like few had ever had it.

Possibly what our young hero felt was History, which, even in Scalvusia (or possibly *especially* in smaller countries) will sometimes fill a room and those inside it with a quiet awe and sense of wilder weather on the way.

Aksamit: "Very well, von Grushka, you have made your point. I'll know it by tonight if there are Germans in the Wheat Belt. But answer me this. If this boy spied on the Germans, who is *this* man?" He pointed a *kielbasa* of a finger at Volodek who sat with his head between his legs.

Volodek glanced up, saw the finger aimed at him, and stood. "Assembled mechanisms of the State! Though it was Barnabas Pierkiel, factotum of pigs, who saw the Germans speaking German in the woods, it has been Volodek Starykapelush, Cassandra of men, who, for years, has predicted, and prepared for, the apocalypse. Hold on to your wives and children, throw your thallers out the windows. It has arrived."

CHAPTER XXXIII

The Battle of Odolechka

ON THE SECOND OF JULY, JUST PRIOR TO DAWN, FROM THE MIST IN THE potato fields and turnip fields and cabbage fields and corn and wheat, the first Panzers emerged. Like demonic leviathans in one of Apollonia's dreams (that is, before she gave up Christianity for fascism), they rolled forth from the Exterior Darkness and approached the western edge of Odolechka. Few villagers were awake.

Artur the greengrocer, it pains to me say, was spiritedly unloading the first crate of oranges Odolechka had welcomed in a decade.

Yany had just awoken for a moment and nudged Sabas, who had told him to remind him (Sabas) to remind him (Yany) to wake him up again in several hours.

Six houses away, in a rather deeper sleep, Apollonia muttered like an idle machina, Boguswav having slipped out of her bed and, unbeknownst to her, out of her house and town, into the misty fields, at four a.m.

The Mayor was awake, but barely, on the sofa in the ofuce in Town Hall. The Police Chief was asleep beside him on the floor, an empty earthen jug of Kashak's moonshine on its side beneath his arm.

The lead trio of tanks were flattening Yayechko's wheat when Yoosef, on his bicycle, delivering the mail, rolled to a stop and stared, as mystified and frightened by the dark oncoming shapes, I like to think, as any pre-Columbian on Hispaniola's beach the day he ceased to be a pre-Columbian.

The Germans, so my records indicate, had no intention of destroying Odolechka. Odolechka was to be a grain depot along the way to Krool. But as the second group of tanks, a line of nine behind the leading three, emerged into Yayechko's wheat, to Yoosef's disbelief, a thing more frightening and mystifying than the tanks themselves occurred: an antitank grenade sailed from the woods and blasted open the front end of a tank in the second line.

All Odolechka lurched awake at once, except for Grandmother Pierkiel, who flirted with deafness, and the two town elders, who were committedly deaf. Confused and sleepy, most still in pajamas, Odolechkans exited their homes and stood in yards and fields and in the square.

Dozens of grenades flew from the woods. A burning Panzer sped across the last rows of the wheat into the town and knocked a horseless horsecart on its side. By now, the whole southwestern quarter of the wheat field was on fire, and from the smoke and mist behind the veering tanks, a figure, two, and then a battalion of German infantry appeared and ran toward the woods.

Yoosef, in his stupefaction, did not realize his trousers had been set asmolder by burning bits of chaff drifting from the field. He and the gathering others now saw hundreds of Scalvusian cavalrymen streaming from the woods. With rifles, bayonets, and even sabers, the Scalvusians overran the German infantry and disappeared into the mist.

A second burning tank crashed through Yayechko's silo and continued into town. The first tank into town had stopped beside the tavern, where it burned matter-of-factly; to the Odolechkans, it was as if burning-by-the-tavern was what this alien apparatus had been designed to do. At this point, the assembled still had failed to understand they were in danger. They observed the burning tank with wonder and approval.

I will now shift our perspective to reveal that, among the Second Cavalry, a few irregulars galloped toward a regiment of German infantry. These were Barnabas Pierkiel, firing wildly, Karol von Grushka, firing (we must grant the man his talents, whatever other flaws he had) very accurately, and Volodek Starykapelush, peeling off the column back into the woods, whence he returned via a thoroughly roundabout route to his bunker, into which he pulled his wife, who had become entirely real, as people often prove in situations such as this.

As the Fourth and then the Second Cavalry (having shot or scattered some two thousand Germans on foot and in trucks) approached the ruined wall that once had been the fortress of the Siege, a new and ten-times-larger echelon of Panzers emerged from the meadow, firing shells that decimated man and horse at once. If you have never seen a rider and his horse explode together, you are, perhaps, a child of better days than I. Your mind must be a pretty place. I hope it's clear I write such things with admiration, not to condescend.

The First, Third, and Fifth Cavalries by now were closing on the Panzers from the north. Though widely reported, it is not true that, in this war, our fellow trampled Slavs the Poles attacked the German tanks with cavalry. This much any Pole will tell you. For better or worse, the same cannot be said of the Scalvusians. It should be understood, at least, that we did win one battle, this, our first and last in the Second World War. A frontal charge is not entirely suicidal when the cavalrymen carry antitank grenades.

No one remembers when and from what direction he had joined the Cavalry, but it must be also noted that one rider, neither cavalryman nor irregular, would probably have led the charge, had it not been for the short legs of his horse. He rode not more than a meter or two behind the bravest of the Fourth and swung a stolen violin string like a morningstar about his head, prepared to wreak the impossible upon the impossibly real. A Panzer fired, and, in a burst of unsought glory such as only animals and innocents achieve, thus ended Barnabas' mare Wilhelm/Lyubitshka, and thus ended Yurek Pierkiel, Sir Simeon the Holy Fool. As for the nannygoat Nanushka, who had once belonged to Celestyn the barber, who can say?

By this time, the town square was a chaos of enraged and terrified Scalvusians attacking, and/or running from, several dozen of the German infantry vanguard who had survived the Cavalry's initial ambush. Panzers also had survived and were demolishing the church, Yolanda's well, Town Hall, and many houses. One tank, stuck between two crumbling houses (belonging, respectively, to Kryshia and the Doctor), finally uprooted one and tore the kitchen off the other.

When the front wall of Town Hall collapsed, the Police Chief, coughing and coated in powdered stone, emerged from behind the sofa in the ofuce, looked out at the square in disbelief, and lumbered to his cabinets, from which he gathered five old rifles (loaded, naturally, for this was Odolechka, and according to the logic of this town, by now familiar to the reader, rifles never used must be stored loaded). As he prepared himself to keep the peace, he remembered something and squeezed through a hole in the ofuce wall into the pantry.

He swept from a shelf a mess of broken glass and pickled cabbage. "This will shoot them in the eye," he said, shaking cabbage off a pellet gun and loading it with tiny metal pellets from a box beside it. "But who is attacking us, after all?"

Stinging bits of brick from the exploding well struck Grunvald who, still in the stocks, stoically accepted this new assault. Basia, Daria, and Zhmiya pressed against the ruined entrance of the church, holding hands, looking from left to right as Dudrovski and a German shot at each other and ducked behind rubble piles.

At the entrance of the tavern, Kazhimiezh the shepherd, employing quite effectively a rifle that, until this day, had been fired only at wolves, "died like a man."

The Police Chief stumbled down the Town Hall stairs and around the side of the building, where a group of Odolechkan men had rallied to the Mayor, who was covering his ears and rocking back and forth in a squatting position. Here the Chief distributed his rusty police rifles to those in need (though most Odolechkans did not own firearms, more than a few did, as they were necessary to play *paranchak* cards). He gave one to trembling Dzaswav, one to whimpering Kowalchyk, one to Yany, one to Sabas, and the last to the Mayor, who promptly gave it back. With an apologetic shrug, the Chief presented Yayechko with the pellet gun and led the men (not the Mayor, he stayed) along the square's edge to where Burthold and Matteush were expertly kicking a German on the ground.

On their way, the men passed Apollonia. She stood in open combat, heedless, hypnotized. The elegance, the industrial virility of these tanks . . . how could machines so beautiful destroy her beloved Odolechka?

The little battle in the village and the hellish battle in the meadow and along the ruined wall continued as the sun came up. It is said that, at one point, the Police Chief and an unknown man (Gavazyl Andryoshka possibly?) dragged the large sheet-metal rectangle that had been the front of Artur the greengrocer's store (which had been crushed) and upended it against the statue of the old Mayor or Police Chief in the square, protecting the statue from further bulletholes. The identity of the man who had inspired this statue remains as obscure as that of the man who helped the Police Chief save it, but the statue stands there to this day. It is surrounded by a different town, which has but little memory of Odolechka, a town with no Police Chief, no Mayor, and no Pierkiels.

EPILOGUE

THE INTENTION OF THIS BOOK WAS NOT ONLY TO CHRONICLE A FEW WEEKS IN the lives of Barnabas Pierkiel and his contemporaries, but, perhaps far more importantly, to enlist the help of Odolechka, touchstone for a hundred towns, in a depiction of the last days of Scalvusia.

If this has largely been a lighthearted chronicle, my reasons are twofold. First, this may be considered, in its modest way, a document of protest, as lightheartedness has become rather rare in this part of the world, even now, eleven years after the war. And second, because, although we mourn Scalvusia, we had our prejudices and stupidities, and such, in any time, in any people, serve as worthy targets for a bit of mockery.

The causal mechanisms of this world possess sometimes a certain baffling beauty. A boy dropping his handkerchief outside the house of his inamorata can result in the destruction of a town. The archives show that the Scalvusian government debated but decided not to warn the Odolechkans, as evacuation would have made the Germans wary, thus the Cavalry's attack would likely have been neither a surprise nor a success.

The Germans were defeated in the Battle of Odolechka, but at such loss to the Cavalry (Scalvusia had no air power, no navy, and no infantry), that subsequent German armies found the road to Krool unguarded. By the time the Russians annexed us in 1945, we, as a people, were so beaten, so exhausted, that we might have been compared to Barnabas when he lay curled in the ferns at Umarlu Grove, defeated by the Devil's Armpit's rhetoric.

As I have come, despite their faults, to care perhaps too much about the Odolechkans, I will not report who died and how. Suffice to say, the survivors were few. It is impossible to say what happened to the Papusha sisters, but I'd like to think they're catching parsley frogs in the Caucasus.

ABOUT THE AUTHOR

MAGDALENA ZYZAK was born in Zabrze, Poland, and moved to the United States in 2002. This is her first novel.